MESSAGE FROM FOREVER

MESSAGE FROM FOREVER

MARLO MORGAN

Cliff Street Books
An Imprint of HarperCollins*Publishers*

 For information address HarperCollins Publishers, Inc., 10 East 53rd Street, New York, NY 10022.

HarperCollins books may be purchased for educational, business, or sales promotional use. For information please write: Special Markets Department, HarperCollins Publishers, Inc., 10 East 53rd Street, New York, NY 10022.

FIRST EDITION

Designed by Liane F. Fuji

ISBN 0-06-019107-4

98 99 00 01 02 ❖/RRD 10 9 8 7 6 5 4 3 2 1

This novel is dedicated
to Burnum Burnum,
Elder of the Wurundjeri Tribe

Photo courtesy of Don Kellogg

ACKNOWLEDGMENTS

I wish to thank my editor Diane Reverand, my agents, Candice Fuhrman and Linda Michaels, and two special people who helped in editing and writing, Jeannette Grimme and Elsa Dixon. Thanks also to Rose Carrano and Cate Cummings.

To Russell Thomas Moore, I wish to say, love and support on your journey.

This story is also writen for Sean, Michael, Karlee, Derrell and Abby.

MESSAGE FROM FOREVER

1

The brown-skinned face of the eighteen-year-old pregnant girl glistened as perspiration rolled down her face and dripped from her quivering chin. Her naked squatting body straddled a smoldering bed of herbs, allowing the smoky essence to curl around her body and be absorbed into the dilating birth passage. Both hands squeezed the sturdy wooden stake that she had pounded into the ground, her aching arms enfolding her protruding belly. The deep, panting breaths momentarily seemed to ease the rhythm of pain. It was her first childbirth, an event not intended to be experienced alone.

When she looked up, she saw a vision of heat-wave ripples, caused by the stifling temperature in the desert. The wavy pattern ran from the brown-red earth into brown-blue sky, blending the two without any clear line of demarcation. The air had not begun to cool, even though the sun was beginning its daily descent beyond the horizon. Back and abdominal pains had made every step she took toward this sacred place progressively more difficult to withstand. Arriving at the birthing tree brought her more pain and disappointment. The tree she sought was dead. There were no leaves, no shade, no sign of any life remaining in the tall gray shell that was hollow where the hungry white ants had stripped the core. Only giant boulders lining a dry creek bed provided a small, shaded rim of protection from the sun. It had been necessary to pound a stray limb deep into the earth. Young women always used an anchor when delivering a child. They held another woman's hand or caressed the trunk of a tree, but she had neither. Seeing the lifeless family tree with the empty space inside where once its heart and lifeline had resided confirmed that it was destiny, or in the hands of Oneness, that she found herself alone at this life-projecting moment. It was an omen of great loss. She acknowledged her sad feeling that the tree spirit was gone. Part of her religious belief was based on the earth's being the school of emotion. Her people never hid or denied feelings. They were responsible for how they felt, and learned to discipline all accompanying action. She felt sadness not only for the deteriorating shell of the once stately shade- and oxygen-producing friend, but for what other deaths it might symbolize.

The birth contractions became severe. Her strangely totemed child with its violent motion was resisting arrival. She moved from the herbal smoke and dug a small depression in the warm sand, where she squatted again, placing her back against a boulder. As she began to push, she thought about the time, months previously, when she and her husband had agreed to stop chewing the contraceptive plant all couples of their desert nation used until they were ready for the responsibility of the journey of a spirit. Together, they planned to provide the outer covering for a spirit by conceiving a child. Her husband had dreamed of a strange wounded one-winged bird that could not fly and could not build a nest. It fluttered on the ground so rapidly, frantically flapping its wings, that it became a blur, a doubled image. It had been a confusing dream. As his wife, she had gone alone into the arid wilderness seeking a spirit sign for better understanding. Since no special animal or reptile appeared, the couple consulted with older, wiser community members and learned that the dream was the voice of a Forever spirit asking them to become its parents. As usual, the unborn spirit first made its request known; the act of conceiving came later. Her tribal people were keenly observant of the desires, messages, and awareness levels of the yet unborn. She came to her family's sacred spot because where one was born was important. Not only was the consideration of the place of birth determined by the footsteps of the mother, but the unborn had no control over birth location. The child speaks by making the first movement, which the mother cannot control. Where that first flutter is felt is a significant factor. The location of the first life signs together with birth place determine totem and song line relationship. The placement of the stars overhead tell the character and personality of the yet unseen tribal member.

The first movement of this child had not been a gentle nudge. It had started with a jolt months ago and had continued until this moment. The young woman's whole abdomen often rippled from side to side and top to bottom, which was not considered to be normal by the other women and the group healers. She was a petite female who bore a very large protrusion that seemed rarely to be still. Several observers had noted that the force within her stomach was constantly battling either to get out ahead of schedule or to demand more room than the skin could possibly stretch to allow. During the past months the young mother had looked for guidance. She was not yet a master at understanding the messages from the stars, but she was learning. Often at the time of extreme activity within her body she would look up at the heavens to study the configuration, but she became light-headed. Her vision was blurred and everything blended together into big lighted masses instead of clearly defined mapped-out points. If she did not lower her head, she became dizzy and felt she would pass out. Everything about this child seemed abrupt, constantly changing, and confusing.

The last year had been, in many generations of remembering, the most difficult physically and spiritually for her people. Message sticks carried by runners for several years had brought news of white ghost-skin people doing great harm by killing and kidnapping whole tribes. This year, neighboring groups and, recently, her own people had been rounded up and imprisoned behind fences and walls.

Pain struck again. In her struggle to blow out short puffs of air to control her level of discomfort, she managed to think, Welcome, little one. Come now, today is a good day to be born. A few more panting breaths, one great groan, and out she came, the perfectly formed infant girl with the characteristic broad nose of her racial ancestors.

The mother scooped the slimy newborn into her arms. Holding the baby out in front, she looked directly at the glossy black eyes of the silent child and said, "Know you are loved and supported on this journey! I speak from behind my eyes, from the Forever part of me to behind your eyes."

She shifted the child to her right arm and with her left hand picked up warm sand and began rubbing it on the babe. As the dust fell away, the coating of mucus and bloody matter disappeared, revealing tender newborn skin. The child began to stir. Mother inspected her creation as she gently continued to rub, first noting the round bald head large enough to house learning and a peaceful mind, next the little protruding chest and stomach to house a warm heart and healthy appetite. She had long runner's legs with good wide toes and tiny hands powerfully moving in new freedom. The body was perfect. There were no physical flaws to challenge this life.

She placed her mouth upon the tiny lips and sent the thought, I mix my air with the air of all life to enter your body. You are never alone, you are connected to all of Oneness. As she gently stroked and removed the birth matter from around the infant's eyes and nose, she said, "You will sleep tonight upon the graves of our ancestors and someday you will walk upon them. The food that you shall eat is grown from the bones and blood of our grandparents' grandparents." Then, looking at her baby's genitals, she thought, Forever spirit, you have come to a daughter-mother experience. I honor your decision to come through me.

The baby made little gurgling sounds as if to try out her vocal cords, while the mother continued to rub the warm sand all over the tiny piece of life until the newborn was spotless and every nerve had been stimulated. Picking up a small wooden board with curved sides she had placed nearby, she lowered the child into it. Next she placed the gathering bowl turned baby bed into a hollowed space on the ground, with the child's head lower than its feet.

At that point she found she must again use shallow

breathing as the remainder of her womb contents was expelled. Rather than expelling the expected waste, out came a head, arms, and legs. It was another child, slightly larger, a boy. She thought, Where did you come from? but aloud, as if programmed automatically, she repeated the ancient greeting that since the beginning of time had been used as the first sounds to be heard by all tribal members. "Know you are loved and supported on this journey!" She breathed into the mouth of the newest arrival and briskly rubbed him with sand. Her thoughts and her facial expression shifted between a smile and perplexed wonder. Two babies at one time. They are beautiful! But two babies at one time. That is not the human way. As she continued to rub the warm earth on the unexpected child, he held his head up with exceptional strength and determination. His body, too, appeared to be without physical challenge. He was flawless. The man-child stretched out his arms and hands and kicked his feet in the same graduation ceremony reserved for a worm turned butterfly. He loved being unrestricted in his range of movement. Her pre-birth abdominal commotion had obviously been instigated by this little fellow and not his sister.

The young mother reached for a bag, normally carried around her waist but now placed on the ground nearby, and extracted a thin black human hair braid. Separating the life connection with her teeth, she proceeded to tie a knot around the umbilical cord of the firstborn, leaving a long section that would dry, fall off, and become a future tradable commodity. "The hair of your father's people releases you from the cord of your mother's people. My daughter, you share life, companionship, and purpose with all our tribe."

To the son she said, "Why, after I give my heart to my

firstborn, do you slip out, not in the lead but as a follower, not on your own path and in your own time, but following another? This I do not understand. Why have you chosen to come through me? I honor your decision, but I do not understand it. You are the largest, yet you come as if time, place, and circumstance mean nothing, only arrival counts. You continue to move as though you need proof that it has actually happened. Your spirit has arrived in this human experience. I honor your decision, but I do not understand it. I have never known one baby to follow another at the same birthing. I am not equipped for your ceremony. I will use a part of my bag. It is made from many people's hair, and animal parts. It is bigger, stronger, coarser. Perhaps you need that to separate yourself from my stomach and prepare you for the world. It seems you may want or need more of everything in life, since you enter in such an uncommon manner."

She suddenly thought of the first major problem presented by this abnormal situation—names. All her plans were disrupted. She would need counsel on what to do, but there was no one left she could turn to for help. Her momentary worry and concern were swiftly pushed aside as the remainder of the birthing process continued.

When her body released the final waste, she buried it as mother animals had taught her people. For the safety of the newborn, all signs and smells must be removed. Then she lay down with her children. She looked over at the boy and thought, I hope you have chosen wisely, your being here may prove uncomfortable for many. In moments, the exhausted mother was asleep and the firstborn began to drain her of life-giving fluid. The sun set and the sky darkened. The universe recorded this to be the first, last, and only night this mother and her children would be together.

• • •

In the morning, as the color of the sky was changing with the emergence of a hint of light, she picked up the babies, faced the east, and said, "We walk today to honor whatever is out there for its purpose for being. Whatever is in our highest good, and the highest good for all of life everywhere, we are open to experience." Having concluded her morning ritual, she began to walk back to the place she had just escaped. There was no other place to go. Her nation had been destroyed, her husband killed, and now she had two children born at one time. The weary girl wore only what looked like a well-worn rag, draped around her and held in place with a little hair and kangaroo-skin pouch tied to her waist. As she walked, she felt her breasts fill and placed the babies one by one to nurse.

She walked for hours, first carrying one baby in the wooden bowl and the other in a sling made from the rag. Then she put both in the bowl. It is true, she thought, people are not meant to have two babies.

When the heat was at its peak, she stopped and draped the rag over her head and sheltered all three. She left the two crammed together on the wood because the sand was too hot for their touch.

At midday, a scaly gray eight-inch lizard came darting past and returned to pause near her foot. She gripped it with one hand and twisted the reptile's head with the other. In an instant, it was dead. She spoke to the creature with her thoughts: Thank you for coming to me. You were born that we should meet today. Your life will blend with my white water to nourish these two little ones. They are grateful for your flesh. Your spirit of endurance in this time of no sky water will strengthen them for days to come. They will carry your energy in respect and honor of your purpose. She bit into the rough sawtooth-textured side of the lizard and sucked the moisture as she nibbled at the flesh.

When the sun began to slide to the far side of the sky, she stood up and journeyed once again. It was almost dark when she arrived at the outskirts of the mission settlement. One of the children in the camp, climbing on the water tower, had spotted her and called out the announcement of her return. The rag was placed to cover her breast just as her three sisters came walking forward in welcome. It was the custom of her nation for all women of the same generation to refer to one another as sister. Although they were not blood relatives, these women were the only family she had left. They had been out together looking for desert yams when white government officials found them and forced them to come to this place. That was five months ago. Since then she had been told that her entire community was dead.

When one sister saw she was returning with not the gift of a child, but a bowl containing two heads and multiple arms and legs, she stopped. Her hand went down as a signal to stop the others. They complied.

They have seen the two babies, she thought as she straightened her back and walked past them with confidence into the stockade.

Inside the compound Mrs. Enright, the minister's wife, approached her and took a child. Without any expression at all, she simply took the larger of the two babies and walked to the corrugated tin shed called "the white man's place of illness." The young mother followed.

By then, the word had spread. Faces began to appear, peeking in through the door and the holes that served as windows. "Don't bother Reverend Enright," the white woman commanded a set of eyes looking at her from a crack in the corner.

"Now let me see what we have here," she remarked as she lit a lantern and laid the child down on a bare, crudely constructed table and took the second baby to place by his side. "Two of them, boy and girl. Well, it could be worse. I've heard of blacks having three. They seem healthy enough."

"This is the firstborn," the mother uttered.

"What?"

"This one is the first one!" she repeated, pointing to the smaller female child.

"Oh, that doesn't matter, my dear," the fat placid-faced woman said. "Doesn't matter at all."

You don't understand, the mother thought. You don't even try. You come to our land bringing others like you in chains. Then you say our ways are wrong. You push my people over cliffs to die on the boulders below, or they become ill with your kind of sickness and die. The few who live are forced to speak only your words and live as you do. Now you say it doesn't even matter to identify my babies. These are such strange and difficult times and you don't even try to understand!

In the corner was a rusty folding cot with a stained and ragged olive-green canvas center. Mrs. Enright's eyes looked toward it, and she gestured with her head for the young girl to go over there. Being indoors was a dreadful feeling. Since the new mother had to stay near her children, she staggered to the white man's idea of a resting place and fell asleep.

Mrs. Enright left the exhausted girl lying on the old faded green army cot in the corner of the mission compound infirmary. She wasn't certain if the girl was sleeping or had lapsed into unconsciousness. It didn't really matter. Beads of perspiration covered the young face and chest above the rag clothing. Rivers of sweat ran down the grooves around her nose, trailing to her neck and dripping finally onto the smelly canvas. "I'll tend to her later."

In the night the new mother remembered her breasts becoming full and was certain the babies were next to her, feeding. She heard voices. First there was the voice of one elder in the room, then the voice of another from a different tribe. Neither man was from her own nation. Minister Enright's raspy voice also hung heavy in her drifting mind. She woke in the middle of the night, confused for a moment about where she was. Her chest ached. It was dark in this room and smelled like a bat's cave. She could make out the open doorway where the moonlight shone in a rectangular pattern and knew the table was to the right. She found it and felt for her children. The table was empty.

3

The mission was a church compound. It had been constructed jointly, first by the religious missionary members who had volunteered to come to this godforsaken portion of the Australian continent to save the souls of the heathen indigenous blacks. Later, it was funded by the government as a part of their program to make all citizens conform. There was never any intention of providing the first continental inhabitants with actual citizenship; they were instead legally voted to be included in the Flora and Fauna Act. The compound was a holding camp complete with fence and corporal punishment for noncompliance. Any tour of the facilities for visitors began with the structure that was simply a roof upon rough wood pillars, referred to as "the outdoor school." They were proud to say it was required that all natives of all ages attempt education. The Bible was the basic text. The main focus was on making it clear that tribal customs were the work of the devil and were forbidden. Next, visiting dignitaries were escorted to the little chapel. It was a three-sided construction. The front was completely open, making the first view one saw a large figure of the bleeding Christ hanging on a cross and, immediately under it, a tall wooden lectern centered between four red-and-chrome kitchen chairs. The members of the congregation were expected to stand or sit upon the earthen floor. Visitors would next tour the infirmary, where there were no medical instruments or medical furnishings whatsoever. All bandages, salves, and ointments were carried in and out as the occasion warranted. The building was for show and was marked as a special place, a white X painted on its door. The tribal people had begun to notice that most walked in but were usually carried out. There were also two small cabins in the compound for associate ministers' families and one large residence where the Enrights lived.

In the 1930s the farther away from civilization any dwelling was constructed, the further the appearance and structural material differed from the creamy-yellow sandstone squares so traditionally seen in the city. Nothing ornamental was used in the architecture of missionary settlements. The house was a square one-story with a slanted tin roof that extended to cover a verandah on all four sides. The Enrights had been told one needed the porch roof to shield the windows, which must remain open for the hot air to circulate. Since they didn't know enough about the seasons and wind and what directions it might come from, they merely had the laborers cover all bases by constructing a porch that extended to complete a square.

The first room inside the front door was the drawing room, where a black foot-bellows organ, originally intended for the chapel, was the main focus of the decor. Before the musical instrument had arrived, delayed due to size and a crate marked "Fragile," the administration had determined that this masterpiece would be wasted on indigenous people, who, as far as the white clergy could tell, had no true sense of tone and rhythm. In fact, this race had no songs of any religious nature. In all their history, they seemed to have developed little culturally. Since the only words the natives set to music seemed to be absurd stories, the organ remained in the protective custody of the white drawing room.

The house had bare wooden floors and contained an array of European furniture. In both bedrooms there was the traditional washstand and pottery bowl, but only in the guest bedroom did the chamber pot display hand-painted roses matching the shaving mug for male visitors.

On the north side of the house was a water barrel on a tall stand and pipes running from it to the house. The kitchen had running water, a modern advance for such a remote location. Though the water tower for the population of the entire community stood higher and could accommodate more volume, the Enrights' personal supply was always greater.

In the center of the complex there was a barren four-post roofed area where an attempt had been made to create a single central public eating zone, but it hadn't been successful. The foreign administration did not understand that one could not force together small nations of tribal people, some archrivals, and achieve overnight harmony and the white man's standards of peace. To the Enrights and their European friends, all blacks were alike regardless of the tribe. It took the same degree of patience to teach the use of spoon, fork, and bowl. Knives weren't allowed.

Throughout the fenced area were the scattered dwellings the natives had constructed, which the whites called "humpies." They were crude round structures that appeared as if a pile of cardboard, tin, or sticks had merely dropped from the sky in a heap. Rooms or walls were of no interest to the natives. The dwellings provided shade and shelter from the sky. Historically, nomadic tribes rarely built anything, because theirs was a life of continual journeying. This settlement had the remnants of ten different groups of people, each with its unique customs, beliefs, and language. The captives didn't understand one another very well, and few knew English, which was the only form of speech allowed. Some, like the young mother, were exceptionally bright and quick to learn, though most didn't seem to grasp knowledge readily. They had easygoing natures, congenial personalities, and most proved honest and trustworthy.

What the white world did not understand was that these tribal people knew they were in another tribe's nation, on land that was marked by song lines, and where the caretakers had disappeared. The whites were now in control, but were obviously not caretakers. The indigenous people knew they were captives, but still believed they must act as guests who had been invited into someone else's circle. It wasn't difficult to convert them to Christianity when they understood it was the new law and it was further explained that Jesus was a hero. Unbeknownst to the church staff, the Aborigines were very respectful of heroes. Their songs and dances, which had been passed on for thousands of years, contained many heroic people and deeds. Jesus was a great healer who could bring people back from the dead. They were familiar with raising the dead from the work of their own healers.

Since Jesus's father created the world, this father must have been one of their ancestors. Reverend Enright, with his red hair and full red beard, proved to be powerfully persuasive when he stated that there was only one choice regarding forever. One could end up in heaven because of Jesus's intervention, or, if opposed, be cast for all eternity into hell. The people understood how long forever is, but they had never entertained any suggestion of a place like hell.

The young mother spent the morning distraught, in total confusion. She could not find her babies or her sisters. There was no one to speak to about it. She was barred from entering the white picket fence around the Enright home. She began the day running from place to place and person to person, frantically searching. Eventually she began to walk and look for clues to the disappearance of everyone she loved.

She ate nothing that day and spent her hours in physical and mental agony. Her breast milk dripped. A score of flies collected and walked across the bare and covered areas of her body with equal ease and interest. She could not fathom what was taking place. It was in total conflict with everything she had ever been taught by her people. She remembered what Old One had once said: "The white skins are not bad. They only use their free will to do things that do not smell and taste right for our people." But it was very difficult for this young girl not to judge them. Old One had also said, "I believe they are an earthly test. We must support each other in passing it!" But she had no support. She was alone!

By the end of the day she was in an emotional and mental state she had not known existed. She had discovered she could live in the past. The present was of no interest. Everywhere she looked she saw less of what she knew life was meant to be. But I will not become less, she thought. Yesterday I said, "Whatever is in the highest good, my babies and I are open to experience." Now they have been taken from me. Everything has been taken from me. I will be sad, I will mourn. It is right to do so, because that is how I feel, but I shall always hear my heart repeating, Forever is a long, long time. My children and I are forever spirits. Somehow there is unseen and unfelt love and support on this mysterious and painfully complicated journey. What is the purpose of our lives? I do not know! But I do know there is a perfect purpose and I accept it in sadness!

She was sent to work on a cattle station a few months later and spent her days wearing a calico dress, with a starched apron tied behind her neck and at the small of her back. Black shoes were put on at dawn and carried her from stove to laundry to clothesline to vegetable garden to kitchen again. Her daily routine varied little over the years. She was a quiet person who never again greeted a day with her ancestral morning ritual. For her, there was no new day. She no longer spoke, or dreamed, or participated in activity except her employment. On the surface, she appeared to have given up all hope, all interest in life, perhaps at times to have lost her sanity. In actuality, she was merely surrendering to a situation she could not conquer and, true to her religious beliefs, she would not put energy into something she didn't want to grow. She honored her emotions of grief, and neither influenced nor hindered any other life. She lived only in the silent, peaceful events of her past memory, assuring that her spiritual involvement would be preserved. It became her only reason to continue to exist. She didn't feel that what was happening was right. She did not understand it, but it went beyond having faith in something that conflicted with feelings. The step beyond faith to her people was *knowing*. She accepted what was happening because she knew that heaven's perfect purpose was in charge. Only over time would history record that goodness for all of life everywhere was somehow being given an opportunity to play itself out in this tiny segment of the world.

4

The night Mrs. Enright left the exhausted new mother alone on the green army cot, not caring whether she lived or died, the minister's wife busily bustled about, trying to decide what to do with the babies.

I need a basket to put these children in, Mrs. Enright thought. There was one in her kitchen that would fill the purpose. She started for the house, then came back to pick up the two newborn infants. They were too young to roll off the bare wooden table, but the boy seemed unusually strong. "One never knows about these strange natives. Can't really compare them to us. Better take them to the house."

It was a short walk across the barren dusty compound to the wooden-picket front gate of her residence. Struggling to juggle her load of babies, she managed to unlatch the gate, and pushed it shut with her rump. Once inside, she stepped into the bedroom, hesitating a moment before putting the bare children down upon her most prized possession, a multicolored hand-sewn quilt given to her by her grandmother when Mrs. Enright had left England for Australia four years previously.

The basket she was seeking was stored high up on a kitchen shelf, so she climbed up on a chair to retrieve it. Carrying it ceremoniously to the guest room, she grabbed a pillow from the bed and lined the empty basket. On the back verandah was a cardboard box from the last delivery of flour and sugar, and she brought it inside. She released a deep sigh as she took the other guest pillow and prepared the box for housing and transporting the second infant. Replacing her wonderful goose down pillows would not be easy, but that was a problem to be solved on some future day. Diapers were fashioned by cutting a tea towel in half and folding a half around each of the sleeping infants. She had never seen an Aboriginal baby wrapped in a blanket. There was no need this time.

Alice Enright had taken on the responsibility of handling the troubling little matters that arose from time to time. Her husband the reverend was busy with the overall politics of religious life. He reminded her often of how important it was to his future professional progress that he not be burdened by trivial situations. She worked hard to make his life as comfortable and stress-free as she could in this remote and alien land so far away from their beloved Great Britain. When they had married, there had been concern that she was too young and not emotionally mature enough to deal with an older man, not prepared to represent her half of a religious pair. She tried daily to prove her worth. She knew her husband had never really loved her. He was a male without sexual passion, but, she had to admit, she didn't really love him, either. She was young and had wanted desperately to leave home, to travel, and to see the world. Marrying Reverend Enright and traveling to Australia was an opportunity that presented itself at a perfect time.

She walked to the telephone and picked up the receiver. With phone in hand, she clicked the side switch until the operator answered, then asked to be connected to long distance. Alice knew the local operator remained on the line to listen to the latest events coming from behind the mission walls. Thank heaven they were so remote that most of the juice from her gossip dripped on ears more interested in the nearby community's sinners. "Birdie, it's me. Alice Enright. I'm sorry to be calling you again for help, but I have such an urgent need. I have a newborn boy to be disposed of. Actually, there are two children, twins, but the Catholic orphanage will accept the girl. I had a conversation with them last week when I confirmed that they have room, but of course we were planning on the birth of one, not two. Our weekly mission supply run is scheduled to leave in the morning, but I can have Alex leave tonight and go the extra distance to your place to deliver the boy. Can you get rid of him for me? Can you find someplace for him and help us out?"

The Birdie on the other end of the telephone conversation was the wife of Reverend Willett, a colleague of Reverend Enright's and an elder in the church. She was accustomed to receiving calls from Alice and the other church wives. After all, her husband was the senior member of England's delegation assigned to this tour of foreign duty. That automatically made her the most important matron. She prided herself on never turning down or being defeated by a challenge. She loved it when the younger women said, "There isn't anything that Birdie Willett can't handle."

For forty years the church had been building mission stations to house, civilize, educate, and save the souls of the adult indigenous people extracted from the wilderness. The Catholics had established orphanages for the children. At this point, there were some adult Aborigines who had been reared in institutional enclosures and then been released into society upon reaching age sixteen. So far, there was no sign of the project accomplishing any social success except in the biblical sense of feeding the hungry and giving water to the thirsty. But after age sixteen, the Aborigines were still hungry and thirsty and still looked to the white community to provide for their needs. No one could predict when the end might come, when the last of the savages would be brought to civilization, their heathen ways overcome and some control over their population miraculously administered.

The phone call concluded when Birdie agreed to find a place for the child.

Alice went to the door and waved her arms. "Go get Alex," she shouted into the black night, knowing that one of the detainees who wanted to make a good impression would jump at the chance to please by doing as she commanded. It didn't matter which one. There were always one or two lurking outside her fence. In her mind they were all lumped into one strange and challenging unit of almost human packaging. Shortly thereafter, Alex knocked on the kitchen door. He was thin, looked older than his sixty years, and gave the appearance of always being in need of a bath. Alice told him of her plan. He agreed to take an hour's rest and then embark upon the long drive to Sydney. Alice fixed a glass jug of honey water. Using a baby bottle recently located to save the life of a dying kangaroo joey, she fed the twins before loading the basket and box into the front cushion of the Ford, its rumble seat converted to a carryall.

Alex was a former convict, the son of a convict, the grandson of a convict. When he was released from prison, after serving a sentence of eighteen years for theft, he found himself homeless and with no particular trade and no friends or relatives to call upon. He got into trouble drinking too much, being involved in too many bashings, and was constantly tempted to remove the cash box at pubs and taverns he frequented. Then he found the Lord, or at least he found people who had found the Lord. Apparently he gave the right responses to their questions, because they offered to take him in and find him employment. In the middle of nowhere, when the mission needed a driver, he seemed like a good solution, even if a temporary one. He purchased whiskey on his trips into town, but never drank in the open. So far, everything was working out okay.

With the two babies loaded, the girl for the orphanage in the box, the boy for the city more impressively riding in a basket, Alex began the eight-hour drive. He paused about a mile from the compound to stuff both his ears with sheep's wool. Even though the infants were sleeping, he anticipated a noisy trip. He reached under the seat and rescued a bottle from the dark, took a couple of hearty swigs, and set it between himself and the little people. He drove out across the barren wasteland on the one-lane partially paved trail. Shifts in the air current would cause wind to march through the vehicle's right-side windows. Then there would be no breeze at all. A few miles later the wind would blow through the left windows. The invisible world seemed to be circling the occupants of the car. The terrain remained silent except for the roar of the automobile engine. The black of night was disturbed by a swirl of fine red dust, like a child's spinning top, following the car. Overhead, clouds sailed faster than the earthly vehicle. When a dark cloud periodically covered the moon, the only source of the night's light, the vast flat horizon would vanish into total darkness. It felt to Alex as if a giant hand in the sky was covering the beam of a heavenly flashlight. The cloud would pass quickly and the source of light would once again appear. "It's almost a Morse code, dot, dot, dash, coming from nature." He took another drink of whiskey. He didn't like the eerie feeling that thought evoked. "I hope it's not an SOS distress signal!" he remarked to himself.

The box containing the female child was delivered first, as the orphanage was located about halfway through the journey. Alex accepted the cup of tea and the two Arnott biscuits offered by the Sister on night duty, but he didn't linger long and was careful to stay smelling distance away. When he returned to the vehicle, the other child appeared to be sleeping satisfactorily, but the dust, contaminating fumes, and lack of food were taking their toll. The child did not utter a peep for the remainder of the drive and only slightly stirred as the sun broke into dawn. Finally, the automobile wound its way up brick paving on an exclusive street in front of a row of magnificent homes built on the cliff overlooking the world's most beautiful harbor. The Willett residence was a hand-hewn quarry-stone mansion fronted by four tall, white columns. Anyone strolling along the walk front could hear the distant sound of the ocean as it crashed against the shore in the cove below. The spectacular view was reserved for those privileged enough to peer out the upper-floor rear windows or be invited to relax on the pristine stone patio carved out of the cliff. The expanse of grass and the flowering borders in the front led to a line of tall trees that marked the driveway entrance, which then circled past two storage garages and terminated under an ornamental portico on the north side. Alex drove into a circle drive and then to the side of the property, where the carved wooden door was inscribed with a brass plate that read DELIVERIES. The baby was now gasping for clean air, his stomach distended with fluid he could not digest and his body twisted with pain, but he arrived in silence, surrendering to the environment.

Birdie Willett considered herself the most powerful woman of the church organization in all of Australia. She had everything under control. The ministers' wives were all her juniors. She made it a practice not to let any one of them be chairman of a committee for a second time. They could get a little administrative experience, but not enough to build confidence, attract a following, or enjoy it so much they might volunteer for more. She was involved in overseeing Sunday School curriculum statewide and in setting up all new mission locations, including the building sites. All programs for the elderly, all charity campaigns, all church outings and decorations were channeled to her for approval. She controlled everything except how ministers and their wives dressed, but she made up for that by ordering absolutely everything Reverend Willett wore, from head to toe, including his gray socks and undershorts.

She was so busy serving on garden committees and choir robe committees and planning holiday menus months in advance that she really couldn't be bothered trying to place a stray Aboriginal baby. She would ship it off to the country and tend to it later, but, to uphold her reputation, she must appear to Alice Enright as absolutely 100 percent efficient.

She advised her husband that he must perform a baptism that day. It could be done in their kitchen sink. She saw no reason to waste a Christian name on a savage, so she decided on Geoff. That was neutral enough. A last name would come later, if it ever proved necessary. Most of the time it didn't. Aborigines weren't involved in legal matters.

Reverend Willett said the prayers and poured water over baby Geoff's lifeless head. Neither adult knew why he appeared so unresponsive. Many native babies died, so this one probably would too. The minister was in a hurry. He recorded the entry in the church log and then left abruptly, knowing Birdie would handle everything that needed attention today and love doing it. He was on his way to minister to a poor lost soul named Shirley who was trying to change from a life of prostitution to being a good girl. It was his sixth visit. So far, she was losing the struggle and seemed to be taking the dear reverend along for the ride.

Geoff remained in the glorious house only as long as it took to perform the baptism and to locate a country family, on their semiannual shopping spree in Sydney, who were willing to add the Aboriginal child's basket to their other parcels being loaded onto the train for a return trip to a country community. The Hanovers had a nine-year-old daughter, Abigail, who took over the feeding and caring of the little brown boy with more devotion than that given to her lovely china doll. He responded remarkably. In spite of the long train ride, soon after they reached their home, a workman was dispatched to transport the almost recovered child on the next leg of his journey. At the age of seventy-two hours, the twin had severed all connection to his blood heritage, traveled four hundred miles, received the name Geoff, and would now become the ward of a wealthy white rural family. He was to go to Birdie's sister and brother-in-law, Matty and Howard Willett.

5

Her earliest memory was looking up at the white flesh under Doreen's chin as she was plucked off the tile floor and deposited in a round tin tub of cold water. Standing up, holding onto the side, she was fascinated by the scum surface that was level with her throat. The oily content made the water appear to be of glistening rainbow colors. She had either lost her grip reaching for the shimmering image or had tried to take a step when her feet suddenly slipped and she was underwater. She later remembered the struggle to breathe, to find something to grasp, and recalled the gray-blurred view as fear of the unknown filled her heart and lungs. Miraculously, she found the ledge. She coughed and cried until Doreen returned to the room. Her first memory of this world was of terror. It was registered at the age of two.

She was the last of a group of little girls in the care of the Mercy Sisters Orphanage to be dunked or, more appropriately described, bathed. Doreen said she was always last because she was the shortest, but the other kids said it was because she was the ugliest. They were all ugly. She knew that from repeatedly hearing the adults say so. She now began to understand what it was to be singled out as the ugliest. They were all different colors, different degrees of black, like the tea Doreen drank each day, adding drops of cream to vary the shade, only the shading was the result of a lost mother and an unknown father.

She became a ward of the church only hours after her birth. Their procedure was to name girls in alphabetical order, starting with the letter "A" each year. Since it was January and she was the second arrival in 1936, her name became Beatrice. She never knew anything about her parents or the rest of her family. In later years, she tried to imagine what it might have been like to have parents, a loving mother, a caring father, maybe even a sister or brother, but trying to picture that was more difficult than sleeping with her eyes open. She had lived her entire existence as no one's daughter and always felt very old.

When they prayed at Mass or at meals, she would study the backs of the other little girls' hands, folded in prayer. They had lovely smooth skin, but her hands had veins rippling on the surface, like the elevated terrain around the institution, and matched those of old, withering Sister Agatha, the superior in charge. The nuns wore long black habits, their heads covered by a black veil held in place by starched white trim. Sister Agatha's hair was not visible, but she had an old pruneface and white eyebrows that gave away her vintage.

From an early age Beatrice somehow seemed to know her role as peacemaker. When arguments started among the children or someone was left out and felt lonely, it was natural for her to step in to soothe, to try to bring understanding to both sides. She had always been aware of other people's feelings; she could tell from listening to their voices, not necessarily to their words, and by paying attention to their eyes. She was able to sense how others felt long before understanding this sensitivity and accepting it as a gift.

There were always others around her. Rarely did she find herself in a room alone, but it did not fill the void she felt. She didn't know what was missing, or why she felt lacking, but she did. A visitor one day commented that it was good that orphans didn't miss the things they had never known. Beatrice absorbed the remark, but it wasn't true. She could not identify what was missing, but she certainly did feel incomplete.

One day she overheard a Sister suggesting to someone else that Beatrice was strange because of her peculiar interest in other girls. The nun implied that she would turn out to be a lesbian. The remark embedded itself deeply, although Beatrice had no idea what the word meant. From the adult's demeanor, she knew it couldn't be good.

Reverend Willett's brother, Howard, and his wife, Matty, owned an enormous sheep and cattle station. Respected and feared by everyone, Howard was head of his family, his station, and the surrounding area. He was a tall, muscular man with a thick head of sandy blond hair always in need of combing. His legs seemed bowed, from straddling a saddle. Because he spent every day out in the open air, regardless of the weather, his skin appeared more like creased leather than human flesh. When they had married, ten years earlier in England, Matty had been a short, fragile, perfectly shaped woman whom men and women stopped to view a second time. Now, after years away from luxury, a daily routine of farming chores, and the birth of her two sons, Abram, three, and Noah, seven, she retained only the original physical characteristic of being short. She was a warm and pleasant person whom neighbors believed helped balance the hard, ruthless, male head of the Willett dynasty. She had agreed to take the native child, whom she was told had been abandoned, after having told Howard it would be temporary, or at least the child would be welcome only if he caused no trouble and eventually did his share of the work. They had no experience with the Aboriginal race of people. After all, they lived in a part of the country where no Aborigines lived. The Willetts had heard stories from others and had already formed a negative opinion. In summation, they believed what they had heard, "There are no smart Abos. Most are lazy, and as adults they remain like carefree children. It is a race of people who never grow up, never become responsible."

In the case of Geoff there was no consideration of adoption or even any official paperwork registered. In the 1930s a child's fate was managed by phone calls, handshakes, a three-line entry in a mission journal, and one line in a church baptismal registry. When Geoff arrived he was given to a kitchen employee who began to feed him a series of every sort of animal milk available until, on the fourth day, his digestive system finally adapted. Thereafter, each day he was bathed, his diaper was changed, and he was put in a crib in the shade of a large old pepper tree just outside the kitchen door. He spent every day there from dawn to dusk, employees passing by and talking to him, until he learned to climb out of the crib. At that point he graduated to a blanket on the green ground cover with one end of a rope tied around his waist and the other to a tree trunk. At age two he deliberately made it a goal and mastered untying the knot that held him captive, even though the tree was his only dependable friend. He had learned to run and crash into the arms of the tree that hugged him and cradled him when he napped. He had outgrown the fifteen-foot area in which he could roam. When he was found freely exploring his new world, one of the middle-aged employees, a woman named Maude, introduced him to farm chores. He helped her pull vegetables in the garden, gather eggs from the henhouse, and stack little pieces of wood. She gave him a broken handle broom, short enough for him to manage. He was a busy and happy two-year-old, left on his own much of the time.

Maude had worked for Howard Willett before he returned from England a married man. They had grown up together, she liked to think. In reality, Howard was six years her senior and had always been wealthy. He had taken over the family property when his father died, because Birdie, his sister-in-law, was in the driver's seat at his younger brother's home. She had no desire ever to leave the metropolitan life, so she forced her husband to forfeit a large portion of his inheritance in exchange for family jewelry, fine china, delicate linens, and imported cloth. Howard had given her free run of his parents' quarters after their funeral and she managed to find enough wonderful items to fill the back of a truck that she'd hired to deliver them to her in Sydney.

Maude was from a much less affluent background. Her parents had homesteaded their property next to what developed into a regional cattle-drive trail. The location had been beautiful originally, next to a river lined with magnificent shade trees and plenty of water for irrigating crops. It also proved to be in the way of a natural, almost straight line for the already existing cattle barons in that part of the country to use to move herds to the railroad and on to the market. It was all the young couple could do to try to protect a small area for their own vegetable garden. They constantly had to contend with hooves trampling everything around the house and between their front porch and the river. It was almost impossible to keep even chickens alive.

The problem was compounded when it didn't rain for two years and the water level severely decreased. The other settlers won the favor from the government barring any dams or irrigation off the river. Maude's parents' crops barely survived with water used from buckets on each plant. They had no money to move from the area or to build another house. Maude, their only child, attended church and school with the Willett brothers. She probably fell in love with Howard when he was fourteen and she was eight. There weren't many other boys to make the choice difficult. Over the years, new prospects didn't arrive. When Howard's mother became ill, Maude was summoned to work for the family and stayed through the matron's death and, later, her husband's.

Howard had always been polite and formal to Maude. He stopped swearing when she entered the room to serve his male friends, depending on the group, either tea or rounds of beer. He had not made any advances toward her. Before his trip to England there had been one occasion when he'd come into the kitchen and, while conversing with the household help, told a funny story. Maude was certain he had winked at her. When he came home from the motherland with a bride, it had been a surprising, shattering experience. She was left with maternal feelings but with no marriage in sight. Her interest in little two-year-old Geoff was natural. She couldn't quite force herself to accept him because of his black skin, but she did her best to keep him busy and out of danger. She did believe he was happy being able to wander freely and never seemed to miss not having a mother or a family or a warm hand to hold. He never learned to kiss or hug another person.

As an infant Geoff was fed in a high chair. Later he learned to feed himself by climbing onto a stool in the kitchen of the main house and using a pull-out bread board as his personal table. He heard Abram and Noah call Matty "Mum" and Howard "Dad," but he was taught to address these two station owners as everyone else did, calling them ma'am and sir. He had little direct contact with the family members. They usually shooed him away like a pesky insect. There was no one individual ever relegated to be responsible for Geoff. Since female workers came and went with the seasons, there was a continual flow of motherlike guides. He was always alone, yet somehow physically cared for.

At the age of three he began to eat all his meals with the other hired hands either in the large outer shed or outdoors under the trees on crudely constructed picnic tables. He loved to hear the stories of what had happened each day. Many times there were visitors who dropped in for a meal of lamb stew, fried potatoes, fresh vegetables, biscuits, and jam and honey in exchange for a day's work and a night's lodging. Strangers always told fascinating tales of faraway places and exciting events. Most of the travelers were drovers, men alone on horseback with a sleeping roll and a tin frying pan tied behind their saddles. Occasionally, travelers arrived in an automobile or a horse and wagon loaded down with pots and pans hanging off like metal fringe and sounding like an untrained drummer. Drovers sometimes were accompanied by a rugged female companion who looked as if she could use a good scrubbing and a change of shoes. If there were children with them, they seemed to be extremely withdrawn and would hide the entire time the couple visited.

On one occasion two children came for the day to work with their father, but Geoff could never get them to speak. Even when the man sat drinking beer, telling tales, and promising to look for relatives of the Willett employees to relay a message, the children stood behind a tree and refused to come out. They didn't even acknowledge Geoff's offer to show them some magnificent rare black tadpoles. It was his earliest memory of studying such sad eyes and hearing in silence the moan of another human being.

The Willett station was a place of continual activity. The house was three stories high; the top floor had six small dormer windows that provided light for a giant ballroom that was rarely used. It was an impressive square building with long narrow windows on the two lower floors, each marked by a set of green wood shutters for closing against the summer heat and the eventual wet season's torrential rains. Across the front, a verandah reached from corner to corner and European chairs provided two separate areas for tea party gatherings. The house was bordered on all four sides in brilliant color. Roses gave it white, pink, and red tones. Marigolds blended bright lemon with pale yellow. The entrance was a gravel drive through fifty-foot-tall ghost gum trees. Two massive water tanks stood behind the house. They were used for drinking, cooking, and the Willett family wash. Rainwater was too scarce and precious to be given to the animals or to be used for irrigating the fields, so deep wells pumped fluid that stank of highly concentrated sulfur. This water was used for the livestock and crops. Humans could not consume the well water, but they were forced to deal with eggs and slaughtered meat that contained the residue. The property actually had a constant rank odor that, according to the season, was rotten or slightly less rotten.

The house had twelve rooms to keep dusted, five bedrooms to keep in clean sheets, and there were always more new modern gadgets to be incorporated, like the first electrically powered washing machine. Dust was a major factor with which to contend. In the dry season it was so fine it was impossible to remove. It collected on the floors and furniture and in the folds of the curtains and towels. A sleeping person's head was outlined on the pillow when he arose.

A daily duty was to change flypaper. From the ceiling in each room a long spiral of sticky paper hung that captured the body of any fly daring to come within touching distance. The strips were changed each morning, because there was never any room left for another creature by the end of the day. Most flies died quickly, but Geoff was always saddened when he observed paper that continued to wiggle after he deposited it in the trash container.

To the rear of the main house, behind the water towers, was the remaining Willett empire, almost a town of its own. There were streets separating sheds for blacksmithing and repairing and storing machinery; there were food storage bins, stockmen's quarters, a horse barn, a dormitory for household help, dog kennels, pigpens, chicken houses, donkey pens, separate slaughter buildings for pigs and cattle, miles of animal pens. The sheep were housed in their own buildings, and in another section there was a full dairy. The structures had been strategically placed as they were constructed over the years, with pepper trees providing precious shade.

The sheep required permanent employees dedicated to handling breeding, lambing, and disease control. Shearing season required additional helpers and was the year's greatest athletic feat. Overall, complex administration was necessary to oversee the food that must be planted, harvested, canned, and stored to feed all the personnel and the Willett family.

Geoff followed men and women workers as they did their chores and observed each facet of station life. He helped when possible and loved all of it, from seeing baby chicks crack out of the shell to mixing and stuffing intestinal tubes with sausage. He had no supervision, so his time could be spent sometimes watching the kangaroos jump fences with ease, or gathering up a green-and-black football-shaped emu egg and struggling, until it broke, to cart it home. He sat mesmerized watching termites build tall sculptures and spiders spin webs, and capturing lizards, grasshoppers, and dragonflies. Each time a snake was discovered in the populated area of the station, he listened carefully until he could recognize the difference between the harmless and the deadly ones. Adult caution was gruffly barked out, so he preferred being self-taught. He often wished he had someone he could tell about his day's great adventure, like the morning he discovered a little spider that ran from him and entered a hole in the ground complete with a closing trapdoor. Or the time he found a big hairy spider larger than his hand sitting next to him. In the paddock there were birds of all colors that changed with the seasons. He learned to imitate their sounds. He knew their favorite feeding spots. With his pocket filled full of delectables, he could entice a brave few to take the riches from his young, innocent, extended palm. He was born with such great patience and adaptability that he managed to blend in with a mother duck and swim with her ducklings.

He found that when he stood in the right spot, out of anyone's way, and remained silent, he could observe any activity and was not questioned or even noticed. During sheep-shearing season, while thousands of sheep had to be separated and graded, there were lots of extra people around. The kitchen was filled with stomping feet, splashing water, potato peels, and wondrous smells. The actual shearing took place in a large, specially designed shed and was a contest of speed and skill that lasted for days. No one was held accountable for Geoff. No one looked for him or made any inquiry into his whereabouts. For days, he received kitchen handouts whenever he wanted, joined the cheering crowd, or climbed into a quiet corner and took a nap. He had learned to be totally alone in a crowd of people.

His education came from experience, not from a book, like the day the ground and air were so dry the energy created caused the sky to darken, as if a tremendous rainstorm would soon occur. Continuous lightning bolts lit up the black heavens. As Geoff stood looking out across a field, a tree only a few yards away burst into flame. The animals screamed and ran for cover. The air seemed to be sucked in one direction and then propelled back with ten times its original force. Geoff, too, ran and hid under a canvas tarp hanging from the tailgate of an old wagon. The storm lasted all day, but not one drop of water ever arrived. Finally, when hunger would no longer allow him to honor his fear, he ran to the kitchen. There was no offer from any adult to console the youngster, and no one asked where he had been, but he did learn from listening to the conversation that a dry storm had occurred. He was becoming more and more self-sufficient by the day.

Geoff loved the baby lambs and watched as they were

born. He observed as each was identified and marked. They squealed as their tiny tails were put into a ring of thin metal, which was then clamped shut. The ring was designed not to expand. In a couple of days the little tail would swell and look infected, but, after a while, it would begin to shrink and would finally fall off. At the age of four he became a participant in one of these bloody ordeals, with the result that he had nightmares for months. All of the male lambs, with the exception of a chosen few, had to have their testicles removed. There were hundreds of animals and only one day allotted for the work. The employees used the method most common on sheep stations. They grabbed each creature, turned it over, and bit off the protrusion. It was Geoff's job to collect the piece as it was spit out upon the ground and put it into a bucket. He suffered alone as he did what was asked of him. He had no one to turn to for answers to his questions. His emotional experiences of sympathy and horror were never released or shared.

At the end of the day, his toes were stuck together with matted mud and blood. The worker who seemed to notice him most and helped him on this occasion was a man named Roger. Rogg, as he was called by his friends, set little Geoff up on the picnic table with his feet soaking in a bucket of soapy water; he remained there for over an hour until Rogg remembered and came with a towel to rescue him and tell him he could go. It seemed he was too small to take a shower and no one paid any attention to a detail such as how the child would clean the blood from his body.

The sheep also developed dags, the excrement that stuck to the wool on the rear of each animal and attracted blowflies. Geoff was assigned to help pick up the filthy mass as the sheep were crutched and the dags sheared away. He was involved in sheep dipping, done for medical purposes, and called upon to join the dogs in moving herds from one paddock to another. The part he hated most was the ultimate slaughter.

The remote Australian station was a place of wonder and beauty for this little boy, but it was also a place of horror where headless chickens tried to walk with blood spurting from their severed necks until they finally flopped back and forth over the ground until dead. It was a place where he saw animals shot, throats slit, and testicles bitten off. The same people who committed these acts would motion for him to come sit down with them while someone played a banjo or a harmonica and everyone clapped their hands and sang songs. At times it was very confusing. Nothing was ever pointed out to him as good or bad, right or wrong. He only knew what he enjoyed and what he wanted to avoid.

7

As a youngster barely of school age, Beatrice's sense of being old was already so strong that one day, after acting as the go-between in a fistfight between girls two years older, she was absolutely certain her face had turned into that of an old lady. She broke the rules and entered the forbidden front entrance hall without permission. She knew there was a mirror on the coatrack and she had to see what she looked like. When she saw that her appearance hadn't changed, she rejoiced. There was still a six-year-old face staring back at her. It was a great soul awakening, to know that she could feel so strongly that she was something which by observation she was not. She had discovered living in two worlds, being two people, and it became a guarded secret that served her well the rest of her life.

The orphanage maintained a military life. The girls were taught to stand straight and tall and marched everywhere—to eat, to bed, to church, to school, everywhere. They always marched behind closed doors, in long hallways, or in the fenced-in outdoor grounds. The army of barefoot little girls usually marched to music played on a wind-up Victrola. It was an atmosphere of "Get up, stand up, hurry up, line up, and shut up!"

For Beatrice, childhood was a series of memories linked to the whirling blades of a fan. The schoolrooms where she spent 80 percent of her young years were long rooms with open glassless windows on each side. Wooden shutters were pushed outward by protruding boards. When visitors arrived, the occasion was always marked by the arrival of an electric fan, which gently pushed the warm air. The dining hall had an overhead ceiling fan that remained motionless unless some outsider was staying for tea.

Life at the institution was so rigidly scheduled that each day and each year remained basically unchanged. There were only a few incidents that stood out vividly in Beatrice's mind.

It was extremely hot the summer she was six. For days there was no breeze, no relief from the heat whatsoever, as if God had turned off an electrical switch in the heavens and all of life had been put on hold. The sky remained pale blue from horizon to horizon, not one cloud daring to break nature's pattern. There were no birds making sounds and the ground was already so dry it had cracked open to reveal mini-caverns she could drop a stick into and watch disappear. It had been a week since a worm or beetle had crawled out in the open, and even the pesky flies seemed too hot to bother irritating her skin.

Late in the day, just before bed curfew, she came upon an old dented delivery truck bringing water to the compound. It had an open cab attached to a flatbed, with the round metal fluid container precariously held in place by aged ropes. The truck was parked outside the office building and was unattended. She saw a tin cup wired to a little spigot, probably used by the driver for an occasional drink. There wasn't a soul in sight. With a minimum of struggle she freed the cup from the grasp of the metal fingers. Placing it under the nozzle, she filled the container. The first mouthful tasted warm and murky, but still refreshing, so she drank it all, and had another cup, and another cup, and then another. Her heart was beating so fast she was certain anyone could see it by looking at her chest. She was experiencing a new feeling, a sense of power, for the first time in her life. She was in control and could drink an unlimited amount of a beverage, all of it if she wanted. She had no feeling that what she was doing was forbidden, even though the long list of "you must not" items didn't mention water trucks. No one saw her. She didn't get caught. She refastened the rusty cup and slipped into the dormitory room just before bedtime.

A few hours later, in the dark of night, she was awakened by a very warm, soothing sensation that quickly changed into something cold, wet, and odoriferous. She had wet the bed. She lay there for what seemed an eternity, even though it was difficult to lie still. It seemed worse to have the wet mess touch a dry place on her skin. Just before dawn, the smell and the crime were discovered. Young pimple-faced Sister Margaret screamed as if a fire were erupting, waking all those sleeping in the room. She shoved Beatrice into the center of the aisle that separated two rows of iron bunk beds and continued screaming at the top of her voice. "You little demon, you did this on purpose. You won't get away with making me clean up that mess. You'll regret this stunt. Believe me, you'll be sorry for this prank. Full of the devil, you are. The devil's child."

Sister Margaret pulled her by the hair into the door of Sister Agatha's quarters, awakening the nun from her sleep. Beatrice stared at the old woman with the short white hair. When informed of what the fuss was about, Sister Agatha delegated the responsibility of punishment to Sister Margaret and then the Mother Superior returned to her slumber. As Beatrice was being dragged away, her mind was temporarily diverted from concern about punishment for the crime. She thought to herself, I knew she had white hair!

Outside, at the rear of the complex, were two metal doors guarding entrances into separate earthen holes. One chamber was about five feet by five feet and the other three by three. In less than five minutes, Beatrice found herself, still wearing the urine-soaked underwear, being forced, along with her soiled bedsheet, into the smallest of the hand-dug dungeons. She had observed the doors in the hillside and known of other girls who had disappeared and sometimes returned very ill, saying they had been punished. She hadn't realized anyone was ever put into the hillside coffins. Inside it was pitch black, and there was no fresh air. When she touched the wall or ceiling, dirt fell, so she sat curled in a ball, motionless, afraid she would soon be buried when the cave collapsed. She held her breath as something crawled over her leg and prayed not to be bitten by a poisonous creature. Before long she was gagging on the stale, putrid atmosphere and searched for a crack of fresh air around the door, but there was none. During the day the inhuman hole became an oven, and the stench caused her to gag and vomit. It was so hot that she collapsed. When she passed out from exhaustion after hours of crying and pleading for help, her face was blistered from having been pressed against the burning heat of the metal door. She woke to find herself on a cot with a visiting physician who told her she must be suffering from some rare and probably contagious disease, so all the others would be kept away from her for thirty days. Everyone was forbidden to touch, to look, or even to speak to her during the next month.

The lesson extracted from that experience as a child was to believe that God's vengeance for the sin of taking too much water or for urinating in the wrong place could only be satisfied by personal, physical torture. The man in the sky became the first on her list of what brought apprehension.

At the age of six she was also removed from the adoption rolls. Periodically she had been given a nice dress to wear, her feet had been temporarily encased in shoes, her short, snarled hair had been brushed, and ribbons had been added to cover the mass that couldn't be untangled. Hand in hand the girls would be paraded before Anglican couples who studied them carefully, as if they were specimens on exhibit. After one woman commented about the disfiguring scar left on Beatrice's burned face, it was decided there was no longer any point in offering her to the public.

8

Geoff was seven when he first discovered the art of drawing. There had been no previous occasion for him to observe pictures or writing. He saw the cooks refer to written instructions periodically, knew the supply driver was handed a list of objects to obtain weekly, and had seen from a distance the Willett sons turning the pages of books. He didn't understand what was happening, and it held no interest for him until he discovered a magazine.

One day he was following a puppy that went inside the community dormitory, which contained beds for the female hired help. When the pup disappeared under a bed, Geoff went crawling after it. A stack of brightly colored magazines caught his eye. He pulled one out. As he thumbed through the pages he became deeply entranced by the places and things shown in each picture. He was still sitting there an hour later when Irene, a housemaid, came in. She saw the child and invited him to sit upon her bed as she explained what each photograph represented. Then she took out a pencil and paper and printed the alphabet. She told Geoff that when he learned to read, he could find out for himself why the pictures appeared in each article.

The boy started to copy the letters as Irene had demonstrated, but soon became more interested in drawing duplications of the strange animals pictured in the magazines.

Irene provided more sheets of paper as the child escaped into the world of an artist. Later that day she encouraged him to look around the station and draw the creatures he liked most. Two days later Irene approached Geoff on the front lawn with a handful of broken crayon pieces. She explained that he could add color to his drawings and showed him the techniques for lightly adding a finish or pressing harder for deeper tones.

The seven-year-old Aboriginal boy obviously had natural talent. Without any instructions, he was producing framable art. He could observe a horse in the corral and copy his mental picture down to the smallest details. When Irene pointed out that the horse was not alone, that there were trees in the background or a building also in view, he immediately incorporated her suggestions. He seemed automatically to understand dimensions viewed from a distance. After only a few unsuccessful attempts, his pictures became alive. He taught himself to show shadows and shades of color, matching his personal vision. Irene told him she had heard that Aboriginal people were very artistic. He didn't know what she meant by Aboriginal people, but he smiled and accepted her comment because it seemed she was telling him something good about himself.

In the back of the magazine, Irene saw an ad that said,

"Copy Me." There was a simple line drawing and instructions to all interested parties to submit their artwork to a correspondence school for a free evaluation. She asked Geoff to copy the pattern without explaining why and bundled up the copy along with six other drawings. They were submitted to the school address under her name.

Only seventeen, Irene was a youngster herself. She was one of twelve children belonging to the Foley mob. She was accustomed to working hard, helping to raise her brothers and sisters, doing the household chores and the gardening. When the Willetts mentioned needing a maid and offered to pay a salary plus room and board, her parents readily volunteered their daughter. Irene didn't mind. The work was easier than it had been at home, but she did miss the little ones. She had seen Geoff running around the vast estate, but had not spent any time talking to him except an occasional salutation in passing. She knew enough about children's abilities to recognize that he was exceptionally talented in drawing.

The reply from the correspondence course arrived six weeks later, just as a monumental decision regarding Geoff's future was taking place in the Willett household. An American minister, Albert Marshall, and his wife, Nora, had been visiting Australia and had been sent by Reverend Willett in Sydney to visit his brother, Howard, on their country station. The Marshalls were considering adopting an indigenous orphan, but didn't want to travel with an infant. Geoff immediately popped into mind. He was a quiet child, no trouble, self-sufficient, and in need of an education. The Willetts and the Marshalls sat in the parlor discussing the possibility on the very evening Irene had received a glowing report on the artwork she had submitted as an adult entry.

Irene called Geoff into the kitchen to tell him the art school felt this artist should have lessons to further his natural talent and had sent a gift. The school had no way of knowing the drawings were the work of a seven-year-old. The gift mailed to Irene was a metal box, brightly painted in primary colors, which contained ten colored pencils, a paintbrush, and ten watercolor paints. Geoff's eyes were as big a hen's eggs when Irene handed him the box and told him it was his. Enthusiastically, he opened the case and stared at the bright colors and the blank paper Irene was offering him.

Geoff was sitting on his favorite stool, a saucer of water at his side, exploring the world of watercolors, when he was summoned into the parlor. He clutched his prize and first personal possession in a tight fist as he slowly walked into the red-wallpapered room with its polished floors and thick-cushioned furniture. He was more apprehensive than he would have been approaching an unidentified snake. The Marshalls introduced themselves and Nora held his shoulder firmly as she patted his head. When they asked what he had in his hand, he reluctantly released his grip and opened the metal snap to reveal the colored jewels. The prize was quickly dismissed with a mere, "That's nice, yes, that's nice." To his great relief, he was soon dismissed.

9

Freda came to the orphanage when Beatrice was seven. Since she was the sixth arrival that year she received an "F" name, even though she was nine years old and had been someone else all those years. There were no exceptions to administrative rule. Freda was slow, her entire body moved slowly, and she spoke with hesitations and stuttering. Beatrice was the only girl in the institution who offered her friendship. The two developed a true bond of sisterhood. Freda could learn her school lessons and avoid the punishment of being deprived of a meal or having her hands slapped with a ruler if Beatrice diligently drilled her on the material over and over. They were both so proud when she finally got something memorized.

All the girls had to learn the prayers and memorize the answers to the First Communion catechism questions. Once in class Beatrice asked what the term "Holy Ghost" meant.

"Your friend's stupidity is rubbing off," the angry nun teaching the class shouted in disgust. "Go sit in the hall before you infect everyone else."

Making your First Communion was not something ever to be questioned. Church rules and house rules were to be followed to the letter and never doubted for a moment. Freda did not master getting the catechism answers out fast enough, even though she knew them correctly, so she failed to receive the body and blood of Jesus. The girls believed his dead body was taken off the cross and that part of it was made into a loaf of bread. Then it could be sliced into paper-thin wafers and gently placed upon an extended tongue by the priest during First Communion.

The girls wore small black veils on their heads during Mass each day, but for First Communion they received white ones. It was an act of humiliation to sit wearing a black veil after the age of Communion, but Freda bore the degrading mark with only an occasional quivering lip.

One day Beatrice discovered that Freda seemed to be able to sing without stammering over words. Together they developed a method where she silently hummed musical notes in her head while she spoke. Even though she continued to have small pauses in her speech, she became able to communicate more directly and clearly. The following year she could pass the verbal test. Without doubt, acquiring the white chapel veil was the highlight of her entire life.

Freda was different from the rest of the orphans in her appearance. She was tall, a few pounds overweight, and had straight auburn hair. She was much lighter in complexion, with very green eyes. Beatrice could never figure out why her friend was so despised by the adult administration of the school. They called her "Stupid" so often that it became a title she acknowledged. Beatrice was the only person who used her name. Freda couldn't see anything well, neither at a distance nor close up. In all her years of living with the Mercy Sisters, Beatrice never saw a child obtain eyeglasses. They were considered too much of a luxury for orphans.

The fence around the asylum was made of chain. Large bushes had been planted that matured to cover the wire completely with dense foliage of several feet on each side. The land throughout this part of Australia was of such high mineral content that almost any vegetation could grow if it received adequate water. The greenery made the school yard a more attractive enclosure when visitors viewed it. For practical purposes, the institution was almost escape-proof. The Mercy Sisters rarely ventured out into the schoolyard. They seemed to avoid the direct bright sun. At recess, unlocking the door for a line of marching students to exit was as involved as they cared to be.

One August day Beatrice heard a slight whimper in the far corner of the yard. Crawling under the bushes with Freda at her heels, they discovered an orange-colored dog. It had been shot in the neck and apparently had crawled away to die in peace. The two girls talked about getting adult help for the creature, but both decided that would only result in an instant, fatal blow. Instead, they resolved to do as much as they could. In the afternoon Beatrice managed to look the dog up in a reference book and identified it as a wild dingo.

Each girl was responsible for a tin plate, a tin cup, and a spoon, fork, and knife. After eating, they stood in line, swished the items in a container of water, wiped them dry, and piled them on a table for reuse. No garbage was allowed. Each student ate everything on her plate. If by chance something was left, it was set aside and left for the next meal until it finally disappeared.

At supper that evening Freda and Beatrice put scraps of food into their pockets. They even managed to rescue a soup can from the trash while on pot- and pan-washing duty. Allowed out to the yard before bed, and with Freda acting as sentry, Beatrice put the can of water and the food through the wire squares near the dog's head. The poor creature didn't stir or make a sound, but Beatrice could tell it was still breathing.

The next day, when they went to check on who they now considered their patient, the water can had been toppled over, and the food was gone. There in the curve between the wild dingo's legs were three nursing newborn pups.

The puppies complicated the situation. They decided to confide in three other students for help in caring for and protecting the day-old litter. It became a great adventure. They even managed to smuggle out a bottle of iodine, which Beatrice succeeded in pouring into the bullet hole. They had to feed and give water to the mother, take turns covering up the noise of the squirming pups, and pray that somehow, against all odds, the mother would live long enough to give her offspring a fighting chance of survival. The dog lay there day after day under the bush. One day her head looked as if rice had been sprinkled on it. Beatrice reached through the barrier and picked off a piece. It wiggled in her hands. Maggots had taken up residence in the festering sore. This sad dingo lay in the same position for five weeks, struggling to eat and drink and stay alive to nurse her babies. The pups had become too noisy for the girls to hide. Sister Margaret found them. She immediately called for a child to bring her a box and deposited all three little dingos inside. The girls thought that was the end of their four-legged friends, that they wouldn't see them again, but they were wrong.

Following dinner that evening, Sister Margaret summoned the five girls after forcing the names of each participant from one of the others. They were taken to the laundry room where the pups were being kept in an orange crate in the center of the room. Sister Margaret told Beatrice to fill the laundry tub with water. Freda had to get a flour sack from the corner, put a big rock in it, and hold it open while each of the other three girls put a pup inside. Then Sister Margaret tied the sack shut with a twine knot and dropped it into the water. The pups struggled and cried as the white cloth sank to the bottom. One corner bobbed to the surface. From the sounds and movement, the girls knew the three tiny creatures struggled for several minutes, fighting and clawing one another to get to the top, to stay alive. Finally, in disgust, Sister Margaret went to the kitchen and returned carrying a heavy iron-skillet lid. She rolled up her long black sleeve, stretched out her eerie, ghost-white arm, and put the iron cover over the sack, forcing it to the bottom of the tub. All the while this was taking place, she was talking to the girls, but it seemed more like babbling than talking. She went on and on about wild things, dangerous, infected creatures, about Jesus trying to save their evil savage souls, and suggested that wild people's offspring would be better off never having been born.

At last she took four of the girls outside to dig a hole for the dead pups. Beatrice had to carry the heavy, dripping sack. Freda was left inside to mop the floor. With each shovelful of dirt that expanded the hole, Beatrice felt hatred for this woman, but, at the time, she didn't even know the word "hate." She only felt the emotion.

They were then told that they had to finish the job by killing the mother and burying her body with the others'. When Beatrice crawled under the bush, the dog was already dead. She was grateful it had given up the battle for life on its own. The mother dog was put on top of the sack of drowned pups and the girls were then forced to shovel the dirt back into the hole. The sound of each shovelful of earth as it hit the dog's body was an unforgettable memory. This dingo was Beatrice's only experience of witnessing an actual mother and her children, since none of the orphans had any memories or stories to share of family. The dead dingo became a heroine, and, of course, Sister Margaret was the villain.

10

The morning after Reverend and Mrs. Marshall were introduced to young seven-year-old Geoff, Matty Willett found him sleeping in his favorite place, a pile of hay in the corner of one of the barns, still clutching his new paint box. She awakened him and told him he would be going to America. He had never heard the word; it meant nothing to him. That very day Irene was assigned to see that he had a shower in the men's bathing area, and was dressed in some of the Willett boys' outgrown clothing. For the first time he found his feet encased in shoes. They were very uncomfortable. When he started to cry, Irene explained that shoes always hurt everyone who wears them, but he didn't see other people crying about it. He was now almost grown up, he was seven, so he must simply accept the necessity, endure the pain, and be quiet.

He would do that.

She handed him a present wrapped in colorful paper

and tied with a bow as Rogg and several other station hands told him good-bye. The little group waved as he, Reverend Marshall, and Nora drove away. Geoff asked what America was and when he would be returning, but the questions went unanswered. As they traveled by car, Nora surprised him by telling him he should take the bow off the package and look inside. Geoff never questioned the fact that the gift was something other than its pretty exterior. It was his first experience of seeing a gift-wrapped present. It was a delight to discover that Irene had provided him with a big pad of sketch paper. He proudly carried it and his paint box from the car into the railway station.

The local station was a small room. It contained a ticket counter on one end and held several long benches with a few people each sitting a comfortable distance apart. It was a very short wait before the train arrived. Geoff had never seen a mechanical structure so big, bellowing smoke and making such a loud noise. The giant black engine, pulling passenger and freight cars, roared into the station past him and stopped farther down the track. He was amazed as he saw that the rows of round wheels passing by were higher than the top of his head. The train ride lasted all day and into the night. The Marshalls occupied double-wide seats facing each other and Geoff had one to himself. It was exciting to look out the window and see the world swishing by, but it made his stomach woozy. He occupied his time by drawing the portrait of a bearded man who was sleeping across the aisle, slumped over his seat. It was late at night when they arrived at their destination and entered another railway station.

The interior of this second station, coupled with the experience of trailing behind two people who continued to act as if he were a stranger, made young Geoff tremble uncontrollably, as if he were standing in the cold. This second station was the most massive room he had ever seen. The ceiling was higher than he could imagine it possible to build. He looked up at the thick black-iron support beams, hoping they would continue to hold the roof until he could safely pass from under it. It seemed there were hundreds of people, most in a hurry. The only ones standing still were a group gathered at the foot of a tall board. There, a man wearing a flat red-striped hat was standing high upon a ladder, which swiveled back and forth. He changed the four columns of numbers on the board. One indicated a train number, the next were the times of arrival and departure. The last column directed people to a specific platform number for boarding. Reverend Marshall announced that they were to proceed outdoors and find a ride to the wharf.

They rode in a taxi to the pier, where Geoff saw a ship even larger than the train engine. He was hesitant, but finally followed as they walked up a long ramp and boarded the vessel. With each mile by car, train, and now a boat, he understood more clearly that he was being taken away from his home. His feet hurt badly for the first few hours in the shoes. After that, they became numb. No one suggested he remove the offending and confining leather, so walking with numb feet made him feel and appear almost crippled.

He was confused about what was taking place. He hurt physically and emotionally, but he could not weep. Instead, he devoted himself to his newfound love of drawing. By the second day at sea, he had come to the last of the clean sheets of paper. He turned to Reverend and Mrs. Marshall, who were seated on deck chairs reading books, and asked for more paper. Nora reminded him of the new rule, the new word "please." He added please to his request and was told that she "would see, maybe later." He asked again that night as he tucked his paint box under the pallet he slept on at the foot of their bed. The first words he uttered in the morning upon awakening were this polite request.

Mrs. Marshall was impressed by how well the child could draw, but her husband thought it was a waste of time. The boy should be learning to read and write instead. There was no place in the world for a black artist. That afternoon, when Geoff asked for the fifth time for more paper, please, Reverend Marshall grabbed the box, walked to the deck rail, and threw it overboard. As the colored metal box twisted and turned in the sunlight and finally splashed into the vast blue ocean, Geoff's world sank with it to the bottom of the sea. Their relationship never recovered from the blow.

The Reverend and his wife meant well. They saw the adoption as providing an education and an opportunity for someone who would otherwise remain illiterate but, most important, they were saving his soul. They believed they were rescuing Geoff from an underprivileged existence and the burning pit of hell.

The view through Geoff's eyes was very different. It was evident that he didn't belong. He didn't understand, in the beginning, why his new parents didn't seem to like him. He didn't know how he was different. On the third day at sea, a new shipboard acquaintance of Nora's pointed out his dark skin and everyone else's light color. Geoff was already aware of this, but he considered it in the same way he thought about dimensions and shading in his artwork. It wasn't good or bad, it just was. On this day he became aware that for some people, shading seemed significant. Later that week the same woman tried to explain the meaning of the words "mom," "dad," "son," and "family," but he felt separate from all those words. Her description was not what he was experiencing.

A few days later the family arrived in the United States, where they were met by a ministerial student in training who had been assigned to drive them home to Vermont. A day later the car pulled up in front of a small yellow cottage surrounded by a fence in front and back. Nora had decorated the home with plaid furniture covers and white ruffled curtains at each window. It was a pleasant sight. The little house also smelled good because the church auxiliary members had prepared a table of fruit and freshly baked cookies and muffins. Geoff was shown to a room that was used as a combination office and overnight guest quarters. He was told they would fix it up for him. Since he had never experienced having a place of his own, he didn't know what to expect, so he was not disappointed when, in the days to follow, the room remained unchanged.

His new family and his new home had in many ways an atmosphere similar to the one he had left on the Willetts' station. He was again left on his own. He stayed outdoors all day long except for meals. Even then, many times at lunch a sandwich and glass of milk were delivered to him as he sat up high in an apple tree, straddling the largest limb and looking around the neighborhood. Once or twice he ventured out the back gate and explored the alley and neighboring yards, but Nora found him and he was scolded for leaving his yard. As in the past, he once again found companionship in birds, and added squirrels and a stray cat to his group of playmates.

One month later, when his new mother registered him to attend school, he knew something was wrong. She held his hand for the first time. Then, without looking his way, she explained to the elementary school secretary that he wasn't their real son, he was an adopted Aborigine. It was the first time he'd heard details about being unwanted and abandoned by his own people, by his own birth mother. She emphasized the fact that he hadn't been wanted anywhere. The Willetts had taken him in and now she and her husband were providing for him. He began that day by calling the minister's wife by her first name, Nora, instead of ma'am. No one seemed to notice the difference. Reverend Marshall was always referred to as sir.

Geoff tucked the words "Australian Aborigine" down deep in his memory. He felt bitterness toward his birth parents. He believed what he had been told. They had rejected him at birth.

Ten months after Geoff's adoption, a son was born to the Marshalls, and ten months later a second boy arrived. The household and church atmosphere changed. He now witnessed the roles of loving, caring, nurturing parents with their two biological sons. He became even more isolated. When there was only one baby, he slept in the parents' room. With the arrival of the second child, Geoff's room was converted into a nursery for the two sons and he was given a bed, chest, chair, and lamp in one corner of the basement.

Reverend Marshall began introducing church members to the two infants and adding, "This is Geoff, our adopted brother of heart." The statement never made sense to Geoff. Sometimes the minister added, "We are trying so hard to save his soul, please pray for him and the other savages around the world!"

When Geoff was nine he found himself in the school reference library with a very helpful librarian, Mrs. O'Neal. She explained that her ancestors were from Ireland and she felt it was important for people to read about their roots. She found two books on Aborigines and suggested Geoff check them out and read them at his leisure. He took the books home, and that night after everyone was asleep he turned on a light and began for the first time to try to make some sense of his heritage. The textbooks said absolutely nothing about land being confiscated, or that the people had been forced to submit to a foreign ruler. It depicted them as primitive people wearing little clothing, eating bugs as food, and living a miserable existence. Geoff felt very mixed emotions. He could find little in the books to build a feeling of any pride in his people. Maybe he didn't belong in the family of the Marshalls, but it seemed he was probably better off than he would have been had he been left with the Aborigines.

11

On a warm day in 1945, when Freda was eleven and Beatrice was nine, the children of the school were given a rare treat. They were taken on an outing away from the compound to visit a nearby stream in a parklike setting. Most years, the channel of water was barely visible, but it had been raining for several months. The creek had swollen into a river and was from four to seven feet deep in most spots. There were numerous craters of much deeper water swirling around in a circular motion. Midway through the day, a fifteen-year-old girl, Hannah, discovered an old tree stump on the water's edge a little distance from the grassy park area. Several of the girls followed to see her jump into the water. Although none had ever been taught to swim, it became obvious that by simply thrashing about, waving arms and legs, one could manage to get back to shore. It looked like such fun. One by one, each girl became brave enough to try. Even Beatrice, with her early memory of almost drowning in the bathwater, couldn't resist the excitement of what looked like more fun than she had ever experienced. It was thrilling and only slightly painful when the water rushed up her nose.

Freda stood in line to take a turn. The group watched her jump in and waited and waited for her head to bob to the surface, but it didn't come up. Beatrice didn't know what to do. She instantly jumped in. As she was descending, she groped around, trying to touch her friend underwater. She felt nothing. She wasn't experienced enough to know how to stay in the water to continue her search. She had to struggle to make it back to shore. Hannah ran for help. One of the Sisters, who was annoyed because she was forced to give up her game of croquet, reluctantly walked up to the old stump and started asking questions. Were the girls certain someone was in the water? Who was it? How long had that stupid girl been underwater?

The Holy Sister walked away and finally returned with two other nuns. After about twenty minutes, they called all the students, telling them to leave. Everyone was instructed to march home. Beatrice couldn't leave Freda in the water. She cried and screamed and tried to get back into the water, but received only slaps to her face and was forced to leave.

Weeks passed before Beatrice could sleep through the night. She had horrible dreams of Freda calling for help, her mouth filling with water. The nightmares were a merger of pups in a white sack and her best friend clawing and crying for help.

Sometime later Beatrice heard Sister Agatha say the deceased had been found with her feet lodged in deep, thick mud. Beatrice's dreams became even worse. Each night her sleep was disturbed by visions of Freda thrashing in the mud, her mouth, eyes, and ears filling up and her feet being pinned by giant boulders.

No one on the administrative staff ever acknowledged the loss of her best friend. There was no memorial or a remembrance of any kind. Beatrice learned to accept that savages were not to be included in the traditional Christian treatment of the departed.

Nightly she talked to her dead sister, telling her about the day. She finally dreamed of Freda's release, as she flew with wings up into the sky. Beatrice continued to feel her presence, especially when she saw one particular white bird that periodically came to sit and sing on the fence during recess and flew over the schoolyard on many evenings.

Each time a girl arrived at the institution, the nuns took away all her personal possessions, burned her clothing, and cut her hair. Haircuts were done in a strapped position in a tall wooden chair outside the Mother Superior's office. Within thirty minutes of arrival, the orphans could count on the show of a screaming youngster harnessed to the chair, and a dramatic before and after appearance. Beatrice learned that this was an opportunity to befriend a new arrival. Over the years she grew to sense how unique everyone was and yet how bonded in needs and feelings the whole group was. But she never considered any other girl as her sister.

Beatrice stayed on the border of trouble most of the time. She wasn't intimidated, but didn't stand bold and hold her ground either. Instead, she had conversations inside her head. She would say to herself, "This isn't right, I know this isn't how it should be. This is like a pretend game." She believed it was not a lie if she knew the difference and was only pretending. After Freda's death, most of her prayers and time spent in church were for show, the appearance of conforming but, in truth, it was pretending.

Reading came easily to her, and she devoured everything she could get her hands on. What was available was limited; when she was nine she began working around the entire building and volunteered for the job of dusting private offices. Here she found wonderful textbooks, maps, magazines, volumes of encyclopedias, even personal letters to read. Once or twice a year, all matron staff went on a holiday and only two nuns were left, so she had access to an abundance of the written knowledge that was not locked behind glass cases. The church held that indigenous females had little use for reading and writing beyond the basic level of understanding street signs, reading labels on cans, and being able, possibly sometime in the future, to sign a legal document. The important education was in learning such practical skills as house care, doing laundry, baby-sitting, planting and harvesting crops, canning food, and, for a few rare and exceptionally bright Aboriginal women, perhaps nursing the ill of their own race.

One cold cloudy day she was taken out of school for the day to help cut and stack wood. During the morning an elderly Aboriginal man came to her and started a conversation. He was the first adult person of her own kind she had ever seen. They didn't converse for long, because the priest in charge of the project, young Father Paul, told him he was interfering with the day's work.

In the late afternoon the man came walking back from the opposite direction, but he was acting strangely and he smelled odd. The priest shoved him, knocking him to the ground. Then he shouted for the man to get up and move on. He kicked the man repeatedly, trying to make him move, until finally the victim managed to stagger off. The beating was followed by a lecture on the evils of drinking alcohol.

Beatrice agreed that it was not a good thing to do and made a promise that night while looking out the window at the stars overhead not to get involved with alcohol. She felt it seemed such a serious commitment that it warranted a special ceremony. Borrowing a piece of a broken china cup the girl bunking next to her had found, she cut herself. As the few drops of blood dripped down her hand, she repeated a vow of abstinence from alcohol. For her, the deliberate physical scar was a glorious new idea just invented, but years later she discovered it had been a part of her heritage since ancient times.

A few drops of blood caused a major disruption in her life. The bedsheeting was changed every two weeks. The following day happened to be the day for Beatrice's dormitory's laundry. The little cut had bled slightly during the night. The stain was discovered by Sister Raphael, in the laundry room. Beatrice was called to the Mother Superior's office, where she was grilled about the blood. She couldn't tell them of her ceremony or why she had done it, but she did show them the tiny wound. The two Sisters exchanged a look that told her they didn't believe her story. She had said, "Here is a little cut and that is where the blood came from." The nuns, however, seemed to share a secret they were not ready to reveal, namely, that blood could come from something other than a wound.

One week later a group of six girls, Beatrice being the youngest at nine, was awakened early and told they had been selected to go for a ride into the city. There was no time for breakfast, they would eat later. Each was taken to the community closet, a row of wooden wardrobes lining a portion of one hall. Clothes were not hung on hangers at

Mercy Sisters, they were folded into neat piles. The girls wore matching uniforms, a white blouse and a brown skirt, but, on a few occasions, like when parading before couples interested in adoption, they were dressed in clothes donated from outside the institution. On this day Beatrice was given a navy blue dress with a white Peter Pan collar trimmed in red rickrack. Father Paul drove them into the city, not for enjoyment but to a health clinic.

A strange, very strong smell rushed into Beatrice's nostrils as soon as the door opened. The waiting room was so immaculately clean that the girls were too uncomfortable to sit down and stood lined up against a wall. One by one, in separate rooms, they were helped to undress and to put on a white shapeless gown. Each was told she was to receive an immunization shot and have a physical checkup. Beatrice remembered a nurse putting the needle into her arm and, later, a mask over her face. She woke up sick to her stomach and had bandages on her abdomen. All six had received the same large incision and stitches. The next day they returned to the orphanage and were kept separate from the others until their stomach incisions had healed. She had become part of an experimental project by a young ambitious parish priest to control the population of the indigenous race down under.

12

At school Geoff was the best ball player, and learning came easily to him. He always won the class spelling bee. But he was a loner. He wasn't liked or admired by the other boys at school. The boys said that their parents had told them he was too dark in color to be a friend.

His one great love was drawing. He looked forward to art class because there was an abundance of paper available as well as crayons, colored pencils, watercolors, and finger paint. His teacher gave him free rein after the class assignment was completed. He always finished ahead of the other students and did a superb job no matter what the task.

There was no art paper at home. He was given no allowance and no means to earn money until Mr. Schroeder came into his life.

Mr. Schroeder was a war veteran who lived across the back alley from the Marshalls' home. His life was spent in a wheelchair because his legs no longer functioned. He lived alone. A depressed and angry man, he drank to such an extent that he had driven everyone out of his life.

One beautiful warm autumn day as Geoff was sitting high in the apple tree, he saw Mr. Schroeder struggling to empty his trash. Although there was a wooden ramp covering the cement steps from the back door, handling the door, balancing the rubbish container on his lap, and descending the semi-steep incline was a challenge. On this day the container toppled over and spilled. A box had fallen in front of the wheelchair and was blocking it, keeping it from moving forward. There wasn't room enough on the ramp to turn the chair around. Mr. Schroeder was stuck and cursing.

He happened to look up in his ranting and raving and spotted the boy in the tree. Geoff was in clear view because most of the tree's leaves had fallen to the ground.

"Hey, you kid. Come here. I need your help," Mr. Schroeder shouted across the yards. "You there, boy. Can't you see I need help? Come over here, or go get someone to help me."

Geoff didn't like the looks of this unshaven and disheveled adult. He'd seen him before and heard him swearing out in his yard as he struggled to do most everything. Since the man was aware of him, he climbed down from the lofty perch and answered the summons. He left the Marshalls' fenced-in area, crossed the unpaved alley lined with trash barrels, and approached the man stranded in the wheelchair. The front wheel had partially crushed the box, jamming a rigid edge so that it had become lodged and prevented the chrome chair from advancing. Geoff tried to pull the box out. He couldn't.

"Get behind and pull me backward," the trapped man said. "Maybe the box will fall away." It didn't.

"Try reaching down and moving it while I pull you backward," Geoff suggested. "This is a two-man job."

It was a heavy weight, but the boy managed to move the chair enough for the plan to work. When the chair was free, it picked up momentum immediately and went sailing down the ramp. Working together, man and boy brought the chair under control. The man was the first to laugh.

"You were right. That was a job for two men. Thanks for saving my life. What's your name?"

"Geoff, sir. Geoff Marshall."

"Glad to meet you, Geoff. You're a strong lad. I was in quite a predicament until you came along. Come on in," the crippled man said. "I'll give you a reward."

"No, that is not necessary," the boy answered.

"Sure it is. Come on in. Or are you afraid of me? My name is Schroeder. I won't bite you. I promise, I won't bite you."

Geoff pushed Mr. Schroeder back up the ramp and into the kitchen. There they exchanged stories and got acquainted. The boy explained that his father wouldn't like it if he took money for helping a neighbor. Schroeder explained that it could be like a salary. Maybe Geoff could come over a few times each week after school to help. He could earn some money.

It ended up that Reverend Marshall was opposed to Geoff's being paid, but he did like the idea of the boy helping a crippled war veteran. In fact, he could use the subject in one of his upcoming sermons.

In turn, Schroeder did not give money directly to the young boy. He learned about the things the child wanted. He purchased art paper and supplies and kept them at his home for Geoff to use anytime. They became good friends. Schroeder enjoyed the artist's work and his company. He had some of the drawings framed. Geoff held the wooden frame against the wall as the veteran sat back a short distance and gave instructions about where to pound the nails. They laughed because almost every project they encountered became a two-man job.

Schroeder seemed to mellow under the influence of the adopted child and the boy responded favorably to being called a man. Schroeder began taking more interest in his personal hygiene and appearance. He taught himself how to bake cookies in anticipation of Geoff's after-school visits. And the two became partners in creating a garden.

It was Schroeder's idea that Geoff look carefully at his name. One afternoon after a particularly stressful day at school, the young boy complained about having no friends and not fitting in. The man explained that he, too, had no other friends and did not fit in socially. "You can't change other people," he said. "You have to change your way of thinking about yourself and become comfortable with who you are regardless of others' points of view. When you are proud of who you are and feel good about yourself and what you represent, it won't matter how many people call you a friend. And for some strange reason, confidence seems to draw followers. But you can also minimize how you differ and that might help a little bit. For instance, your name. It isn't spelled the same way Americans spell it. I am sure when people first see it without your pronouncing it, they have difficulty in trying to decide what to call you. Why don't you ask your parents for permission to start writing it as Jeff instead of Geoff? Or maybe you can think of a nickname that you really like and we could all start calling you by that new name."

His parents did not agree to allow him to change the spelling of his name, but he did it occasionally anyway. He used the new spelling when he signed up for a neighborhood baseball team even though he knew his family would never attend any games. Schroeder started called him "Slugger" after seeing that Geoff was the sole member on the team to hit home runs. Geoff told his older friend it was a good feeling. He felt as if maybe he had outgrown his Australian birth name. But his family would never recognize or fulfill his need for a rightful place.

One cold and snowy winter day Schroeder had a surprise for his young friend. He had gotten a ride to the library and had checked out a book about Australian Aboriginal art, which they studied together. The art form was unique. It seemed to be all symbols. People were represented by a mark that looked like a capital "U," rivers were wavy lines, and the backgrounds of all the illustrations were covered in dots.

Geoff thanked his friend for finding the reference book. Though his outer appearance was one of interest, inside he felt quite the opposite. To him, the information was simply more proof that his heritage was primitive, uneducated people. He did not understand what the pictures were meant to say, and nothing about their artwork made him proud to be an Aborigine.

13

Ten-year-old Beatrice loved nature. She read all the books she could find describing the trees and flowers of her native land. She was fascinated by photographs showing the rain forest, the waterfalls, lime-rich sand dunes, and the coastal shores in all four directions. She read of animals, insects, birds, and sea creatures. She longed to see these things for herself and dreamed of the wonderful world outside the walls of the institution. When she turned eleven, she developed an interest in astronomy and would study books about planets and patterns in the sky. After sneaking outdoors after dark, she searched for their actual locations in the heavens. By her twelfth year, she was studying complex scientific theory, experiments, and proofs. Of course she had no laboratory and no instructor. But on the pretext of having an interest in one day becoming a medical nurse, she managed to receive permission to make selections from the public library's supply of knowledge. Twice a month Father Paul brought new volumes and returned the ones already read.

During that year Father Felix arrived at the orphanage for a six-month period, while Father Paul returned to his original seminary. Father Felix had been briefed on his specific duties and had also been told about such extra activities as Beatrice's interest in reading. The difference between Father Paul's delivery of books and Father Felix's method of handling the transfer was apparent immediately. When Beatrice entered the priest's private office, he locked the door. The new books were sitting on the edge of his desk. He took the tall leather office chair behind the desk and asked her to sit opposite him, where she could reach the reading material. He asked her to look over each volume and tell him if she liked it or not and what she hoped to learn from the contents. As she followed his instructions, she could tell he was doing something behind the desk. His hands were not visible, but his upper arms seemed to be moving.

After the second set of questions, he smiled and told her to come up to him. She did so reluctantly, not knowing what to expect. Something in the pit of her stomach was warning her that his actions were not proper. She walked to the side of the desk as she'd been told and discovered that he was sitting in the chair with his trousers unzipped, exposed and clutching himself. He joked about her interest in science and biology and added that she needed to also understand anatomy. He made no overture toward her, but continued to enjoy what he was doing. When Beatrice looked away, he laughed. As he repositioned his clothing, he told her it was for her benefit to see what she would be missing for the rest of her life. No one would ever marry a woman with such a badly scarred face, as well one who had also been surgically prevented from ever having children. He unlocked the door and warned her not to speak of their conversation, threatening to discontinue giving her library books if she did. Beatrice left the wood-paneled office in a daze. She didn't really comprehend what had happened, what he was doing, and what he had said. She was shocked by his actions, was shocked by actually seeing a male reproductive organ exposed. And she was especially shocked to learn that her surgery at the age of nine had been to eliminate all possibility of childbearing. She had never contemplated any of these things, had never thought about boys, or getting married, or having babies, and certainly never about a priest undressing. She didn't tell anyone what had happened, but she did manage to get Sister Margaret to confirm that the scar on her abdomen was from female surgery. She was afraid not to do as Father Felix instructed. Two weeks later she returned the books, leaving them outside his office door and receiving new ones in the same way thereafter.

At the age of thirteen, had she been given an intelligence test under nonprejudicial circumstances, she most clearly would have ranked at graduate school level. But the Mercy Sisters weren't interested in Beatrice's intelligence. They settled for a student who quietly kept herself entertained and no longer caused problems.

14

Reverend Marshall's family spent every Wednesday night at church fellowship. The weekends and summers were times for tent revivals. Life was continually filled with loud singing, boisterous praying, sinners crying, and the saved shouting. Geoff's adoptive father called his well-groomed family up onto the stage early during each session. Nora held the youngest boy, dressed all in white, while the older one, leaning against her legs, still immaculately clean early in the evening, usually wore a white shirt and tiny bow tie. Reverend Marshall introduced each family member and always ended up with Geoff, pointing out how godly they were to include one offspring of foreign pagan savages into his otherwise very white fold. Geoff served as an example for the congregation. He learned to stand tall with a smile while the master of his household and the church pointed out repeatedly that everyone must love the enemy, forgive ignorance, pray for heathens, convert the savages, and stamp out evil wickedness and Satan's ways by eradicating uncivilized cultures. It was very confusing for Geoff, who felt on Monday and Tuesday that he was making progress and had become a part of God's family, only to be exhibited each Wednesday as the example of lost souls around the world. It became a game, a joke, a role he played that was every bit as compelling as the voices over the radio Nora faithfully listened to on "As the World Turns" and "The Life of Stella Dallas." By then he had learned of monkeys' being the attraction for organ grinders and compared his situation to that of the captured beasts. As far as he knew, there was not another dark-skinned person in all of Vermont.

One Wednesday night Geoff realized that the reverend had been studying library books about the indigenous people of Australia. His sermon that evening referred to people so primitive they had no written language, did not know how to build houses or grow food, and had no concept of the love of Jesus and the salvation of heaven. Geoff felt humiliated. He wanted to explain to the Marshalls that his interest in the Aborigines was not about finding out what they were like, but was about letting them know who he was and what he was about. But he remained silent. Australia was across the ocean and he was sure he would never return to those shores.

His two brothers were never close to him. They were, of course, much younger and stuck together. When one of them broke a toy, Goeff was always blamed and it was their word against his. He couldn't defend himself. No one would listen to his part of any story, so it was a continuing losing battle.

As he got a little older Geoff was no longer good at his schoolwork. He understood the lessons, but he had no interest in what he was expected to learn, so he did the minimum required. He never questioned why his clothing came from secondhand shops while the Marshall boys wore department store items, or why his sleeping quarters were in a dark corner of the basement while the other two boys slept in the sun-filled corner room. He never asked because he knew: *He did not belong here. He did not belong anywhere.*

When he was fourteen the Marshalls moved to Texas. Geoff was speechless. Apparently the family had talked about it and the sons were gradually coaxed into acceptance, but Geoff knew nothing until the day they left. He was not permitted to tell his only friend, Schroeder, goodbye. In Texas, Mexicans, Indians, and Negros comprised a large portion of the population. Geoff was often taken for one of the local people of color, since it seemed no one in the state had ever heard of an Australian Aborigine. He felt that the years in Texas were his best in school, not in terms of academics but because he was accepted, and it happened to be by the toughest and most feared group of students. Secretly, one by one, each of his friends confided his desire to know how to read, write, and do mathematics. They were perfectly normal kids, but there was so much prejudice against them that only a rough appearance got any attention from school officials. Geoff found it best to conform to the new lifestyle, which included learning how to curse, smoke, drink alcohol, and steal, but he also tutored his pals.

He was in trouble with the law as soon as he had friends. At first it was just for missing school, then for being caught drinking illegally. He was caught driving before he was of legal age to obtain a driver's license, and was arrested for breaking that law. He refused to attend church anymore, and would no longer tolerate the remarks and physical abuse from the two Marshall sons. He kept to himself, stayed away from the house as much as possible, and mentally divorced himself from his adoptive family.

By age sixteen he was addicted to alcohol, and one rainy Thursday night he simply didn't return home. He drank so much he passed out in an old shack that his friends used for meetings. He had been able to hide his alcoholism from the Marshalls because he never drank so much that he became drunk. Instead, he drank a little bit constantly and so lived under the influence of alcohol hour after hour, day after day. The break from the Marshall family was swift and uncomplicated. They didn't look for him, and he didn't miss one of them.

15

In January 1952, Beatrice turned sixteen. Her actual birthday was an unremarkable event; the day came and went without recognition. There had never been a birthday celebration held in the Mercy Sisters Mission.

In the first part of February she was summoned to Father Paul's office. At a long table sat Sisters Agatha and Margaret, Raphael, the priest, and a middle-aged white woman wearing a blue dress with a small matching veiled blue hat.

"This is Mrs. Crowley," Father Paul said, introducing the stranger. "She has come to offer you employment. We are only obligated to care for you up to the age of sixteen, so now it is time for you to be on your own. Mrs. Crowley has a rooming house and needs help cleaning it, preparing meals, and waiting on the boarders. You should be able to do that, don't you think?"

"Yes," Beatrice answered shyly.

"Good. Well, then, you and Sister Margaret go fetch your things, and after lunch Mrs. Crowley will take you with her." He stood. Beatrice knew from past experience that she was now dismissed. She walked to her place in the dormitory and sat on her bed. Her pulse was racing. She hadn't allowed herself to become a close, confiding friend to anyone since she'd lost her sister Freda. Still, she would miss the other girls, especially the younger ones. She took out a cigar box from under her mattress and held it lovingly. It contained everything of importance she owned: an empty iodine bottle, Freda's white veil, a shiny rock, and several notes Freda had written. Sister Margaret came in carrying a paper sack. Beatrice folded and put her undergarments and her sleeping shirts inside, then added the cigar box. She was allowed to go to the community wardrobe and pick out two cotton housedresses to add to her sack of possessions. There had been no occasion for Beatrice to wear shoes during the past few years, but they did find one pair discarded by one of the nuns that would fit well enough to make her presentable in Mrs. Crowley's home. Beatrice hated how shoes felt on her feet.

At noon Father Paul announced her departure. She said good-bye to the whole school from her seat at the dining table. By one o'clock, she was sitting in the backseat of a sedan between fresh vegetables, two sections of a metal lawn chair painted blue, and a wooden hall tree with four of the original six coat hangers still attached. While Mrs. Crowley drove, there was very little conversation. It didn't matter because Beatrice was too busy looking out at the world she knew so little of. The fact that she was free from the orphanage walls for the rest of her life left her almost breathless. She had no idea where she was going, what was going to take place, or how she would handle it. All she knew was that this morning she had belonged at the mission school, and now she was on trial to see about belonging to someone named Mrs. Crowley.

16

For Geoff Marshall the years between sixteen and twenty-three were a blur. He bounced between alcoholic highs and deep depression, standing on highways and rural country roads in rainstorms, falling snow, pelting hail, and steaming heat.

In January 1953, he opened his eyes the morning of his seventeenth birthday to see an overcast day. He woke in the front seat of a grocery delivery truck. The driver had taken pity on the young boy after almost running him over as he stood in the rain on the edge of the highway. The truck was traveling from a factory in Wichita, Kansas, to make deliveries in Nebraska and Iowa. It had been raining for hours. The heat in the driver's warm cab, connecting with the icy-cold rain on the windshield, had caused him to wipe the glass periodically for a clearer view. Coming around a corner he'd made a wide turn and there in front of his headlights stood the black iced-over figure. The boy wore blue jeans that the rain had soaked and turned to black. He had a flimsy navy blue jacket pulled up around his ears and his skin was dark. Ice had collected on his clothing and hair. When the driver brought the truck under control, he put on the brakes and rolled to a stop. The kid came running.

"Get in," he told the young man. "What in the hell are you doing out here? It's forty miles to the next town."

Geoff explained that he had been hitchhiking and that a local farmer had brought him this far. The farmer had turned off here to go to his own home. It hadn't been raining four hours earlier when he'd climbed out of the farmer's car to hitch his next ride. Traffic had been slow and the cars had passed him by.

The driver told Geoff to take off his wet jacket and shirt and handed him an old bath towel from behind the seat. Geoff wrapped it around his shoulders. There was also a little coffee left in the thermos, which they shared. Neither party had much to say and Geoff fell asleep in a short time.

There was no sunshine when he opened his eyes. It was a gray day, but he was warm. His shirt was dry, and although his jeans were damp, they were much less uncomfortable. The driver had parked the truck in front of a roadside diner. When he turned off the engine, the silence woke the hitchhiker. "Let's get some breakfast. You got any money?" the driver asked.

Geoff shook his head no.

"That's okay. I'll buy." The two went in and sat in the nearest booth. It was upholstered in worn and faded yellow plastic. A waitress watched them from behind the counter. She had a puzzled expression on her face, as though she wanted to ask some question of these two. But she didn't. A few minutes later the driver shouted, "Hey, can we get some service here?"

"What you want?" the woman asked without lifting her head from the position she had taken to read the newspaper.

"What you got?"

"The usual—eggs, bacon, toast, pancakes, cereal. What you want?"

"I'll take bacon and scrambled eggs. I want hash browns too. How about you, kid? Want bacon and eggs?"

Geoff nodded a yes.

"You paying for him?" the waitress asked.

"Wait and see," the driver snapped back. He winked at the boy across from him and added, "No need to be nice to nasty people. She ain't figured out what the world of tips is all about."

As they were being served their breakfast, a man came in and sat at the counter. He was a tall, thin, balding man in his late forties. The waitress called him Lyle. She poured a cup of coffee and sat it in front of him without his asking. Lyle and the waitress seemed to continue a conversation that was being carried over from the previous day. He still hadn't found anyone to help him clean out a big storage barn and the sale was scheduled for Saturday. She offered sympathy but no solution to his dilemma.

"My friend here is a good worker," the truck driver, continuing to chew his food, said to the man, and pointed to Geoff by nodding his chin. "You got room and board and a salary to offer?"

"Yes, we have a room," Lyle answered. "But it's only till Saturday. Nothing permanent. I'm paying ten dollars a day for five days."

The driver grinned and replied, "Throw in this breakfast and you've got a deal. Okay, kid?"

Geoff was startled by what had taken place so quickly.

He had been invited to breakfast, and then his labor for five days had been offered and sold. He was now bargaining for the breakfast he had just eaten. He didn't say a word until the man came over to him, extended his hand, and said, "I'm Lyle Moore. What's your name?"

"Geoff Marshall."

"Glad to meet you, Geoff. Is this job all right with you? Your friend seems to be the only one talking."

"Yes, it's fine with me," Geoff said. "I'm free till Saturday."

So Lyle Moore and Geoff Marshall left the diner in Mr. Moore's Ford. The Moore farm was only six miles out of town. It consisted of a two-story white frame house, a horse barn with eight stalls, a barn used for hay and machines, and another very large barn full of items the recently deceased Mrs. Moore had collected over the years. She and her husband had gone to farm auctions almost every month during the summers. It was their social outing. Farm people had sales to dissolve estates when they wanted to purchase newer replacement items, or sometimes simply because antiques had become popular with city residents. "The problem Momma had—that's my wife," Lyle said. "I always called her Momma, like the kids. Well, her problem was she bought things but she never sold them. I just have to get rid of the stuff now. There's an auctioneer coming Saturday and I have to see what we have. I need to sort it and put it in piles. There's only my youngest daughter, Nancy, at home now. It's just too much work for the two of us. If you work real hard, I know it will be a big help. You just passing through? Know you're not from around here. How old are you, anyway?"

"I'm nineteen this month," Geoff answered, adding two years to his age. "I'm traveling around the country right now, trying to decide where I'd like to live and what type of work I'd like to do."

"Good idea. It's a big world. Lots of opportunities."

The guest room at the Moore residence was the bedroom that had belonged to Lyle's son in his youth. He was now grown, married and living in Oregon. He seldom visited the Midwest.

The first sound Geoff heard from daughter Nancy was a scream. She had not responded to the "Hello, I'm home" her father had uttered when they'd first entered the front door. Lyle had shown Geoff the bedroom and bath. They were coming out into the hall when Nancy came bounding down the stairs, her hands up to her head, drying hair wet from a shower. When Geoff came out of the room, she looked up and screamed. It was embarrassing to everyone, but understandable. Mr. Moore explained who their guest was and the situation seemed calm.

The day was spent with the younger worker moving items into specific sections of the barn's open central space. It became fun as he quizzed Lyle on what some of the objects were. There were hundreds of unusual things, including a wooden horse-drawn sleigh with seating for six. There were saws with handles on both ends so that two people could jointly cut a tree. Geoff moved large iron pots for melting wax, and molds to form candles. They found old radios in big cabinets, boxes of dishes, different styles of butter churns, and at least fifty ornately carved picture frames. The stories were fascinating about how the old items would have been used, but the young man could not imagine why anyone would buy such old junk.

That evening Mr. Moore gave Geoff some of his clothes to wear while he put both of their dirty clothes into the laundry. He also prepared the evening meal while Nancy sat in the living room and called for Geoff to join her. It seemed Mrs. Moore had never required her daughter to help around the house and the idea had not yet entered the girl's mind. The three of them ate together and then the younger two went out to the barn to see what had been uncovered that day. "I don't really care about that old stuff you're working on. My dad has a stash of home brew in the other barn," Nancy said. "He doesn't think I know about it. Come on, I'll show you."

They went into the hay storage building. She walked over to an old wooden cabinet with paint peeling from the surface. Opening the door, she took out a bottle.

"We can sit over here," she said, walking to a corner piled with hay as she twisted the top and opened the bottle.

"This might not be a good idea," Geoff offered, looking around at the unfamiliar setting. "Your dad might get mad."

"No. I know my dad. He'll do the dishes, listen to a radio program, hang the clothes on the back-porch line, and go to bed. He won't even look for us. He never does." She was right. They drank the home-brewed beverage and Nancy told him how boring and miserable it was to live in the Midwest. They opened a second bottle. Sometime during the night Geoff woke up to find that Nancy was gone. He made his way into the house and went to bed. He hoped she had done the same.

The following day was a repeat of the first. The only difference was in the stories Lyle told about each antique item. There were three beveled mirrors, each six feet high, that had been rescued from a hotel, as well as a walnut bar with a brass foot rail that the mirrors had enhanced. There were dirty blue-velvet upholstered chairs, the horsehair stuffing breaking through the surface of the fabric. Lyle blew thick dust off a black case, which he opened to reveal strangely shaped guns. They were dueling pistols. He explained the practice of men settling disputes by shooting at each other.

At lunch they went into the kitchen and Lyle fixed sandwiches and opened a can of soup. He stared out the window as he ate. The room remained silent until finally he said, "I've had a good life, young man. Yes, I'm very fortunate. Own the roof over my head. Had the love of a good woman. All my kids are healthy. Farming is hard, but I can go fishing most anytime I want. I hope you find your calling. I hope you have a good life too."

That afternoon the yellow school bus stopped at the road to the Moore's place and Nancy slowly walked into the house. She saw Geoff looking at her from the barn but she didn't make any gesture of recognition. When the men finished for the day and came in to clean up, she was up in her room. Loud music could be heard and it sounded as if she was dancing. She made no attempt to help her father, who once again prepared the evening meal and put the day's dirty clothes into the washing machine.

After dinner Nancy and Geoff headed for the hay barn and the corner cabinet. Nancy was in a good mood. She hated school, hated this farm, hated this town, but today had been a good day. She had been chosen to play a role in the spring school play. "Why didn't you tell your dad?" Geoff asked as he tipped the bottle for his first swallow.

"He's not interested. You don't know my dad. My mom was the only one who cared about stuff like that. She would have come to see my performance. But she can't see me now. I don't think dead people know what is happening to us, do you?"

"I don't know. My stepdad was a preacher. He talked

a lot about dying and going to heaven or hell but he was such a hypocrite I stopped listening. I haven't thought about it for a long time."

"Well, I don't think anyone can see us," Nancy continued. "But I would like to give them something to see. How about you?" She unbuttoned her blouse and started removing it. "I've never seen a Negro before. Take off your clothes."

"I'm not a Negro," Geoff answered. "I'm Australian."

"Oh, I don't care where you are from. Black is black, that's all I mean." She grabbed his hand and put it on her body. "Come on, let's have some fun," she whispered.

When he was in Texas, Geoff had listened to his friends talk about their times with females but he had not been with a girl. He was hesitant and proceeded slowly. Nancy was in charge. They finished drinking the bottle and he wasn't entirely sure what was happening. It was not anything like the guys had described. She seemed to be finished. She put her clothes on and walked to the house. He waited a few minutes and followed. She had gone to bed.

The third day of the barn-cleaning project, Lyle discovered a slotted wooden egg crate in the cardboard inserts of which Mrs. Moore had carefully placed pieces of antique jewelry. He told Geoff to take it to the house. They would look at the contents more closely that evening.

After dinner Lyle remembered the find and asked Geoff to take the crate to his daughter. He told her to look through each separation carefully so they didn't miss anything and to see if there was anything that appeared to be of value. He would join her after he finished cleaning the kitchen and tending to the day's laundry. Geoff watched as Nancy removed the first layer. She took each item out of the indentation designed to hold an egg. There were rings, earrings, necklaces, and bracelets. Neither youngster knew enough to determine value, but Nancy held up a pearl necklace and instead of returning it to the crate, she put it in her pocket. She continued to scan the pieces and had added a diamond ring, an emerald brooch, and a pair of diamond cuff links to her pocket before her father joined them in the living room. He seemed amazed at the collection Mrs. Moore had acquired and felt certain the jewelry would command a good price at Saturday's sale.

Midway through the following day, the two men had completed their task. Lyle told Geoff he was free to leave if he wanted or he could spend the night and start his travels in the morning. Lyle had located a gym bag that had been discarded by his son and he put a change of clothes inside for Geoff. He handed the young man a ten-dollar bill for each day's wage. He also held out his hand and said, "These are for you too." It was a tie bar and matching cuff links. "I think the red stones may be garnets or even rubies. I'm not sure, but they are nice."

"They are nice," Geoff commented. "I don't know where I will wear them, but they are nice."

"Every young man making his way across the country, seeking his destiny, can use a good set of cuff links," Lyle said jokingly.

The following morning as they rode together back to the diner, the young passenger glanced over at the driver, concentrating on the road he had driven thousands of times before. He's a good man, Geoff thought. Fair, perhaps even generous. It's too bad his daughter doesn't see that, but who am I to judge? I've only known them a few days. Maybe the old boy feels his wages were too low, and he is just glad I didn't spend much time with my hands on his daughter. He felt the cuff links in his pockets. These are useless to me, he thought. They were probably given as a payoff, not out of sincerity. But he is an okay guy.

At the diner Lyle said good-bye and went in for a cup of coffee. Geoff stood in front, his thumb pointing out for a ride. In five minutes he was on his way.

He continued to hitchhike around the United States and learned it was cheaper to drink than eat. In Detroit he worked for a month as a dishwasher. In New Orleans he was employed by a trash collection company. In Miami he worked doing lawn and garden work. Everywhere he went he seemed to be a magnet for unhappy people who habitually stole from each other. The dishwashers stole the waiters' tips, the trash collectors stole bicycles sitting out in yards, the lawn service people asked home owners if they could use the bathroom, then stole anything they could stick in their pockets. He understood the thefts. He, too, felt denied and deprived and was envious, but the overwhelming feeling that dwarfed the others was guilt, because stealing was wrong. He hated seeing it done by others, and he hated knowing he was capable of it himself. Geoff had no ambition. He could think of no occupation that held any interest, and he found he could escape feeling anything by drinking himself into intoxication. It was always a welcome relief. He became addicted to alcohol.

In Arizona, at the age of nineteen, he was put in jail for stealing checks off the front seat of a parked car. He was sent to a rehabilitation center. It looked as if he was on the road to recovery when he was hired by an insurance firm as a mail clerk and copy boy. Unfortunately, part of his duties was to obtain alcohol for the agents' desks. They offered the clients a complimentary cocktail. Access to the beverage was too easy, and he soon lost his job. Later, in San Francisco, California, he was introduced to smoking a special weed that wasn't readily available in other states. The added addiction of this illegal substance to his already existing alcoholism was his ultimate downfall. He lost track of time, of where he was and how he had gotten there. He went for months never coming out from under the influence of addictive substances.

17

The Crowley boardinghouse was a two-story clapboard building, the only one in the nice neighborhood badly in need of a coat of white paint. There was an extension of the roof line, the width of the door, over the front entrance, as if to represent solidness and strength. The two pillars holding it in place were made of paver brick. Small windows dotted the front, and, in each, curtains of different colors hung. There was a grassy area the width of the house in front, surrounded by a waist-high iron fence. The gate had rusted, and was stuck in the open position. Untrimmed bushes and a few brave flowers lined the base of the house. Mrs. Crowley pointed out the residence as she drove by and circled to enter the rear alley, where she parked the car near the back entrance. Five steps led to a partially screened door that opened into a five-foot-square back porch.

"Put the furniture on the porch and bring the vegetables into the kitchen," Daphne Crowley barked as she slammed the right-side driver's door shut and disappeared inside the house. Beatrice looked around. There was just the faintest fragrance of sweetness in the air. She had to discover from where it was coming. She followed her nose and found a neglected and forgotten fruit tree growing between the house and its next-door neighbor. She immediately returned to her chore of unpacking. She did not want her new employer to be angry at the start of their relationship. She removed the chair parts and the long wooden coat stand and made a pile in the porch along with a dull-metal milk delivery box, a lopsided base from a wooden funeral wreath, and numerous empty crates.

She got the food from the car. Walking in the door she found herself in Mrs. Crowley's kitchen. It was a cluttered room with a black-and-white imitation tile floor and dishes piled high in the sink and on a table nearby. The cupboards that surrounded the room had no doors so the room appeared to have no walls, only slots everywhere filled with glasses, cups, bowls, boxes of all colors and sizes, and foodstuff in varying degrees of spoilage. A yellow cat peered out from under the table where it had been napping on a stool. Beatrice didn't know where to set the groceries. The only clear space available was on the floor, so that's where she deposited the sacks.

"Clean the dishes first," came the woman's voice from beyond the next door. "Wash them, wipe them, and put them away. I'll be out to help you in a few minutes. I'll show you your room later." It looked like a monumental task, but Beatrice was actually glad to have something specific on which to concentrate. Her mental questions needed a rest. She had to rearrange the dirty dishes on the table first in order to remove and stack the dirty ones from the sink. Then she could fill the sink with soapy water. Two hours later, and after two refills of soap and water, her task was complete. The yellow cat had by now accepted her and was purring and rubbing itself against her legs.

"Oh my, it's getting late," Daphne Crowley said as she came bustling through the door. "We must get ready for evening tea. Get those potatoes peeled; here's a peeler. I'll make the biscuits!"

The preparations went smoothly. Daphne made specific demands and Beatrice was able to comply without question or comment. "Now wash your hands and put on this clean apron. I want everyone to see you. Here, carry this into the dining room with me."

They went into the next room where four men were seated at a table. "Gentlemen, this is Beatrice. She's a trained darkie from Mercy Sisters Mission. She will be helping me and I'll keep her out of your way, so I hope it will work out all right for all of us. Beatrice, bring in the soup tureen."

That is how the first day and most of the following days went at Crowley's Boardinghouse. Beatrice changed linens on beds, used the dust mop and dust rags in the guests' rooms and in the dining hall and living area. She cooked all the meals once she learned how Daphne wanted each dish prepared. She waited on the table, cleared the dirty dishes, cleaned the kitchen and the bathrooms, and even helped pull weeds in the yard. She pruned and nurtured the neglected fruit tree between the houses. It responded with shiny new leaves, and the limbs began to uncurl and stretch toward the sky.

Her room was in the attic, which was entered from a door opening off the back stairway to the kitchen. The large attic was filled with storage items, but one center portion had been partitioned off by nailing old quilts to the rafters to make fabric walls. The quilt room contained only a single-size bed and a small dresser, but she had access to other pieces of furniture stored among boxes with contents probably long forgotten. When she had been there a week and was feeling very brave, she rearranged the attic, without permission, repositioning the quilts and adding a small red table and black spindle-backed chair, a rocking chair, and a cracked mirror to her new domain. By enlarging the space, she had included a rear window which, when opened, looked out onto the roof. It was wonderful. She could climb out through the window onto a flat portion of the roof and not be seen from below. The very first night she discovered that she could sit out under the stars and felt it was a time to celebrate. The city lights made viewing the heavenly bodies more difficult than it had been in the country, but still, she could manage. She actually preferred sleeping under the open sky. The hard surface was not a great deal different from the hard beds in the orphan school. After a while she was able to tune out the noise that continued all night long. Beatrice could not remember a time in her life when she had been so happy.

Guests at the boardinghouse were like the ocean tide, in and out, come and go, but some stayed longer than others. Andrew Simunsen was considered a long-term boarder. He was twenty-one, tall, lean, handsome, and fully focused on success. He had completed his primary education in the rural area where he had been born and his family still resided. He had come to the city for higher education and had remained there. His interest was not in agriculture, like his grandfather, or in his father's general merchandise store, an investment his father hoped one day to pass to his son as an inheritance.

Andrew was farsighted. He studied economic trends and was absolutely certain a fortune was to be made from minerals: iron, lead, or petroleum. He had the habit of staring at his hands and envisioning a ring of highly polished gold with a flawless white diamond in the center. He did this several times each day to remind himself of his goal of wealth. He had designed and redesigned the ring again and again in his mind. He knew one day it would be his, and mining seemed the best road to success. Unfortunately, he had no money for investment and knew absolutely nothing about the field. He took a job in a local bank where he had access to the most affluent and powerful men in the state.

He lived at Mrs. Crowley's because it was cheap and convenient to the bus line. He tried to save part of his small salary, but it was difficult because he had to keep up appearances and good clothing was a necessary expense. All noonday meals were eliminated. He walked much of the time instead of taking the bus. He hadn't even been tempted to look toward eligible young ladies, although his male desires were not exactly put on hold. Instead, he had gone one step farther.

He had made himself available to a wealthy and lonely bank patron whose husband traveled a great deal of the time. She enjoyed his company to the extent of subsidizing his income in return for personal attention. Her name was Mrs. Henry Holmes, Elizabeth, actually. They had never discussed money. After their first time together, he found dollars in his coat pocket as he was leaving. Now, he could pretty well judge what amount she would slip into his garment by what request he had fulfilled for her.

He remembered as a child when his grandmother was helping him pack for a short trip. She held up one of his stockings. "Hide your extra money in here," she said. "Thieves don't think to look in rolled-up stockings." So as silly and feminine as it sounded, he never discarded his worn socks. He had half a dresser drawerful and each one was stuffed with the dollar-bill gifts from Elizabeth.

Crowley's Boardinghouse had five rooms for rent. Each was furnished basically the same, with bed, dresser, end table, desk, chair, and lamp. Nothing matched, but the furniture was sturdy and would hold a man of considerable weight. There was a shower, bathtub, and separate toilet area on the first floor and a toilet and washbasin on the second. Daphne Crowley's personal bedroom was off-limits. She carried the little brass key tied to a string that was safety-pinned to her pocket.

John Ramey, another boarder, was a man in his fifties with gray beginning to spread from his temples to other parts of his head. He had piercing blue eyes with lids that never quite opened fully. His home had caught fire six months previously, and his wife, son, and daughter-in-law had all perished. He had been devastated. At first he stayed at the home of some friends, but finding privacy was difficult. They wanted to talk when he didn't. When he couldn't sleep at night, he needed to walk, leaving at midnight and sometimes returning around three A.M. He tried to be thoughtful and not wake anyone, but he also wished to avoid receiving a barrage of questions and advice.

One day he looked at the newspaper ads and found Daphne's place. He didn't care what it looked like, or how the food tasted. It was simply a place to stay until he decided what to do with his life.

He worked for a cement company that, until the tragedy, had boasted of his twenty-two years' perfect attendance. He went to work every day, but he was making mistakes, too many mistakes. The supervisor didn't know how to handle it. He was ten years younger than John and with half his experience, and had sympathy for the terrible loss, but he knew something had to be done. He called for a meeting with the plant foreman to ask for advice. The foreman and the supervisor tried talking to John, but it was like talking to an empty shell. He only smiled and nodded in agreement.

The largest room available for rent in the Crowley boardinghouse was in the front corner and was occupied by a bartender, Kenneth, and Charles, a young man who entertained by playing various instruments and singing in the same establishment where Kenneth worked. They worked nights and slept during the days. The room had twin beds, and each paid a full week's fee, so Daphne was happy with the arrangement. They seldom ate any meals with the others because of their work schedule, so the fact that two men were sharing one room hadn't become an issue.

Bright-red-headed William Brawley was the other boarder. He was a muscular two-hundred-and-twenty-five-pound thirty-five-year-old who worked at the brewery and was the product's greatest mouthpiece. He had been thrown out of more taverns, off more ball fields, and out of more hotels and rooming houses than one could imagine. He didn't look alcoholic. The typical puffy face and red nose were not apparent because his light complexion was covered in a deep, golden tan dotted with darker brown freckles, and contained wrinkles on every inch. People didn't realize when he was drunk because they never saw him sober. Brawley, as he was called by everyone, displayed only one personality and it was kept afloat by drinking three beers faithfully each morning for breakfast and at least twenty more by bedtime. He was loud, crude, argumentative, and a know-it-all, but he paid his rent in full and on time each Friday. That's all that mattered at Mrs. Crowley's.

"Beatrice, can you iron?" asked Daphne as the morning sunlight made a pattern on the kitchen table where she sat dipping a two-day-old biscuit into her mug of hot tea.

"I've done some, but not much."

"Well, it isn't difficult. You must pay close attention to what you are doing so you don't leave the iron in one spot too long and scorch the material. I'll show you today. All the boarders pay extra if we do their washing, and so far everyone has been satisfied except Andrew Simunsen. He prefers a Chinese laundry. Strange young man. Acts like he thinks he is important. Chinese, can you imagine!"

Later that day Beatrice was instructed on how to fill the electric washing machine, how to feed the soapy garments, after a time of sloshing around, into a set of rollers that squeezed them into the rinse tub, and, finally, how to wring them out once again and into a laundry basket. Daphne provided supervision and exact instructions on how the clothes should be arranged on the rope clothes line. A split-tipped pole had to be inserted to hold up the sagging weight and bedsheets had to be placed carefully so they did not blow against the side of the sedan. Then Daphne gave folding instructions, followed by ironing lessons.

At the evening meal Brawley complained about the bread. He called Beatrice into the room and began grilling her about the baking she had done. "It tastes terrible; it is tough, and even the honey wouldn't soak in and ran off onto my fingers. I'll tell Mrs. Crowley when I see her. She better teach you, darkie, what to do or she'll need to give up and buy commercial bread. If things don't change around here, someone will be leaving and it isn't going to be ol' Brawley."

The girl was shaken by the insulting remarks. After all the day's chores were completed, sitting high up on her roof perch, Beatrice questioned for the first time what would happen if Mrs. Crowley no longer wanted her. Where would she go? What could she do? She had been gone from the institutional home for two weeks, and it was the first time the question of the future had ever entered her thoughts.

18

The following weekend Beatrice was cleaning the second-floor bathroom and found a gold watch lying near the washbasin. As she headed downstairs to ask Daphne's advice on what to do with the jewelry, she walked past Andrew Simunsen's room. The door was open, and he was sitting at the desk reading a book. When he saw her he smiled and said, "Hello." Then he folded down the corner of the page, closed the book, and continued, "I'm sorry, I have forgotten your name."

"Beatrice," she answered, holding out the watch. "Is this yours? I found it while cleaning."

"Why, yes, it certainly is," he acknowledged, placing the book at the back of the desk. "I'm pretty bad at taking it off and forgetting I've done so. Thanks for finding it."

"That's okay. I hope I didn't disturb your reading," she said as she took a few steps forward into his room and handed him the watch. "I love to read too."

"Really. I never think of Aborigines as being scholars. What do you read?" he asked as he put the watch around his wrist.

"I love science, physics, biology, astronomy, that sort of thing. Of course I haven't read anything since I left school and came here."

"There's a library downtown. They have volumes of books I'm sure you haven't seen yet. It is a mammoth place. You should get someone to take you sometime." Then, listening to his own suggestion, he quickly added, "Better still, I can give you directions." He took out a piece of paper and a pencil and started writing down the information. While he was doing it, he asked, "What are you going to do with all this science knowledge?"

Beatrice looked at the cleanly shaven young man and said, "Do? What do you mean, do with it?"

Andrew sighed and let out a strange little noise that accompanied a blank expression. Good question, he thought. Never heard of a black scientist, let alone a black girl scientist. What occupations did Aborigines have? He hadn't a clue. They certainly weren't hired at the bank to do anything, not even to empty the trash. "I don't know any Aborigines personally. Except you, of course. I don't know anything about your people. Tell me about yourself."

"Well, okay," she replied. "I don't really know what to say," but she then proceeded to tell him the story of her life. At the conclusion, Andrew knew that she didn't know much about her race.

Beatrice asked Daphne about the library, about taking an afternoon to go there, and the answer was always the same, "We'll work it in." A month later, on an outing to the grocery market, Beatrice once again reminded her employer, so they parked the car. The two women climbed the cement steps and entered between massive pillars and two lion statues. The request from an Aboriginal person to borrow library books came as something of a shock to the elderly woman behind the counter. Could she read well? Would she understand to care for the books and return them on time? What sort of books would she be interested in? Maybe she should come and sit here and read. Then there would be no worries about the books not being returned or being mishandled. Yes, best that she come here and sit and read, the clerk repeated several times, speaking to Daphne and not to Beatrice.

Beatrice wasn't refused a lending card. She just wasn't given one, Daphne explained on the ride home. To this new employee, it was a very disappointing experience. She was sitting on the porch as the street lamps came on and Andrew Simunsen was leaving the house. She stopped him and tried to tell him of her day's misfortune, but he was in a big hurry and merely grunted, "Sorry."

The following Wednesday he called Beatrice to his room and handed her three library books he had checked out under his name. That was the beginning of a long-standing and complex relationship. He still couldn't see what possible good all that studying could do for this black maid, but he felt guilty about the treatment of her people. He felt guilty that she had no future, and down deep, his guilt about how he was earning money from Elizabeth was gnawing at his soul.

The arrangement with the Mercy Sisters was for their former ward to receive a small salary and room and board for her services. Ten percent of the salary was to be sent directly to the school and would be considered Beatrice's Sunday offering. The details of the arrangement were not revealed to the orphan, so she waited and waited for the day Daphne would give her some money.

Beatrice had been employed for five months and Daphne was actually on the verge of releasing a little cash to her employee when something happened that made her change her mind. The future boardinghouse finances would be affected on the day the telephone rang and the secretary at the cement company told her John Ramey was dead.

His absentmindedness and lack of concentration finally caught up with him. He pulled a machine start lever, and dropped a live wire on the watery floor he had just cleaned. Now Daphne had an unrented room to deal with.

"Beatrice, bring a cardboard box and help me pack up John's things," Daphne said as she unemotionally returned the telephone receiver to the cradle. "He's dead."

Mr. Ramey had two leather suitcases under his bed, so they didn't need the box after all. He had very few possessions, mostly clothing. There was no photograph album, no jewelry, only a few toilet articles and two cartons of cigarettes, which Daphne took downstairs. There was also an ashtray that she hadn't seen before. She left it on the bedside table and added it to her inventory. The packed suitcases sat in the hall for two days and then were moved to the attic to be stored until someone called to claim John Ramey's personal items. No one ever did.

Brawley continued to complain about the food. He criticized the condition of his laundry, the dust on his bedroom furniture, and every other thing he was aware the dark-skinned woman had a hand in. Mrs. Crowley had her response down to a fine art. She always shook her head in disbelief, put on her best listening expression, and promised to fix it or get rid of the girl. Beatrice initially took all his comments to heart and felt bad for not pleasing one of the boarders. Little by little, however, she came to the realization that the only thing she could ever do to satisfy Brawley would be to disappear or paint her skin white.

John Ramey's room was finally rented to a working lady referred by Kenneth and Charles. She worked at a clothing store downtown and paid two months' rent in advance, which put an end of any questioning by the landlady. Helena was very tall and thin. She wore the finest of clothes and had so many she had to bring two iron racks from the store on which to place her shoes, hats, and garments. She wore very heavy makeup foundation, deep scarlet lipstick, and had long fingernails. There was a full set of costume jewelry to match every color in her wardrobe. She had an active social life. Beatrice heard her high heels clipping along the front walk at all hours as she came and went from Crowley's Boardinghouse.

Beatrice was spending so much time on the roof that she could report on everyone's arrival and departure. She recognized each one's footsteps. She even knew that the man who delivered the milk each dawn, putting it into the metal box to preserve its cold freshness, was the same man who quietly came and left from the back porch and was admitted through the door that dear Daphne guarded so diligently with her brass key.

The first year working for Mrs. Crowley came and went. Daphne finally began paying her employee. No one ever asked Beatrice if she was happy or not, and she rarely questioned it herself. She read the newspaper and listened to the boarders talk, so she was aware of world events. But any racial tensions in the city went unrecorded. Indeed, the entire continent of Australia seemed not to be aware of any black and white conflicts.

19

The taillights glowed a cherry red on the speeding 1953 Chevrolet sports car as the driver slammed on the brakes and skidded to a halt. White vapors of smoke still clung to the tires as it was put in reverse and moved slowly backward, closing the distance between the vehicle and the hitchhiker running to catch a ride. Geoff half-expected the unseen driver to stomp on the gas pedal, for the car to leap forward, leaving him spinning or sprawled on the ground. It had happened before. He opened the passenger door cautiously. The driver was a young man with a golden tan and pale blond hair cut very short. His index finger motioned for Geoff to get in. The car was so new it still smelled of a factory assembly line.

"Where you headed?" the blond asked.

"No place in particular. Where you going?"

"Fort Irwin, California. Just got drafted for a two-year hitch. Got myself a present here. Ain't she a beauty?" he said as he patted the leather-wrapped steering wheel. "The Burks own most everything where I come from, including the car dealership. Their son, of course, doesn't have to serve military time. I figure the Burks are paying me to do his job. Pretty slick, huh?"

Geoff smiled but didn't reply. He had already sized up this guy. All that was needed was to become a listener, which would be good for a ride from the Midwest to the West Coast. He recognized someone in love with himself. He wasn't sure if the car was stolen or if somebody named Burk had given it to him. It didn't really matter.

"Harry. Harry Tull," the blond said, extending his right hand in introduction.

"Jeff," the hitchhiker answered.

The two teenagers had been in the car, which was again traveling at a high rate of speed, for only five minutes when Harry asked his passenger to reach back onto the rear seat and hand him a beer. "Help yourself. It's going to get too hot to taste good. We'll stop somewhere and get a cooler."

They spent the day drinking the remainder of the beer even though it did get warm, and finished off a pack of cigarettes that amused them by sliding back and forth across the front dash as the car turned with each curve. The driver talked and the passenger listened. Periodically Harry would pull over. They would quickly urinate, each opening a door and challenging the other to see who held the most to be eliminated. By eleven P.M. they had exhausted all their supplies. In the distance the headlights, on high beam, exposed a diner with a single gas pump bearing the symbol of the Mobile Oil Company flying red horse. Harry elected to pull in. Both boys laughingly left the car and staggered into the building. A CLOSED sign hung on the door, but the door was unlocked. Inside they were greeted by the strong smell of cooked meat and grilled onions.

"I'll take one of those," Harry said to the round pink face looking out from the kitchen. The cook did not immediately reply, but somehow sensed trouble and finally answered with, "One of them what?"

"Whatever smells so good. Hamburger, isn't it? Make it two. No, make it four. We're hungry, aren't we, buddy?" Harry commented as he drummed his fingers on the pink counter, not taking his eyes off the kitchen. The cook put up no argument and placed four beef patties on the flat frying surface of the stove he had just cleaned. He took a match and lit the gas burners.

"Wait here," Harry instructed. "I'm going to get gas." He walked to the cash register and, feeling on the shelf below, extracted a strange-looking key. Stupid people, he thought. Always leave the key in the same handy place. He walked outside, put the key in the pump and turned it on, filling the Chevy's gas tank. He had replaced the key and joined Geoff, sitting on a stool at the counter, just as the sandwiches were served by the fleshy pink arms belonging to the round kitchen face.

"Gimme a beer."

"Me too."

The cook took beer from the beverage cooler and placed it before the customers, then walked back into the kitchen. The two ate in silence. When they had finished Harry went behind the counter and, opening the cooler, removed two six-packs of beer.

"Take these," he said as he took two more and carried them to the car.

Geoff knew the cook wouldn't do anything. He wouldn't call the police and probably wouldn't even tell the owner unless he was confronted with a need to explain four missing six-packs of beer. In Texas he had witnessed bullies and victims so many times that he could easily predict their behavior. It seemed that more and more of his life was spent observing other people and very little of it doing much of anything himself.

The next few days were repeats of the first. Harry pulled off the highway and they passed out or slept, neither was quite sure which. They stole and changed two sets of license plates and only paid for filling the gas tank once. Harry seemed to love the thrill of almost being caught.

On the morning of the fourth day they were on Highway 66 in front of a grocery store, the Cottonwood Market. The town was Linwood, California. There were two metal signs posted. The top one read LINWOOD, POPULATION 37, and the bottom one said FORT IRWIN, with an arrow indicating a turn off the highway.

"Guess this is where you get off, partner," Harry said. "Take the rest of the beer."

"Thanks," Geoff answered. "You sure you are up to being in the army?"

"Well, we will see. Maybe I will make it a lifetime career. I heard before I left home that as long as I am in military service, I can't be arrested for any civil matter. Sounds like a license to steal to me." Harry put the car in gear and peeled out of the dirt-and-gravel parking area, never looking back.

Geoff went inside and purchased a sack of potato chips. Outside he walked slowly west, alternating between nibbling on his breakfast and raising his thumb at passing motorists. Linwood, they had been told by the grocery story clerk, was still in the Mojave Desert and to reach the coast was another two hundred miles. Geoff had walked fifteen minutes before he heard a car slowly pulling up behind him. As he turned he recognized the insignia on the side of the car. It was a unit of the California Highway Patrol. He stopped and the officer got out and walked up to him.

"What you doing, boy?" the uniformed man asked.

"Just walking to Los Angeles."

"Let me see your identification."

"Don't have any."

The officer looked him over and finally said, "In that case, I'll just have to take you in for questioning and check out your fingerprints. Get in the car."

Geoff did as instructed without comment or protest. He was driven thirty miles, to the city of Victorville where the highway patrol had an office. There he was told to empty his pockets and a set of his fingerprints was made. He was put in a room containing a table and two chairs, and was left behind the locked door for the next two hours. He didn't know why he had been picked up. He didn't know if being with Harry was involved or not. Finally, when a stranger came to talk to him he answered all the questions as evasively as possible and insisted he was merely walking to Los Angeles. They didn't seem to be able to find any reason to keep him, so by the afternoon he was released.

When he asked that the contents of his pockets be returned, two officers looked at each other and shook their heads. "Your pockets were empty. Remember?" Suddenly the roles were clearly defined. He was no longer a bystander watching a bully and his victim. For years he had believed others to be weaklings and couldn't understand why they let themselves be abused. Now he was in the position of either standing up for himself or submitting. The jewelry didn't mean anything to him. He didn't feel he had earned it, and almost felt it had been a payoff to keep his hands off the farmer's daughter. It probably wasn't worth much anyway. He would just consider the cuff links and tie bar as payment for his freedom. It was an easy decision. He chose the path of surrender and walked away.

For the first time in his life he considered the word "coward" in a new light. Maybe, under certain circumstances, it was more intelligent to let the other person win. Perhaps coward should be thought of as "co-ward." There were two directions, inward and outward, which meant thinking of both sides of a situation, looking both inward at oneself and outward at the situation and acting with wisdom.

Geoff frightened himself. When he wasn't drinking he was a deep thinker. Too deep. He found himself asking questions and looking for answers he didn't even realize he was interested in. He knew he had a five-dollar bill in the bottom of his shoe. He had kept it hidden from Harry. He stopped and removed it.

I'll buy a beer or two, he thought. That will stop all this thinking going on in my head. And he did.

20

During her second year of employment, at the age of eighteen, Beatrice had perfected a routine for doing all her work. She found that, so long as it was disguised as work, she could spend the extra time as she pleased. She began walking to the market by taking different streets and venturing farther and farther into other sections of the city. She was no longer intimidated by the bus service. She carried the fare in coins, and always counted it out exactly, so when she boarded she could sit quietly alone, look straight ahead, and get to her destination without incident. During one of these explorations she discovered a section of the city where only Aborigines resided. There were no manicured lawns, no flower boxes, no colorful borders to greet visitors approaching a front door. The entire area consisted of old ramshackle buildings, with many windows broken. There were splintered wooden crates and pieces of metal thrown about. Bread wrappers, empty cola cans, and other waste lined the walls and curbs, indicating from which direction the wind had last blown.

There were always people sitting on steps, under trees, and on the sidewalk. When she saw a group of children playing, she sat down to rest and observe. A young woman who appeared to be near her own age came up and asked, "One of them yours?"

"No," Beatrice answered. "I haven't any children."

"That one's mine," the woman said, pointing to a small boy wearing short red pants and displaying a mass of curly hair. "I don't think I've seen you around here before. New, are you?"

"Yes. I work at a rooming house and I haven't seen much of the city so I was just walking around."

"Working, you say. You have a proper job?" the girl inquired.

Through this connection with Pansy, the young mother, Beatrice became acquainted with a whole segment of society she hadn't known about. There were second-, third-, and fourth-generation people, born here in this isolated community or nearby. Great-grandparents had been displaced from the land as the white settlers moved in. They were given tea, sugar, flour, and tobacco in exchange for giving up the land, their way of life, and all their beliefs and practices. They camped on the outskirts of the city and watched it develop. Over time, the white population had moved, leaving behind their abandoned buildings. Since the lowest classes of the white culture would not live with the blacks, the area became totally Aboriginal. Beatrice saw that, in 1954, there were schools set up to teach her people, that the orphan missions were closing, one by one, and that Aborigines were subsidized by a welfare system. There was also talk of equal rights by making legal the sale of liquor to the Aborigines. Equal housing rights, equal employment opportunities, and a campaign to overcome racism were still far in the distant future.

Beatrice worked hard at Mrs. Crowley's in order to complete her chores and spend time in the Aboriginal section of the city. She made friends and listened for hours about historical events, but most of all she enjoyed cornering the very oldest people and having them tell her about life before the white man.

Her longing to know of her roots began to dominate her thoughts. She learned what she could of the old languages. "Farther north are people who still live in the old way," she was told. "They hunt and fish and live in bush dwellings. There aren't many left, but there are a few."

"Where in the north?" Beatrice asked a very old man.

"Don't know. Just go walking about. You'll end up right. That's the way. Have faith in yourself and trust in the path. I'm too old. Been sitting in this place too long. I don't know why my people have been made to suffer so, and I see no way out, but I do cling to the old law that says with each incarnation the world is given an opportunity to demonstrate that we are caretakers and live in the Oneness as we were meant to be. Maybe young people will make it right. I don't know. It hasn't been right for a long, long time. You are young. You try. You try to make it right. You go north and learn."

The sun was peeking through a cloudy sky the next morning as Beatrice made breakfast, cleaned the kitchen, washed and hung the clothes, and pulled weeds in the garden. As she was dusting and cleaning Helena's cluttered room, the phrase "have faith and trust" kept welling up in her mind. Were there really people out there somewhere who could tell her who she was? Perhaps her own mother and father were living with these people up north! Her thoughts were interrupted as she moved Helena's many medicine bottles to clean the desk surface. The woman must be quite ill. She had every possible over-the-counter feminine-related tablet and two prescriptions for female hormones. Beatrice felt sorry for her. Even though the lady looked and acted healthy, it was evident she wasn't. She needed all this medicine. Looking at the floor, which again required her doing the tedious work of picking up hair, she could tell the poor thing was spending a lot of time removing unwanted hair growth. It must be terrible, she thought, to be a woman and have as much hair on your arms, legs, chest, and face as a man.

One day at the breakfast table as Beatrice was serving the daily routine of tea and beer, Brawley was, as usual, reading the morning newspaper and interpreting the articles to give his own personal slant on each event. He read the report of a woman's murder. She was a wealthy woman in high society, one Mrs. Henry Holmes. The husband had been questioned and released. He had just returned from an out-of-town trip. He didn't fit the description of a man seen accompanying her earlier in the day. Andrew Simunsen, as he continued to add cream to his tea, asked if there was a photo of Mrs. Holmes. He might know her from the bank. And was there any description of the man they wanted to question? Brawley told him, "No. But they have a piece of evidence they are checking out. It doesn't say what, only that it is jewelry."

That evening Andrew added a large paper sack to the trash barrel in the alley and set it on fire. Normally, it was Beatrice's job to dispose of all the household rubbish. She watched from the roof and thought the behavior curious for this houseguest. The bin was nearly full, so she would have burned it herself by the next day. One of the pieces that fell out of the mesh trash barrel and was not destroyed was a portion of a torn photograph. It was a picture of two people with big smiles and their heads touching in a playful manner. The man in the photo was Andrew. The woman's face was the one Beatrice had seen in the newspaper. It was Mrs. Henry Holmes. Beatrice also noted that Andrew didn't wear his wristwatch any longer. He had apparently purchased a pocket watch. She never asked about it, or spoke of her observations to anyone. The mystery of Elizabeth Holmes's death was never solved. But she suspected she would recognize the watch connected to the case.

Beatrice had been saving her money for over four years. She got a good feeling when she took out her cigar box and counted her earnings. Throughout the year she had offered to help Aborigines who had some sort of immediate crisis, but Pansy had cautioned against it. There was always next time's allotment for them to use, and she reminded Beatrice that she might not always have Mrs. Crowley.

Beatrice was intrigued by the notion that she had a future ahead of her and by the possibility that her entire life might not be spent working for Daphne. She often recalled the old man's advice to just go walking about. With faith in herself and trust in the path, she would end up all right. But she might never have acted on her deep desire had it not been for the fire.

At three o'clock in the morning she was awakened by the smell of smoke and the steady stream of thin gray air puffing out the attic window onto her roof sleeping area.

The commotion began as boarders came running from the building, screaming and carrying some precious item. The neighbors began to awaken and come outdoors. She went into the smoke-filled attic, found her cigar box, and put her hand on a very hot doorknob. She turned the handle and opened the door. The entire stairwell was engulfed in flames. By opening the door she had let in so much smoke that the room was filled with it. She couldn't see the escape window, but she knew the direction. Holding a deep breath, she headed for it. She found the casing and climbed out. The men from the fire department didn't see her at first. They were concentrating on the front of the house. No one had mentioned that anyone lived at the top of the building. Finally, someone spotted her standing on the edge of her perch, clutching her savings. They brought a ladder around. As the fireman was guiding her descent, the roof collapsed, spraying the area with tiny bright sparks.

Daphne Crowley was standing in the middle of the street, her head covered in pink plastic rollers, wearing a black satin wraparound. Brawley was there wearing only his undershorts. His beer belly protruded much farther than it appeared to when he wore a belt. Kenneth and Charles, wearing matching terry cloth robes, were wrapped in each other's arms. Helena was nowhere to be seen, but a neighbor reported that a man with long hair, dressed in a woman's dressing gown and clutching a purse, was seen running off down the street. Beatrice just nodded her head as she listened to the neighbor's comments. It had never occurred to her that a man might try to appear as a woman. It answered the question of why Helena had been such a mystery.

Andrew Simunsen hadn't returned home that night.

Beatrice went over to soothe Daphne, but she couldn't get near her. The property owner was busy telling the fire chief how valuable her house and furnishings were. In a second breath, she confided to the neighbor that it was all insured, that she had wanted to sell it anyway and move away. If the insurance company paid her fairly, she would certainly be better off. As an afterthought, she remarked to the neighbor, "I hope the fire department can keep the flames from spreading to your place!"

Beatrice didn't look any farther. She didn't worry about what to do, where to go, or what would happen to her now. She clutched the cigar box to the front of the cotton dress she wore nightly out on the roof and walked barefoot up the street. Without making a conscious decision she turned the corner and followed her heart. She was heading north.

On July 14, 1960, Geoff Marshall was found passed out in an alley behind a liquor store. He had no wounds, but his clothing was soaked in blood. A knife was found only a few feet away, bearing the fingerprints of someone on file known as Jeff Marsh and matching those of this drunk. Three men were found stacked on top of each other, Geoff on the top. The two below him were dead. He couldn't remember anything, not even how he had arrived back in Florida. He didn't know the dead men but neither did anyone else. Even the court could not identify the drifters and they were referred to as John Doe number one and John Doe number two. The blood on his pants and shirt matched that of both the John Does. It was assumed that he had killed them. He didn't know. His mind was a complete blank.

He didn't bother to correct the authorities about the name Jeff Marsh. Somewhere during the past years, when he had been arrested somewhere, he had apparently given it to the arresting officers. It was okay with him. He didn't care what he was called.

There was no money for a defense attorney so he received the services of a court-appointed lawyer who advised him to plead guilty. If he did, the lawyer claimed the sentence would probably be more lenient than going to a jury trial and being found guilty. Geoff knew nothing about the law and trusted his lawyer. He entered a guilty plea and received the maximum penalty: death.

For Geoff Marshall, the first door in his life blew shut when he was less than twenty-four hours old. The second one slammed shut, cutting off all he had ever known, at age seven. Now, for the third time, a door, this one of steel, had clanked with a resounding final firmness at age twenty-four. He had become prisoner 804781 and was sentenced to spend the rest of his life incarcerated behind prison walls awaiting execution.

His entrance into the penal system was a reenactment of the surrender he had experienced as an infant when taken from his mother and given to the white world. He was issued prison wear. As he walked down the long aisle carrying his pillow, blanket, and towel, he heard hoots and catcalls directed at him from the cells of men on the lower level and on the upper deck. He tried to avoid trouble, but withdrawing from alcohol and drugs made his mind play tricks. For two days he clawed and scratched at nonexistent objects. Finally, on his third day of incarceration, he was put into solitary confinement. When he emerged two weeks later, his head was clear, but the trouble wasn't over. He didn't fit into any of the groups that had formed in the institution. There were self-isolating entities of whites only, Afro-Americans, Hispanics, Native Americans, and Asians, then subdivisions of those with various religious beliefs. There was no place for an Aborigine. He became the target for everyone who, in prison lingo, "felt like punching out somebody's lights."

Toward the end of his first month, someone jumped him from behind in the death row shower room and held his head with the twist of an elbow around his neck. Another spat in his face. As the garlic-smelling slime slid down his cheek, a blow was delivered to his chest that caused him immediately to expel all the air in his lungs. He fell to his knees as another blow was delivered to his right kidney. It was delivered by a steel toe boot and was permitted because of a payoff to two prison guards. He faded into unconsciousness. When he came to, blood was gushing from his mouth and nose as well as from a deep gash on the top of his head. He staggered to the hall, where a guard took a look at him and told him to get dressed. When he emerged the second time, he was asked if he wanted medical attention. The blood was still flowing from the open head wound. He nodded yes.

After that he was alert to every movement around him. He gained the reputation of being a loner. He had to fight others and spent time in and out of solitary confinement until finally he was viewed as vicious, and someone to be left alone.

22

The sun came up shining over Beatrice's right shoulder. It confirmed that after following curving streets, hills dipping up and down, and going through residences and, later, blocks of commercial buildings, she was still going north. Next to a highway ahead a blue-and-white enameled sign indicated four towns at intervals of 20-, 80-, 120-, and 250-kilometer distances. Cars whizzed past, but she didn't look up. Though her eyes were down, she wasn't as deep in thought as it appeared. In fact, her mind was a blank. She was in limbo. An invisible magnet from far away seemed to draw her body forward. Her brain, dulled by the early morning's fire, was being dragged along like a pull toy.

Her feet weren't as tough as they had been before she'd begun wearing shoes four years earlier for Mrs. Crowley. Pebbles and protruding dried grasses damaged the soles of her feet, which began to swell. She didn't notice. Occasionally a car would blast its horn, the driver's signal a greeting or a warning to stay out of the way. Her ears didn't hear. She just walked on.

When she emerged from her self-induced anesthesia she was standing on a railroad track. A train whistle blared and she was startled to see the approaching black monster. The speeding train brought her back to the current moment. She quickened her pace, crossing the tracks, to reach the town ahead. There were houses, each a white square with a green patch of lawn in front, and a park with benches and sidewalks crisscrossing the grounds. She used a water fountain to gain liquid nourishment. She could almost feel it pulsating through her body. Splashing cold water on her face brought her back to reality. She had walked twenty kilometers and couldn't remember seeing any part of it.

The smell of roasted chicken was in the air. Following the scent, she walked across the park and onto the sidewalk fronting the Main Street stores. The milk bar shop was completely open in front, because the wall was constructed to be pushed to one side, shutter style, during operating hours. A sign was posted telling what foods were available and the price of each item, but she didn't stop. Instead, she walked to the next cross street, turned the corner, and there, out of view, opened the cigar box. She took some money out and stuffed it in her pocket, then retraced her steps to the delicious smell of food. The cook behind the counter first quoted his price for a meal and held out his hand. He needed to receive the money before he would box up and hand over her order. She carried the treasure back to the park and sat under a tree to enjoy golden-brown chicken and deep-fried potatoes.

There was a lawn-bowling game just finishing, off to

her right. The court was surrounded by a wire fence and dotted with tall outdoor lights on a timer. Just as she looked that way, the lights snapped to attention. The instant glow made all the uniformed players suddenly look like moving white masses. The people were dressed in white hats, white shirts, white trousers or skirts, with white shoes. Beatrice had heard of the sport, but hadn't seen a lawn-bowling club. It was a part of the white world, not a place she would be invited to join. She was sleepy and looked around for some inconspicuous spot to lay down her head, settling on a corner where large full bushes grew. Shoving the cigar box under the foliage, she lay down and fell asleep.

The sun had already made its appearance when she was awakened by someone shaking her shoulder. "Wake up, got to move on now. Can't live here in our park," said the police officer standing over her, his body shading her eyes. "Got to keep moving. Come on." Beatrice reached under the bush, retrieved her box, and stood up, straightening her well-worn dress. She took a moment to get her bearings, then slipped another dollar from the box into her pocket as she walked back toward the food shop. This morning she would have a doughnut and a carton of milk, then be on her way out of town.

On the highway, she walked just off the pavement. There was a slow, steady stream of cars, one about every five minutes. An old red truck passed her, slowed down, and pulled to a stop a hundred yards ahead. As she approached it, she saw in the rear a middle-aged Aboriginal woman and a boy about twelve sitting among some pieces of furniture that were held in place by rope ties. Another woman leaned out the passenger window to ask if she wanted a ride. When Beatrice accepted the offer, she was told to climb in the back. It was too windy to try to hold a conversation, but the three occupants in the truck bed occasionally smiled at one another and pointed out a sight in the distance. The next sixty kilometers went much faster.

At last the vehicle came to a stop, parking in the side yard of a small yellow house from which several people emerged at once. All were Aborigines. Beatrice was given an opportunity to introduce herself and learned that this was the McDaniel family. The four in the truck had gone to pick up the furniture from the house of a relative who had died. They insisted Beatrice stay the night and visit. The family seemed open to sharing everything they had and to taking strangers in as if they were members of the immediate family merely passing through.

"I'm Pauline," the woman said, descending from the truck. "Here, carry this clock," she added as she thrust the old-fashioned timepiece toward the boy. He carried it indoors.

"My name is Beatrice. How can I help? I really appreciate the ride."

"We can carry this table to the porch," was her reply, followed by, "Freddy, come help!" Two older men walked forward. They maneuvered the pitted and rusted chrome table while Beatrice and Pauline each carried a chair. The table was placed on the porch because there was no room inside. The house already had a table and four chairs taking up most of the kitchen. The other rooms of Pauline's four-room house held beds, sofas, and cupboards, as well as mattresses on the floor. The bathroom was adjoining the kitchen, and the toilet was squeezed in a closet off the center hall.

As soon as they stepped inside they were met by the

smell of wondrous food. "Take a plate," Pauline insisted. "Then we can sit somewhere and you can tell us your story." Beatrice hadn't thought of her life or the circumstances of her travel as a story, but perhaps that was a good term to use.

She told about the fire at Mrs. Crowley's and her interest in learning about the old ways.

"Why are you interested in that?" asked Pauline as she put another bite of sweet yam in her mouth. "That's going backward. We need to go forward. We need more money from the government and more houses and better jobs. If you start talking like old Auntie here you will only make things worse, not better!" Old Auntie was the woman in the corner of the porch, Beatrice decided.

"That may be true," Beatrice acknowledged as she smiled and studied the old woman's face, "but how do we know what to fight for in the future if we don't even know what we have surrendered?" Looking back to the others she said, "I just wish I could spend time talking to someone who could tell me about the past, the way it used to be, why things were a certain way and how and why it changed."

"There are still a few who live in the ancient way," Freddy added to the conversation. "Go to Arnhem Land or to the inner desert. We have friends who live in the Northern Territory and others in western Australia. I can help you meet people up there if you like."

"But things are just as bad there," Pauline interjected. "Everything is so unfair. No one in government is willing to listen to us. No white man cares, and they have all the power. I'm sure they wish we would all move to the desert, leave all the land so that their cattle and sheep can graze everywhere except where they want to cover it in cement and use it for shopping. I have no interest in running away, I'm here to stand up for our rights. If we must accept their ways, then we must be allowed to live their way too. We need our own doctors and solicitors, radio announcers, and factory workers at the brewery and the—" But she was interrupted by a loud laugh from the males on the porch.

"Yes, working at the brewery would sure fix everything all right, Pauline," they jeered.

"That's a dream," said Freddy. "For blacks to have jobs with whites. Get paid the same. Do the same work. Live next door to white people. It's all a dream."

Then came the tiny voice of old Auntie, almost in a whisper. "We are the children of the Dreamtime—the only ones who understand what it is to be human.

"We must live the Dreaming. That's the only way. The only way to help our people, the only way to help the world. The white man thinks all Aborigines came from the desert, but my people stood on this very spot thousands of years ago and this was our land. Our country went from the sea to the mountains. There were no paper maps to unroll. The borders were song lines. Everything was set in place and held in place by music. The neighboring nations knew our song and recognized the trees, and the streams, the rocks and the mountains we sang. Our ancestors made this place for us by their Dreaming, and it was a place of honor, dignity, and happiness. We were good caretakers of our Mother Earth.

"But the white man came, bringing others in chains, and they didn't learn our song. In fact, they made fun of our music and ways. Their minds were closed to our Dreaming." She began to sing, *"Na na num que, num que, num que."*

Beatrice was fascinated by the old language remembered from when Auntie was a child. When she finished, they agreed that Beatrice would stay for a few days and learn some of the words and songs. The few days quickly turned into a month. She helped in every way she could and contributed money toward the group's food. Pauline took her to a thrift store, where clothing previously owned by someone else and given to charity was sold at greatly reduced rates. Beatrice bought two dresses, a pair of canvas shoes, and a small blue tote bag in which to carry her clothes.

In one of the daily talks Beatrice had with old Auntie they discussed religion. "I like Christianity," the elderly woman stated as she stretched her bent and humped back against a tree, settling into a more comfortable position. "I like Jesus stories and the nice organ music. But I have never understood those ten rules they are so proud of. God told a man to write them on stones, but I think something is wrong.

"One rule says to respect your parents. Why would Oneness want that written down when he made us to be born loving our parents? A child has to be taught not to. Maybe the rule really said, 'Don't do things that make your children lose their love for you.' Probably the man thought that was too long to write, so he shortened it.

"There's another one that says not to steal, but everyone knows if you listen to your feelings you would always feel bad taking something without permission. And they say it is a rule to remember God one day a week. I can't believe Oneness ever said to write that down. We honor the Oneness in all things, every day, and all day long. It is too bad that the ceremonies, the dances, and the languages of our people are being forgotten, but somehow good will come, I know. It may be in another thousand years," she said jokingly, "but sometime it will come. We must not give up our Dreaming. Beatrice, if you live the Dreaming, the people you need to meet will find you."

The following week Pauline and Beatrice were cleaning dead chickens in the yard. They had a big iron pot filled with scorching water into which they dipped the fowl and then plucked out the loosened feathers by the handful. When red feathers were sticking to her arms and the front of her dress, and were causing them to inhale the peculiar smell of wet feathers, Beatrice said, "I've got to leave, Pauline. I feel I need to be with the people in the north."

"Stay here. Together maybe we can do something for our people. Two people are better than one. I need your help here, and the people in the north need the same things we do," Pauline snapped back.

"Perhaps finding our roots," Beatrice said reassuringly, "will help us all in another way. Just sitting around complaining doesn't help. I need to know who we are, or who we were. Somehow, getting a proper white person's job and living in that sort of house doesn't feel like the answer to me. I don't know what it is, but I think I can find out if I follow my feelings. My heart tells me to trust in my guidance and believe there is a trail out there waiting for me to walk. I will help you fight, Pauline. I promise. But I have to know what I'm fighting for, not just what I'm fighting against."

23

The next morning Beatrice said her good-byes and began walking down the highway once again. Her cigar box was now only half full and was tucked inside the blue tote along with food the McDaniels had insisted she take. She had an old army surplus water canteen tied to the tote's strap, across her shoulder.

She was given several rides that day. An older white couple stopped first. She rode in their backseat for more than three hours before they came to the crossroad where they were to leave the highway. After that, a lone foreign woman on vacation picked her up and drove into the next city where she dropped her off at the petroleum station. Beatrice ate a sandwich and refilled her canteen with water, then started walking once again. Suddenly there was a loud blast behind her as the driver of a large over-the-road truck honked the horn and pulled to a stop. He would be driving all night and could use some company. She climbed aboard, grateful for his generosity.

"Where you going?" he asked, a cigarette hanging from the corner of his mouth.

"North."

"Lots of you blacks live in the north, don't you? Must be better bush food. I don't see how you can eat some of that stuff. Now me, give me a big ol' slab of beef with plenty of biscuits and homemade jam!" He was busy the rest of the night talking to Beatrice each time another subject popped into his head. Occasionally he asked her a question, but a mere "uh-huh" usually satisfied as a reply. She was really sleepy, but, since he had offered the ride on the basis of companionship, she forced herself to stay awake. She pretended to be interested in all he wanted to brag about and to listen to his personal complaints.

They stopped in the morning to refuel and for him to eat breakfast. She ate from her own supply. They drove on until about noon, when he said he had to stop and get some sleep. Another trucker had been traveling at about the same speed. They had passed each other back and forth several times. He flashed his lights at the other truck and both pulled off to the side. Her driver explained that he had to pull over and rest, but that he had a hitchhiker in need of a ride. Would the second driver give her a lift? It was agreed that he would. Beatrice climbed down from one cab and got into the other.

This second driver was big, six feet tall. When he grabbed Beatrice's tote and threw it on the floor, the muscles of his arm rippled, as if they were disappointed not to be challenged by several hundred pounds of weight. He, too, lived with a burning cigarette protruding from his mouth as if it were a normal growth upon his lip. They rode all day, stopping only to refuel. The owner of one station refused to allow Beatrice admittance to the ladies' toilet. He implied that it was broken. His wife handed Beatrice a paper cup and said, "Here, maybe you can use this!" Beatrice wasn't sure how, so she went behind the building and held the cup between her legs. When she finished she poured the urine on the ground and decided to keep the cup for a possible future reoccurrence of this situation. It was added to her bag.

That night, several hours after sunset, the driver pulled the big truck off to the side of the road and got out, stretching his arms and moving his neck around as if to loosen tight muscles. He opened Beatrice's door and said, "Come on out and stretch. It's a beautiful night." It truly was. The stars were flickering overhead, and without any electric light from the city, kilometers away, the brilliance of the moon as the sole source of light could be appreciated. After Beatrice climbed down from the cab she, too, reached above her head and stretched her arms and spine. The driver grabbed her around the waist and threw her on the ground. He knelt down, one knee on her leg and one hand holding her arm and tangled in her hair. His free hand was groping at her dress and feeling her body. She screamed and struggled to get away but he only said "Shut up" again and again. The weight of his knee on her leg was crippling. She tried to twist from his grasp, but he slapped her. Then, clenching his fist, he hit her with a powerful blow. She went limp.

When she began to regain consciousness, she found that she was alone at the side of the road. The trucker and his truck were nowhere in sight. She was covered in dirt, sweat, and blood. Her left eye would open only to a slit and her leg, where it had swollen to twice its normal size, felt numb. She finally forced herself to sit, then to stand and take a few steps. There was nothing else to do but try to walk. Several minutes later she saw her blue bag where the driver had thrown it from the window, probably having discarded it just as he was driving away. She knew she should change her ripped and stained clothing, but she didn't have the strength. Instead, she continued to force her feet in a shuffle forward, dragging the bag behind.

When she heard the next sound her heart raced. In the wide-open space sound carried far. She could hear a truck long before she saw any headlights come into view. She had to hide. But where? Her impulse was to run away from the pavement and lie flat on the ground, but she couldn't run. She could only turn and walk toward the brush, but it was too late. The trucker had spotted her and began to apply his brakes. He came to a stop, got out, and called to her. "Hey, hey! Is that you, girl?" He ran after her. When he caught up, he put his arm around her to stop the forward movement. She was so weak it took no effort to force her to turn around. When he saw her face, his only words were, "Oh, my God! Oh, my God!"

It was the chatterbox driver. He helped Beatrice back to the truck and up into the cab. She was asleep by the time he'd closed the passenger-side door, walked around to the driver's door, and settled himself behind the wheel. He stopped in mid-morning for fuel and breakfast. Someone in the eating establishment saw her sitting in the cab and began making remarks about his obviously battered passenger. He didn't answer. Instead, he finished the food, paid the bill, and left, bringing her two biscuits, tea, and ice for her swollen face.

By their third day together, Harry had introduced

himself. He hadn't bothered to do that initially when he'd been so preoccupied with talking. Since he felt responsible for and guilty about what had happened, he did his best to make it up to the young black woman, now in the north.

24

For Geoff Marshall, the routine appeal process went on for eight years. It was handled by court-appointed officials and he neither participated nor took any interest in what was happening. At night he often looked at the ceiling, picturing the clear starry sky he had loved so much as a child on the Willetts' sheep station. He longed for a return of that childhood freedom. Even the thought of his own race of people—wild and uneducated, but free—seemed appealing. He yearned to learn more about them but was hesitant to damage his fierce reputation by asking for a book from the prison library.

One day, as the library cart was being pushed past his cell, he spoke to the inmate in charge.

"Hey, man, wait a minute," he said. "I'm interested in seeing if you can get a particular book for me."

"Sure," came the reply from the old man who had held the position for over thirty years. "What's the title?"

"I don't know," Geoff offered. "Once when I was a kid I saw a book that explained about Australian Aboriginal art. I'm from Australia. I'd like to read about that but I don't have any title or author's name or anything. Can you help me?"

"Sure," the white-haired man again stated confidently. "I'll have to order something, though. Will take a few weeks." He took out a pencil and paper and made a note to himself. Then he wrote down the cell number and asked Geoff who he was.

"I'm 804781."

25

The sun was directly overhead and all of God's creatures were without a shadow. As they approached the small community, Beatrice knew this was the place she was to leave Harry's company. It wasn't an impressive place, didn't even look inviting, but somehow it felt right. Dust had settled on every building, showing either a recent storm or a part of the world that entertained wind daily. There was no grass growing between the sidewalk and the street, and the main street looked dead and forgotten, but on a side street she could see a green park with tall shade trees. There were black figures in the park and a few blacks mingling with others on the main avenue, so she knew she had arrived at a place where her race was no longer the minority population in residence. Harry pulled to a stop at the corner, in front of a two-story hotel sporting an entrance through the pub. Several windows were open on the second floor and curtains trailed outside, waiting for another breeze to boot them back into the guests' rooms.

Beatrice climbed out of the cab, said her farewell, and reassured Harry that she would be all right. She had not mentioned the two side teeth she had lost yesterday as she'd eaten a piece of meat pie. Her eye was blood-red and still only partially open, but the leg seemed improved and caused her less pain with each passing day. Carrying the tote, she crossed the street and headed for the park. Right in front of her, an older white woman was inserting a HELP WANTED sign on the front counter of a milk bar shop. Without hesitation, Beatrice walked through the open door, approached the woman, and said, "That's what I'm here to do!"

The startled woman looked up, saw the maimed face looking at her, and was almost frightened by the repulsive eye staring her way.

"What?" she said. "What did you say?"

"I'm here to help you. Like the sign says! I can do most anything if you just show me how." Then, catching her breath and sensing the woman's cautious look, she added, "Please don't worry about how I look today. I had an accident, but it was a first. I'm not prone to trouble and I can help you. I really can."

"I'm just putting this up," the woman said rather indignantly. "You're the first to apply."

"Let me work for you for two or three days and see how I do. If it doesn't work out, you owe me nothing and you can put the sign up again. If I do good, you pay me, and it'll be my job. How's that?"

"I don't know," the woman said with a worried tone to her voice. "Who are you and where are you from?"

"My name is Beatrice and I'm from down by Sydney. I

have an excellent education in English and math and such, and I've had four years' experience working and helping people. I know I look real bad today, but every day it's getting better. By next week it will be so healed you'll be surprised by who you hired!"

The gray-headed woman smiled. She couldn't have thought up a more convincing story herself. "Are you married? Do you have a family? Where are you living?"

"No. No. Nowhere yet!"

They both laughed. It was a silly way to ask the questions and received an equally silly response.

"Okay. Come on back, Beatrice. Let me show you the shop and we will see what you can do in the next two days."

The shop owner was Mildred McCreary. She had been in business in the same building for more than twenty years. At first she and her husband ran the business. When he died, her son became her partner. But he had outgrown this out-of-the-way community. It was too quiet, too dull, too far removed from the rest of the world, so he left. She had received a few letters and one Christmas card five years ago, but nothing since. Every day she anticipated and hoped he would come strolling in through the long plastic fly strips hanging at the front door, but he never did.

The store was a long, narrow structure. The front half was seen by the public. It contained a wide assortment of groceries in tins, wrappers, and boxes. There was a refrigerator where beverages were kept cold. Mildred charged a few cents more when the customer selected a cold drink instead of the same beverage sitting warm on the shelf. She also made food each day for regular patrons to purchase and take away to eat. That was mostly for the noon meal, but leftovers were almost always sold by closing time in the evening. People staying at the hotel sometimes came across to buy groceries for sandwiches instead of eating the higher-priced dinners at the pub. A few blocks away were two commercial pearl-diving operations whose employees had found her food reasonably priced and superior in taste.

In the back half of the store were all the stored cartons of food to replace shelf items as they disappeared, a bathroom and toilet, a small stove, a sink, an overhead cabinet, and another refrigerator. Just inside the door separating the two sections Mildred had a tall old-fashioned cabinet radio where she could sit in an overstuffed chair and listen, within view of the front door, during the slow business hours. To the right of the back door, steps led to the second-story level, the McCreary family residence.

Mildred put Beatrice to work stocking shelves with missing items, sweeping both halves of the building, and cleaning the food preparation area. She was impressed by how dedicated to each task the young woman seemed to be. By the end of the day, she suggested that, as a sleeping arrangement, Beatrice go upstairs to get a folding cot to put in the rear of the store. For the next ten days Beatrice did not leave the store except to sweep the front walkway and shake a rug out the back. She offered to clean Mildred's residence and did a much better job than the owner ever did herself, so that, too, became part of her duties.

The two women got along well. Neither indulged in idle talk, and since Beatrice kept constantly busy, Mildred felt she had found a jewel for an employee. She even taught the newcomer how to keep her record books, balancing income and expenses, and how to handle the ledgers for people who were given credit.

During the fourth month of her employment, Beatrice was trusted to take the deposits to the bank and to deliver an envelope each month containing the money for rent to deposit to the account of Malcolm Houghton.

Mr. Houghton was a second-generation sheep station owner. He owned twenty times more land to run his sheep on than the entire town covered. The building that housed the hotel and all the buildings on Mildred's side of the street belonged to Malcolm Houghton. He sat on the board for the bank, supported the visiting doctors' service by providing a place for their two-day-a-week clinic, and was instrumental in providing for a park and ball field for sporting events. He also employed Aborigines. Beatrice had not seen the man and doubted she would ever be in a position to do so, but she heard his name mentioned almost every day.

When she'd mastered the routine of opening, closing, and running the shop, she found time to finally get acquainted with the other Aboriginal women and families who came to the store from time to time.

It was wonderful to see that at last, in the north, the black children attended the same school as the white children. Although their income was still subsidized to try to elevate the standard of living, far more of her people were employed than she had experienced closer to the nation's capital. She became familiar with an ancient desert tribe's type of artwork and learned some of its historical stories. She continued to voice her desire to know more about her Aboriginal background. One man named Bill, who lived outside town in a settlement with a number of others in makeshift shelters, said that every so often they were visited by a desert dweller. He promised to tell her if one came around again.

One bright Wednesday morning a delivery truck rumbled up to the shop door and left several cases for Beatrice to carry to the back. "These are really heavy. What's in here?" she asked Mildred, who was munching on a piece of toast.

"Empty bottles," she replied as she reached for the strawberry jam.

The bottles sat in the cartons, unpacked, for a couple of weeks. Then Mildred received a package in the mail from a toy manufacturer. Beatrice watched as she unwrapped a carton of colorful balloons. She was very curious about why her employer would order such an item, but asked no questions. Only a few days later the purpose came to light. Beatrice was asked to unpack the glass bottles and wash each of them. She then watched as Mildred added grape juice, sugar, and something mysterious to each bottle. She was asked to put a balloon cap on each. They were making wine, and the balloons would need to be monitored carefully and gas released periodically to avoid an explosion. Part of Mr. Houghton's payroll was met not with cash, but with alcohol instead. He relied on Mildred's expertise to carry on a tradition originated by his father and Mildred's deceased husband. She saw no problem with her participation. The Aborigines were going to drink. They were going to get grog somewhere, so it might as well be hers and she might as well reap the benefits of the sale instead of someone else in town.

Beatrice was disappointed in her friend because she knew drinking was killing her people faster than bullets, but she could do nothing. It seemed that that was the way life was.

She had been working for Mildred McCreary almost a year when, one morning, she was awakened before dawn by Bill, the fringe dweller, who entered the back of the store through the open door. He told her to hurry and take the road out toward the massive sheep station where she might be able to see a desert tribal runner as he had described.

It was early; she wouldn't waken Mildred. She knew she would be back in time to open the shop, so she threw on a skirt and blouse and left.

26

Geoff, now legally known as Jeff Marsh, had been on death row for eight years and all of his appeals had been exhausted. He was a bitter man, but one resigned to dying, when one Tuesday morning, without warning, the guards came to his cell, shackled his hands and feet, and took him to the warden's office. There in the wood-paneled office, the warden, sitting in a tall black leather chair, read an official document to the standing convict. Geoff was advised that the state had passed a law repealing the death penalty. His death sentence had therefore been commuted to life in prison without parole.

It was a shock. He had dealt with his feelings about dying. He hated the Marshalls and he hated their religion, but he had spent hours thinking about all the sermons he had heard over the years. He thought about heaven and hell, the ten commandments, Jesus and Satan. He wasn't comfortable with any of it. There were too many unanswered whys. Now the warden was telling him he wasn't going to die. He was going to continue to live. He was going to continue to be a victim, locked in a cage, until he was an old, old man. The news was unsettling. He couldn't really say how he felt. Something in him felt relieved and something else felt frightened, frustrated, and depressed.

Over the next few weeks all of the death row inmates, who had been isolated, were incorporated back into the general population. In all the years of prison life, Geoff had never shared a cell. Now he was put in with an Italian man who called himself Shorty. The only thing they had in common was their age. Shorty was short, only five feet four inches and weighing one hundred thirty pounds. He wore his hair as long as the prison officials would tolerate, and had more tattoos than teeth. He had a long history of crime, starting as a juvenile. Over the years he had been in and out of prison five times, having been arrested for auto theft, robbery, being part of a gambling and prostitution ring, and now for attempted murder. He loved to talk. Geoff, on the other hand, seldom spoke and was used to not being included in any conversation for days at a time. Shorty was afraid of Geoff. He didn't really trust anyone who appeared to be so quiet. Geoff was sure Shorty would drive him crazy with his constant babbling, but after only a few weeks they seemed to mesh. Shorty instructed his cell mate on how to hot-wire a car so it could be driven without the use of a key, how to break into numerous types of safes, and how to beat the odds at horse races. Geoff listened because Shorty needed someone to listen to him and while he listened he studied the little Italian's facial features. It stirred an interest in drawing that had been dormant for a long time. It was easier in the general population to acquire items like paper and pencils so he began once again to spend time as an artist. At first he tore all the pictures into small pieces and flushed them down the toilet. He didn't know what the reaction to his new hobby might be. But there was a need for patterns to be used by the inmates who tattooed the others. The men wanted pictures of dragons, snakes, or skulls and looked forward to anything new and unique. Geoff soon acquired a reputation as being able to fill individual requests creatively. He also discovered something about himself. For every hideous pattern he provided, he found he must spend time drawing something meaningful and pleasant to the eye. He didn't know where the urge for balance came from, but it was so overwhelming he could not deny its existence. Eventually he openly drew both forms of art. He could create a monster with a long sword-shaped tongue, to be repeated with ink embedded into someone's biceps, and on the same day draw a field of flowers to be mailed home for some inmate's mother's birthday.

During the passing years he did not have a single visitor. The court-appointed legal advisers were finished with him. He had no family or friends outside the prison walls. He received no mail. It seemed there was no one in the world who knew or cared about his existence, but he was resigned to his life behind walls. He made the best of the situation even though he felt in his heart that he couldn't have been more alone if he had been in an outback desert.

27

Beatrice walked along the dusty red road bordering the sheep station owned by powerful Malcolm Houghton. The fence was in good repair, as he demanded, and the pasture of scrub grass was beginning to grow back where the herd had nearly eaten and trampled the ground barren. There was a very slight breeze, which made the morning temperature so perfect it could easily deceive any new Australian arrival into thinking perhaps today would not be as hot as yesterday, but it only made Beatrice grateful that her bare feet were hard and calloused against every change in the seasons. The wild vegetation in the area was green after the recent rains. Ahead there stood a small grove of trees where the fence line curved to end the Houghton property line on the western boundary. It appeared that a motionless blue object was hanging in the midst of the cluster of trees. She thought it might be some sign from the tribal runner she was to meet.

Walking forward, she stared at the blue image until it became apparent that it was not an object and was not actually hanging. It was, in fact, an Aboriginal woman sitting with her back high against a tree trunk, legs propped over a limb, as if she were lounging in a modern reclining chair. She wore only an open blue-plaid shirt exposing her black chest and a cloth tied around her genitals. Beatrice couldn't hold back her smile. It spread across her face as naturally as butter melting on warm brown bread. The grin from the woman in the elevated position revealed a response of childish delight and a mouth with a missing front tooth. The woman's dark eyes, as shiny as highly polished river stones, matched those of Beatrice, but the graying hair on her fifty-year-old head, which bobbed up and down like a child's yo-yo in a silent and enthusiastic yes, yes, was in contrast to Beatrice's dark brown shoulder-length curls.

The young girl voiced a greeting in one of the tribal languages she had studied and waited for an answer. She tried again to no avail as the older woman merely continued her smiling and head-nodding. On the third attempt the woman said, "It is today!" in a native tongue. Beatrice immediately introduced herself and made an attempt to start a conversation, but the tiny female unpredictably climbed down from her perch and slowly began walking away. She was a petite five feet in height, and her short stout legs supported her small yet strong and muscular body. She was heading away from the Houghton station and the nearby community and out toward the outback, where all vegetation grew scarcer until the landscape was a truly barren desert in the heart of the Australian continent. Without turning around, as though she were speaking to the wide-open spaces, she firmly said in English, "We go!"

"Wait," came Beatrice's startled reply. "You speak Australian!"

The new acquaintance paused where she stood and, turning, said, "Yes, I, too, have lived in the city world. But now we must leave, we must go to my country. Our people heard your cry for help. You ask many questions. We'll help you find your answers. Come, we go!" Then she proceeded to move again.

Beatrice had hoped a desert dweller would come someday, but somehow she had assumed they would go together into town, and that she would tell her employer good-bye and find someone who would take her possessions to put in storage. Then, with all the arrangements made, she would follow the tribal woman to her native home. It wasn't happening as she had planned.

She looked down at the flower pattern on her skirt, and from some distant file drawer in her mind emerged a question she had pondered for years regarding a person's last day on earth. When they woke up the morning of their final day, did it feel any different? When they put on the clothing they were to die in, did they have any inkling of the future? She wasn't going to die today, but she was certainly closing a giant door. Somehow the question had formed its own answer. No, she told herself, you don't know when any day is your last day and the best of plans will not be carried out, but you can be in the frame of mind to accept. You can believe something good will come from this!

For sixteen years she had known nothing except life in a mission orphanage, with no family, no heritage, no individuality, one of many Aboriginal baby girls raised within the institution. She spent the following four years without a mentor, a guide, a confidante as a young woman searching without any idea of what she was searching for. She had been someone lost who was no one's daughter. This was the day that was ending. Today there seemed a glimmer of hope that she would finally connect to somebody or something and might actually feel she was where she belonged.

In a voice loud enough for the departing desert dweller to hear she shouted, "Wait, I'm coming. Yes, wait for me, I'm coming!"

They walked without speaking, the younger woman slightly behind the older until the silence was broken by Beatrice asking, "How far away is your country? How long must we travel?"

The woman pointed forward with her index finger, then retracted it back into her palm, pointed again, pulled it back, and pointed once more. Three of something. It couldn't be three miles, it must be three days. Walking for days was no problem. She had certainly spent enough time walking the streets and the countryside during the past years.

Beatrice was amazed that the woman knew in which direction to travel. There were no landmarks in sight and everything looked the same. The earth was a reddish gray, the bushes were in shades from pale to deep green, the rocks were the same as the earth, and the occasional lone lizard blended so well into the landscape that only darting eyes revealed a presence. Once the sheep station was out of sight, Beatrice lost all sense of direction. She voiced her thought: "How do you know which way to go?"

The question was acknowledged with a gesture of a folded hand, thumb pointed down to the ground and smallest finger pointed up toward the sky. She didn't understand the gesture, or why the woman didn't simply speak and answer her question. It probably meant she was following something in the sky and something on the ground, but it didn't matter. Walking away from everything she had ever known felt right. The farther away the tin houses became the more she knew her rightful place was out there somewhere, ahead of them. With each step she felt increasingly confident that she would find it.

Thirty minutes later the woman stopped, turning to Beatrice to say, "Here we thank our mother, the earth. Our body is made from her. She gives us our meals and nourishment, she provides our medicine, and she cleans us with her tears. We sleep in her arms. When we die, she accepts our used bones to mingle with the bodies of our ancestors and the yet unborn. It is time we give back what was taken and we no longer use." She spoke to the ground, asking permission to open it. Then she dropped to her knees and began to dig, scooping out the dirt to make a hole.

"May I help?"

The reply was a nod in the affirmative. Beatrice knelt on the opposite side and they dug together. Finally the woman stripped off her buttonless plaid shirt and dropped it in the hole. She unwound the loin cloth and stood as it, too, was deposited, revealing a rope braid hanging low on her hip with a small leather pouch attached. She offered no explanation for the bag and looked at Beatrice as if to say, You are to follow. All the preaching at the mission school came rushing in, the feelings of shame and embarrassment attached to the naked human body. With only a slight hesitation, Beatrice added the flower-patterned skirt and blouse to the pile. The woman again talked to the earth and said thank you to the clothing as the colors disappeared when the two filled the hole and spread the sand to make it level. Last, the older woman puckered her lips and blew upon the sand, removing all traces of their hand marks and the indentations made by their knees. There was no visible sign that this place had ever been disturbed. She turned and said, "You will not feel so uncomfortable after you join the others and learn more of the ways of my people, the Real People tribe."

"But you had clothes on!" Beatrice remarked.

"Yes, it is necessary to honor that way of thinking. We don't agree with it, but we do not judge. We observe instead. Sometimes, where the weather is cold, it is necessary, but clothing seems to lead to more judgment and separation of people, not less. I am sure you have noticed how confusing it is when judging by the impression given from the outer appearance; the person may be very different from the picture presented. You will discover, as I have, that there is no shame except when groups have made it so. If you were to continue to wear that skirt and blouse, it would only serve to make you feel an outsider in a clan who wish to make you feel a part of us."

They walked on. Beatrice was glad her continent was unique in that a majority of its animals and reptiles were nonaggressive. There were no large man-eating tigers or bears. Instead, they had bouncing kangaroos in all sizes, from that of a rodent to six feet in length; the little koala, who seemed to do nothing productive except remind the world of the wonders of touch; and the emu, with its majestic feathers and flightless running speed. There were, of course, some poisonous snakes, but she felt comfortable with that because her lead companion would certainly know how to deal with them.

They walked for hour after hour through the low-lying bushes and the occasional stand of trees. Finally, later in the day, the woman again spoke. "If it is in our highest good, we shall eat again today, so let us observe what gift Oneness presents. There are things to see and remember with every footstep." She began to point out the tiny marks on the earth, barely visible until Beatrice concentrated. There were marks for paws, claws, slithering-belly, fast-hopping, slow-walking, hungry, tired, old and young exploring creatures. They came across a bed of taller green-speckled plants with a thicker stalk than others they had seen during the day. The woman stopped and spoke to the vegetation. Bending over, she pinched off a piece, broke it open, and revealed seeds inside resembling plump brown berries. She used her thumb to remove the core in the same manner Beatrice had been taught to strip peas from their pods. The two shared the few prize bites. The woman then motioned for Beatrice to break off a piece and shell it. As Beatrice followed the instruction, she asked, "How in the world did someone discover that this was safe to eat?"

"There is a method to tell compatibility when you encounter something different. It begins with your sense of smell. It is very important that you learn to smell everything, not just plants. Smell the air, the water, animals, even other people. Smells are distinct, and you must not forget how something smells. When you have enough comparisons, you will note that poisonous substances often have very strong, individualized smells. If a plant does not smell of a poison you recognize, then next you should break off a portion and rub it upon your body. Use a tender area such as your eyelid, around the nostrils, or under your arm. Wait to see if any sting or discomfort develops, or if itching, any raised marks, or blisters appear on your skin. If not, then you may try one taste, but put the taste upon the side of your mouth or under your upper lip and again wait for the body's reaction. If there is none, you may increase the taste to a slightly larger sample. Gargle some juice at the back of your throat before spitting it out, again waiting to see how it feels before you swallow any. Once you ingest a sample and swallow, you must wait to see if this causes any stomach pain or if your body rejects the food by forcing it back out of your mouth or running out the bottom. Wait long enough to see if it affects your thinking or walking.

"All new encounters are tests—with food, with people, with ideas. Smell everything first. If someone tells you something, smell it! If it smells all right, then try just a little for the taste, but always chew it. Chew for a long time before you swallow. Even words should be chewed for a long time before swallowing because it is much easier to spit something out than it is to get rid of it once you have already taken it in. If you accept words within yourself and the idea is not right for you, it will cause problems. It will cause lumps and bumps and headaches and chest pains and stomachaches and rotting sores until you get it out. Fortunately, with food it is easier to vomit or have running bowels and be over the mistake quickly. Ideas and beliefs are more difficult to expel. You see, there are things the world outside this desert is doing that have caused much of life to become altered. It is best not to assume that something that appears normal or simply looks okay will be, in fact, safe.

"Our most difficult challenge has been to smell and taste the words and beliefs of the European white world and to spit them out politely. There are few free indigenous people left. Each year the number is declining as more and more tribes are forced from their country and must submit to living in the white world or die. I don't really mean the white world. I must correct myself because skin color has no bearing. It is the thinking and the way of life, the change in values from the original laws that have made humans become mutated. Mutants come in all colors.

"Our elders agree, my sister. We have heard your cry for help coming to many of us in our sleeping and waking hours. It is true your life is one of searching and you have the potential to find important answers and to help many lost people to find their way. But it will not be easy for you. Unlike a small child who is eager to learn and has a void to be filled with knowledge, you are already full of information. You will have to decide for yourself what to discard, what to replace, and what to accept. I know because I have been in your place."

Beatrice took the small palmful of seeds. She slowly chewed each one, enjoying the nutlike flavor and wondering about the nutritional value. They continued to walk as she thought very seriously about what the woman had just told her.

"I'm not sure I can do this!" Beatrice finally said in a voice barely above a whisper.

"I'll take you back."

"No, I don't want to go back. I just mean, I'm really uncomfortable without clothes. The thought of meeting other people, men especially, is . . . " Her sentence trailed off to silence.

"That's okay," her escort said, her feelings of concern evident on her face. "We will make an appropriate covering. We will find the things we need as we travel and I will show you how it is done. Real People wear coverings on occasion. It is fine. I think you will still feel better not wearing your skirt and blouse. We can make something more comfortable and much less cumbersome. I understand your belief that exposing your body is shameful, but that really is an attitude you have learned." With a grin that exposed her whole mouth, she added, "I think an opossum skin would be wonderful. Maybe if we send that thought out into the vapors, the opossum born for that purpose will honor us by crossing our path."

Toward the end of the afternoon they came across a small stream of water and both knelt to drink. Just then a brown-striped python with a shiny jet-black head came slithering over a rock to the right of the two travelers. Before Beatrice could open her mouth to speak the woman had grabbed the snake just behind its head. Taking a stone blade from her pouch, she immediately took the reptile's life. She hung the body over her hip belt. Without a word they continued walking.

As the sun was sinking on the horizon they paused for a few minutes. The woman commented on how gloriously each sunset presented itself. Dusk was short-lived once the sun was down; it quickly became dark. The stars stretched out overhead in one massive diamond display. The woman spoke again after they had walked a short distance to announce that they would stop to eat and to rest.

Together, the two gathered and made a pile of dry vegetation including a handful of rabbit droppings. The snake was skinned and cut into pieces that were put on a rock in the center of the brush circle. With two small pieces of flint from the bag Beatrice's companion produced a spark that ignited a fire.

"We must not drain all the water from this meat," she said, "but this one must be heated or we will have little worms form inside our stomachs." She reached into the circle, took a cooked piece of snake meat, and handed it to Beatrice, then took another for herself, saying, "It is our way to be grateful to this snake for being born and being on our path today. His spirit will join ours as his flesh joins our body and we will continue life together." The flesh was still slightly moist, chewy, and remarkably filling.

After they had eaten and were silent for some time, Beatrice asked the woman, "What is your name?"

"On this day I am Benala, which means a brown duck. It is our way to learn from our names. We outgrow each name as we gain wisdom and select a new one periodically that better describes who we are. After living this life I find it interesting that as a mutant I received a name at birth and was expected to retain it my entire life."

"Yes," Beatrice replied. "At least that is how it works for people like myself, who never received a last name. I found that was true for men in the white world too. But when white women marry, they take the last name of the husband. They keep the same first name and sometimes they use a nickname or a substitute name. Mostly people just live with the birth name even though they may not like it, or as you suggest, may believe they have outgrown it. I was told once that there is a way to go to the government and pay money to have it changed. My friend said that it's funny because usually the family keeps on calling the person the original name anyway."

"People who love them?" Benala asked, the orange glow from the coals showing her puzzled expression.

"Yes," Beatrice said, pausing. "I guess they love them, just not enough to address them as they prefer to be called!" Both women laughed and then fell silent again.

They sat, deep in thought. After watching one coal finally burn out, Beatrice said, "You spoke about the necessity of the Real People to spit out the beliefs of the Europeans. How do you know that what they were trying to teach was wrong?"

Benala arched her brow, sighed, and replied, "It wasn't wrong for them, but they seem unaware that life's laws are never changing. They are Forever law. I think your experiences during the first part of your life form what you believe. Later, what you believe determines what experiences you have or how you view the happening. Neither makes it true. People tend to replace truth with belief."

"I don't understand what you are saying. Can you give me an example?"

Benala nodded her head yes. "In the mutant world there is a religious law. I am sure you are familiar with it. It says 'Do Not Kill.' That is clear enough, but still they kill in wars, with transportation, experimenting in medicine, in defense of their possessions or of their own life, in anger or to get even. The interpretation of the simple 'Do Not Kill' is altered to justify a person's thinking in different circumstances. That is all right if a society chooses to believe in such a way, but the truth is a statement, 'You Cannot Kill!', not 'Do Not Kill.' It has nothing to do with circumstances, permission, or analyzing actions already taken. The wording is very clear. It is impossible to kill. You did not create that soul, you cannot kill it. You can stop the human form, but that merely releases the spirit back to Forever. Souls do not stop and start, they are continuous. Death is not final. It is existence in a different form in the Forever world. Certainly there is accountability for taking a life; it is such a precious experience. But the accountability is not in the terms of the European laws. It seems a few men's ideas were presented as universal laws, and millions of humans have propagated these as valid. The laws of our creation don't change over time and most certainly are not different for males or females. Each person has been given the gift of free will. That can never be taken away. So we are each free to travel our own path, seek our own destiny, discover our own highest self. The group you travel with through life will either support you positively or will continually present opportunities for you to reach your own positive level in spite of them."

"But wait," Beatrice interrupted, "I had no free-will choice about being abandoned by my parents at birth and spending my childhood in an orphanage."

"If that is what you believe, that is what you believe," Benala replied. "Does it make it the truth, or just what you believe? Before you were born, when you were in Forever, you were presented with the opportunity to have this human experience. You were aware of the circumstances of your parents and still you saw it as a wonderful opportunity to advance your enlightenment. Why look backward to the 'what if' and seek some logical or rational reasons to explain the past? Today is a new day. We walk forward each new day. Today's choice is today's choice. You have been given many situations in the past to learn tolerance, patience, expression, acceptance, kindness, love, honesty, integrity, and so on. If you didn't learn it as a child in that orphan circumstance, it will come around again, I assure you. If you did learn it, fine! The situations are unimportant. The graduation is what counts. Now it is time we sleep. We will have many more important talks."

Benala showed Beatrice how to smooth an area for sleeping and dig a small indentation to conform better to her body curves. When Benala lay down sleep came almost instantly. Beatrice could not resist looking up at the heavens, thinking about what she had just heard, sorting out questions and arguments to discuss later. Most universities were not outdoors. There were no desks here, no books, no degrees hanging upon the walls, not even a wall, but it appeared to her most certainly as a place of higher learning. Beatrice was distracted by a sudden flash overhead. A shooting star burst into view and zipped across the black sky. Oh, my, she thought, I don't know what that means, but it must be significant! She giggled quietly, thinking, It's what I believe, but it may not be the truth!

Momentarily, peace of mind walked from her head down through her body and she fell into a deep sleep.

28

Benala began to stir while the sun was still hiding on the back side of the earth. The sky was changing from dark blue to a slightly lighter shade with tiny streaks of watercolor pink and orange. Her movement caused Beatrice to open her eyes and momentarily question where she was. She sat up in her narrow sleeping trench and rubbed off clinging sand still embedded in her face and arms. She was surprised at how well she had slept without any separation between her body and the ground.

"Good morning," Beatrice said from her sitting position.

"Top of the morning" was the response. Both women laughed and Beatrice commented, "That is a nice comment. It is the top of the morning."

"Yes, I think people in Ireland say it. I like it too. Now my people would say, 'It is today.'"

"Should we speak in the tongue of your people?" Beatrice asked. "I certainly need the training and practice."

Sadness fell over the face of the listener as she looked away before answering. "It isn't that easy. You see, things have changed a great deal over the last thirty years. At one time there were hundreds of tribes, many different languages, and even more dialects of each language. Everyone knew their territory, honored other nations, others' customs, others' ways, but with the foreign control, some people now find our clan a place of refuge. Our language has become a combination language out of necessity. Our ways have changed to honor the ways of others who joined us. For instance, some never speak about anyone who is not present, and others come from a tribe that does not ever refer to anyone deceased. Of course, we learned about these traditions by first making the mistake of doing something offensive. The others learned by being patient and forgiving us for our ignorance. Today, simply identifying an unmarried woman such as yourself could involve six or seven different terms. I think it is best if we speak Australian; you will learn the necessary words as you need to in the future."

Benala again knelt and restored her earthen sleeping bag back to its original appearance. Beatrice followed suit and found that blowing away her prints wasn't as easy a task as it appeared to be.

"Why were there so many tribes long ago?" Beatrice asked, her head already full of questions.

"Just the way nature works, I think. As people multiplied they formed deep friendships. Primarily because of food, the friends probably walked away together and lived in a way agreed upon by all parties. But values, beliefs, and ceremonies varied somewhat across the land."

The snakeskin from yesterday's meal was hanging on a nearby bush. Benala took it and returned it to the traveling position of hanging from her hip belt. Then she stood, feet apart, arms up over her head, and in silence declared something to the day.

At the conclusion of her morning ritual, she looked at her new traveling companion. With no further comment, walking side by side, they began another day's journey. One woman was retracing steps she had taken many times before; the other entered a whole new world.

This morning's walk took them through heavy brush country where the green branches, sometimes laden with thorns, had to be held out of the way for them to duck under. As they fought the terrain Beatrice posed a serious question to her friend. "Benala," she asked, "why do you think our race of people has lived here for tens of thousands of years and has never developed any alphabet or any written language? I have defended our culture against criticism from those who imply it is because we are intellectually inferior. Do you know the reason?"

"Yes," came the reply from the older of the two Aboriginal women. "The price was too high! Our people told the British, who placed the captives in buildings to force them to learn to read and write, that they would die first. The price was too high! They would die before they paid the price of lost memory. When information is passed on to our children, to a student, it is not done by one teacher. It is done in the setting of a group of teachers. That way nothing is forgotten, nothing is added, and one person's interpretation is not taught as fact. We learn from history put to music in songs and dances, which is not a great deal different from the mutant world teaching the ABC's by its musical rhythm. Things written down rarely go many years without change. In the past our people used silent head-to-head and heart-to-heart communication. You will see that my tribe has not lost that ability, but it is based on having no secrets and telling no lies. When you write something down, you tend to believe you don't need to remember it because you can look it up at a later date. Unfortunately, this leads to a lazy mind. Your power is handed over to the piece of paper. People can't remember the simplest things, like what they did yesterday or what they had to eat the day before. People keen on writing look around and compare themselves to others in their society and come to the conclusion that it is normal for humans to have poor memories. It goes back to the question, Is that fact or is that merely a belief?" She grinned and her parted mouth showed her naturally snow white teeth as she continued, "Our people at age one hundred have retained twice as much as when they were fifty years old. We have rarely relied on passing information on by writing it down. For us, it wasn't necessary and was inappropriate. It works well in many cultures, but it is not a matter of lesser or better. You have been educated and know the value of the written word and also the pitfalls. With my people, you will see life very differently. Then you can decide for yourself. We have used the writing of symbols on our message sticks and to post a notice to a future traveler for thousands of years. We have history recorded in caves and ravines, but our people have always lived their lives dwelling on spirit, not materialistic things. We have never considered manipulating nature, controlling the elements, or advancing ourselves to be superhuman. The world hasn't finished evolving. It is not sensible for man to decide he is the best there is. Plants are still adapting, animals still unfolding, and humans have a long way to go for their spiritual awareness to catch up with their emphasis on things. We, instead, have developed our way because our desire is longevity and harmony for all of life. Beatrice, I'm confident that one day you will no longer feel the need to defend your heritage and will truly appreciate as I do how blessed we are to be Aborigines."

"Yes," Beatrice replied. "I guess there is significance in being a culture where the people aren't farmers, merchants, and lawyers, but are artists, poets, musicians, and magicians instead. You are right. We have reason to be proud!"

Protruding from the brush was a pile of boulders where rainwater had collected in one concave corner. The area was strewn with feathers, and the bodies of two birds floated in the dark liquid. Benala took the dried snakeskin from her belt and with her hand swished the water back and forth, clearing an area of debris. She lifted water in the python skin and told Beatrice to drink the water filtering through. Then they exchanged roles and the leader satisfied her thirst from the steady trickle of purified fluid.

After a rest they walked again, and soon a small flock of colorful green-and-yellow birds flew overhead. They began seeing the same type of bird flying or sitting alone on a nearby branch. Benala kept her eyes searching for a nest. When she discovered it, they took an egg, leaving two others for the continuation of life. Benala poked a hole in the end of the eggshell and sucked some of the contents into her mouth. She then handed it to Beatrice to finish. Benala took the empty shell, wrapped leaves around it, and put it into her hip pouch.

By evening a mature blue-tongue lizard crossed their path and the day's nourishment was complete. That night, as they sat under the brilliantly lit sky, Benala suggested her companion think about a new name. "You can keep what you have if you are comfortable with it, or you can choose something else. There is no limit. You can be called by any name you want."

"What if I want to use a name and someone else already has it?"

"No problem. It symbolizes different things for different people. Your name is how you want the world to address you. It reminds you of any specific issue you are giving attention to on this portion of your spiritual path. My name, for instance, Benala, meaning brown duck, was chosen because I have been too serious most of my life. There must be a balance between lessons and play. I admire the duck's ability just to float for the fun of it, not in search of food, not to escape danger, not to impress anyone looking on, but merely for the sake of pleasure. I don't spend much time that way and I am working on having a more floating personality!" Her eyes twinkled and she raised her eyebrows as she concluded her statement.

"I'll think about it," Beatrice replied.

That night Benala taught her friend how to prepare a sleeping place using some of the soft leaves from nearby vegetation. It was comfortable. Daybreak brought a repeat of the morning ritual.

The terrain was changing slightly and the plants were becoming farther apart. They seemed to be more clustered in certain areas that Benala explained followed an underground river. Periodically they stopped and picked dried leaves and dried berries, which Benala added to her pouch. Looking for the berries, they spotted the opossum. He was a large, fat gray creature casually nibbling on a leaf as if he had been sitting there waiting for the two-legged ones to arrive. Benala picked up a big rock and, throwing it as hard as she could, achieved an immediate kill. She said her words of gratitude as she cut the animal's underside and removed its internal organs. Beatrice offered to carry the carcass. She, too, silently gave her thanks to the spirit of the opossum.

In the early afternoon, Benala guided them to a large pool of water. The rocky bottom and constant trickle from an underground spring provided a fluid so clear it was possible to look down and see the mosaiclike appearance that nature had structured. Just outside the pool, as the water ran off into a dense marshy patch, were brown sausage-shaped growths that looked as if they had been stabbed and run through by the tall reeds holding them up. Beatrice knelt for a refreshing drink as Benala gathered the tall plants and an armload of new, tender shoots. Several feet away, a large flat rock was positioned by itself, obviously not a part of nature's pattern. On top of it was a smooth oval stone much darker in color.

"This rock has been used for grinding powder, like an altar, for hundreds of years by the inhabitants of this nation. Today we will use it to grind our food, and by doing so add our spirit energy to this place and exchange it for spirits already here." She took out the contents of her bag: berries, leaves, and the eggshell. One by one each was pulverized into granules. Drops of water were added to the mixture until a paste formed. The reeds were woven into a container and the paste was put inside. "We will eat this later," Benala said as she cleaned the area and restored it to its original condition.

The day and distance seemed to pass gently as they walked. Benala took long plant leaves out of her pouch and braided them as they talked.

"How many people are in the Real People tribe?" Beatrice asked.

"Nineteen at the moment. You will become number twenty. But the number varies frequently. You will not meet everyone at the same time. It is not possible for us to live together as we once did. There is no longer the food supply available in one location for nineteen people. More important, there is grave danger of being caught if too many of us are seen together. We can disappear and become rocks or tree stumps in small numbers. It was decided that was the best way for us now."

"Why does the number vary?"

"Because many of the members are like you and me. They are refugees from some other nation. There is the life at mission stations available, where food and tobacco are free and nothing is asked of you. The original captives now have children and grandchildren who were born there. All tribal customs are forbidden. There is life outside in the small towns and in the big cities too. The government is beginning to give away money so the people can buy a few things, which is very enticing. But it is a lost existence between two worlds, with both out of reach. A few find us; some stay and cling to us as a support system. We guard our energy to direct our lives to be as positive as is possible."

That evening after they stopped to camp they made a very small fire. Benala waited until it had burned to white coals before she took the seed-powder cakes from her hip pouch and laid them in the warmth. When the food was ready, they each ate two of the plant-stuffed sandwiches. "Here is something for you," Benala said. She handed the project she had been working on all day across the dying fire to her friend's outstretched hand. "Later, I will teach you how to make one like mine from skins, but this will do for now." Beatrice got a better look at Benala's carrying device. It was an amazing invention. Put together in squares, it could fold up as small as a wallet. When needed, it continued to unfold, larger and larger, until it was shopping-bag size. And people think if you don't live in a city you are uneducated and inartistic, Beatrice thought. What a shame the world is so blind to this sort of genius. "Thank you so much," Beatrice said affectionately. "I'm beginning to feel more at ease."

Benala picked up the opossum. After cutting off the head, she stripped away the fur. She placed the meat upon the coals and the hide on the ground. Using a scraper from her pouch, she removed the fat and other tissue clinging to the surface. She removed the brain matter from the skull and told Beatrice it would be needed to rub into the hide as it dried during the coming days. "When we get your covering finished, you will feel at home!" Benala added as they ended the day.

Beatrice smiled, thinking to herself, I already feel more and more at home, and now I am becoming permanently homeless.

29

On their fourth, fifth, and sixth days together, Beatrice woke before the sun and knew what was expected of her. She filled in the sleep trench that had been prepared the night before, leveling and smoothing the sand surface. With puckered lips, she blew away all marks of human visitation. Benala soon joined her. Both women greeted the morning and finished by dedicating the day to Oneness. Beatrice now understood that whatever crossed their path that day—each creature, person, even weather condition—had a unique purpose for existing. Her goal was to honor by acceptance, not necessarily understanding what was taking place. Life in the Australian outback was not complicated. It was a simple matter of honoring the purpose of the Great Spirit.

Beatrice picked up the woven reed belt and pouch her companion had given her and slipped it on. It rode comfortably on her hip over the opossum hide that now hung in two small pieces, one in front and one in back. Her chest remained bare, but that didn't bother her. She shook her head and combed her fingers through her hair. The dirt that had blown during the past few days was mingled nightly with more sand grinding its way into her sleeping head. She didn't know when or how she would be able to remove it, so a good shaking would have to do. Following Benala's example, she pinched two fingers and her thumb together and put sand in her mouth. She massaged her gums and ran the sand across her teeth before spitting it out. Her mouth felt fresher. The two women jointly dismantled the small area that had been last night's campfire and returned it to pristine condition before heading out across the flat terrain.

There was a slight breeze, so gentle it could have been confused with a lover calling for attention by mischievously blowing upon a cheek. The distant blue sky blended into the red-brown earth, making a clear defining line. Identical views of vast flatland and little vegetation were repeated in all four directions. They had traveled to a part of the continent too dry and barren for the big red or gray kangaroos to inhabit. The only hopping creatures were forms of desert rodents and the ever-increasing rabbit population.

After walking two hours they came to an area dotted with scrub bushes. "We wait here," Benala advised. "This is the area of a song line dividing two nations. It is now cared for by my people, but because I bring you, we will stay and wait for permission to enter." They sat quietly in anticipation.

"How long will it take for someone to discover we are here?" asked Beatrice.

"They already know," was the reply.

"How could they know?" Beatrice asked, her brow wrinkled in a puzzled expression.

"They know!"

"What do we have to do? How will we know when we can go on?" the young urban dweller continued to question.

"You will see," came the answer.

They sat in silence until Beatrice asked longingly, "While we wait, please tell me more about our people."

"Well," Benala began with a deep sigh, "Aboriginal people are children of nature. The earth is our mother and we do nothing that would injure her or be disrespectful. We are related to the sky, the stars, the sun, and the moon. We have a kinship with all life—the animals, birds, and plants are blessed to have been born here in paradise. It really was a paradise for thousands of years. All humans everywhere appreciate a place where there is a nearby mountain range, a river flowing down from on high like a lazy fat snake feeding little tributaries into fertile valleys until the stream enters the sea at a shore of golden-white sand and magnificent curling blue waves. That is what our people had on every coast of this land and what the Europeans, coming from a cold, damp, dreary place, wanted for their towns of Sydney, Brisbane, Adelaide, and others.

"We were forced off our land, but Aborigines are not violent people. It is not our nature to be warriors, to try to get even. We do not think like the eye-for-an-eye culture, in fact, quite the opposite. In our history there is much less physical aggression than any other race in the world. When someone committed a socially unacceptable or violent act, it was handled by a method called 'bone pointing.' The offending party made himself sick and sometimes died from self-inflicted psychological illness due to feelings of guilt or remorse. We've never had a jail, a guillotine, a firing squad, or even people in the role of police. Then eighty years or so ago, self-rule was denied us by foreigners who formed a government that never attempted to make any provisions for us. There was no treaty. In fact, the documents on which the entire Australian legal system is based stated emphatically that the continent was devoid of human life. A million people were considered to be nonexistent. Because we were such peaceful people, the culture was dissolved relatively quickly.

"Much of our peace, I think, comes from our methods of child-rearing. There are no unwanted children. We have used an herb for centuries, chewed by both husband and wife, that prevents pregnancy. Our planned parenthood was very different because the unborn soul was in control. When the spirit wished to enter the human school of experience, it made that desire known. Our whole community awaited the spirit's arrival. All other children of a clan became its brothers and sisters, all the women were like second mothers, and all the men were second fathers. Children never lacked attention or love. Each was encouraged and treasured. Children drank from the breast until they were three or four years old, and the pleasure of nursing was shared by numerous women.

"You see, we know all babies, regardless of gender, are born multitalented. All humans are born with the ability to do so many wonderful things in life, we seldom live long enough to explore it all. Everyone is a singer, dancer, artist, healer, teacher, leader, clown, storyteller, and on and on. We may not believe it, may not be interested in part of it, but that doesn't diminish the talent. It only means we do not recognize or honor that part of ourselves.

"I think that is why it has been so difficult for Aborigines to understand racial prejudice. We don't consider one person as more valuable than another. In our clans and tribes, members do what they love to do, not because it looks most impressive or because of some special reward. Everyone contributes what they wish and each is given a genuine thank-you, so feelings of being accepted and worthy are mutual. Even our so-called leadership is basically voluntary, often rotating. Our elders are respected older citizens who are wiser because of experience.

"You have to realize that I speak in generalities. There were hundreds of tribes of people and, like groups everywhere, there were differences in their ways of life. I don't know what tribe my parents and grandparents came from. You and I are a generation of stolen children, taken at birth. I am guessing that you, too, were never informed of birth details."

Beatrice shook her head in agreement.

"For me personally," Benala continued, "the greatest insight into comparing the two societies, the mutant city and our refugee world here in the desert, has been to understand my role as a Forever spirit having a human experience, and to understand the difference between judgment and observation. Growing up in the city world, I was taught to judge everything: to judge people by their appearance, judge possession by the value, judge the day by the weather, judge health by any degree of pain. The world is full of expert judges who can never agree completely. Each person ends up somewhat isolated and separate from even his own spouse, family, and friends in key beliefs that structure his actions.

"Here in the desert I learned observation. Judgment means deciding right or wrong or degrees of more right than wrong. When you judge, you automatically set yourself up for the other half of the equation. You must also experience and learn forgiveness. When you judge, you ultimately spend equal time, moment for moment, in forgiving. If you don't do it while you are alive, you will do it at another time.

"Observation is a one-hundred-percent-different mental viewpoint. It does not require the step of forgiveness. You acknowledge all people as Forever souls, acknowledge all people as being on their journey through the school of human experience, and acknowledge all souls as possessing the gift of free will and freedom of choice given by the Creator. In other words, people different from yourself are not wrong. They are just making different spiritual choices.

"Our body comes with five senses that connect to every inch of us, so observation can be done with your eyes or nose or any of the senses. Each of us must decide what is right for us to help support a positive journey. In turn, we are responsible for serving others who cross our path. Instead of judging the modern value system, for instance, our tribe would say we smell it, and for us the smell is one we prefer to reject. In your case and mine, we have tasted and felt that other world, and for us it is not supportive of our path. We have blessed that way of thinking and walked away. We are not judging it as wrong, irresponsible, or selfish. Instead we merely observed what was taking place and decided we did not wish to participate. It's more involved because it deals with Oneness consciousness, but we can talk about that more when other members of the tribe are present.

"My people are called the 'Karoon,' meaning first, original, unchanged, thinks in oneness, or real. I say Real People tribe. The European-type society is referred to as changed, no longer thinking in Oneness, altered or mutated." Benala smiled her toothy grin and laughingly added, "This is not a judgment statement. It is an observation."

Just then a strange droning sound came in waves across the open plain. The pitch varied from high to bass tones and continued in an eerie, breathless moan.

"What in the world is that noise?" Beatrice questioned. Benala put her index finger across her lips to indicate silence. She studied the sounds until they ceased and then spoke. "It is from our people, telling us to come. For now you are welcome to the outside of their circle. They are using an old, old method of communication, a special piece of flat wood attached to a rope. It is whirled round and round and the sounds form words and send a message. It carries over vast distances here in the open, and is very helpful when it isn't possible to talk head to head and heart to heart."

The two began walking again and stopped once to drink and eat. Benala had guided them to a small row of plants. She knelt down and asked permission of the earth to open a hole that immediately filled as dark water seeped in. She then talked to the water and asked permission to drink. Both women used their hands to form a cup and drank the water gratefully. Beatrice was beginning to understand that water every day was not a guarantee. Benala pulled two clumps of the vegetation, handed one to her companion, and demonstrated how to free the roots of dirt before eating, as well as how to consume the most tender portion of the stalk. After a short rest they walked on.

After thirty minutes they could see the largest mound of earth they had encountered that day. "The people wait for us on the other side, in the shade," Benala commented.

Beatrice wondered what they would be like: Indigenous people, many who had not seen the city, hoping to avoid capture? So-called primitive people who lived their entire lives, from birth to death, without any modern conveniences. Had her parents been stupid, pagan, and not quite human, as the mission school had repeatedly tried to drill into her head, or were they intelligent and peaceful, as Benala had described? What would she find on the other side of the hill, and would she be sorry she came? She continued to ponder the situation the entire distance until at last she saw a tiny speck moving toward them. As it came closer and closer, she recognized it as another Aboriginal woman.

The greeter wore only a warm welcome smile and a pouch, suspended by a braided cord, on her hip. Soft brown skin, taut upon a long slender neck, revealed her youth. The pace quickened as Benala and the girl drew nearer to each other until finally the younger of the two broke into a run.

"It is today," Benala said as she embraced the girl in a hug.

"It is today," the other repeated. Turning to Beatrice she said, "You have come to us. We hope you find what you seek. I will take you to our circle."

The three walked side by side in silence.

Windstorms of wet howling sand blocked by a rocky surface had caused a large protrusion on the earth's surface. As the three rounded the mound they saw an area left open, making a sheltered overhang, and there on the ground sat four people, two women and two men. One man had long white hair and a full beard to match. He had such a soft and gentle presence that in the city he most certainly would have been called Santa Claus. The other man was younger. His hair appeared to be wrapped with some sort of twine, holding it tight to his head. His face was thin, his arms almost birdlike, but his body seemed strong and muscular. It was difficult to tell the age of the first woman. She had no gray in her hair, although she looked older due to many deep wrinkles around her eyes and mouth. The other female had snow white hair. Over her right ear she wore a small bird feather, which, upon casual observance, could easily have been considered a portion of her unruly hair. She had white stripes painted on her chest and dots painted across her forehead. All four smiled but remained seated as the young girl approached and sat opposite them.

"Wait here. You must be invited to join," Benala told Beatrice as she moved forward and took her place next to the young girl. Beatrice remained standing in the sun wondering what was involved in proving her worthiness to join this circle.

The last four days had been completely different from the first twenty-two years of her life. She loved her new friend, who made the travel seem easy. She enjoyed how her explanations answered so many questions, but still she was uncomfortable. Deep down she admitted to herself that there was the fear that discovery of her true heritage might be a Pandora's box she might later regret not having left unopened. She wanted so desperately to be proud of her ancestors, to defend them, to boast about them, but at this moment she was not at all certain that was going to happen. These people did not look like neighbors welcoming someone new into their neighborhood!

30

The woman with the painted body and the feather adornment stood, then moved a few feet away to a flat area where she kneeled to remove the rocks and smooth the sand, using the palms of her hands, until there was a clearing approximately three feet by three feet. Then she returned to the shelter, picked up a short, pointed stick, and handed it to Benala before returning to her seated position. Benala brought the stick out into the sunlight. Giving it to Beatrice she said, "Please use the drawing area and make a picture."

"A picture of what?" the outsider asked.

"Anything you wish these people to see," was her reply.

"But I can't draw," Beatrice insisted.

"Of course you can. Everyone can draw. Don't worry about it. Just do your best. Go ahead, draw a picture."

Beatrice was at a total loss. She had no idea what they

expected, or what they wanted. Was this a test, a game, or a joke?

They all looked serious as they waited for her action. They were pleasant and friendly but definitely serious. "Draw a picture," her friend had said. "Just do your best," she had instructed. So Beatrice picked up the stick and without anything in mind began by drawing a circle, putting another smaller circle on top, and adding lines. She found a very inartistic drawing of a kangaroo emerging. She stood when the artwork was completed and turned apologetically toward the audience, saying, "I've never developed any skill in drawing! Sorry."

The party of six, in line one behind the other, walked around the childish kangaroo image, viewing it twice. Then they returned to their seats. There were quiet whispers for a few moments before Benala turned to Beatrice and told her to come in and sit down beside her.

"Welcome to this circle," Benala said. "This is Apalie, Water Person," she said as she introduced the woman across from her. Then she continued, "Wurtawurta, Feather Ornament," pointing to the white-headed woman. "This is Mitamit, Spirit Wind Runner," she said as she began with the two men, "and Googana, Rain Man," pointing to the white-bearded man. "Our greeter is called Karaween, Reed Basket Maker." Then, turning to Beatrice, she said, "They know who you are reported to be, but you need to tell them personally."

"I am Beatrice and, like Benala, I was stolen from my parents at birth and come to you for help in learning who I am." All the introduced members nodded their heads in understanding and agreement. Googana, Rain Man, spoke in his native tongue, which Beatrice could follow remarkably well.

"We asked you to draw a picture because it reveals many answers for us to unasked questions. If a visitor draws mountains and trees, that person sees our nation as a territory to pass through. If the drawing is of the sky, we have someone who is more aware of our unique space in the universe and someone who may remain for a while. You drew a kangaroo, which came comfortably for you, so it indicates a relationship to this animal and all others related to the kangaroo. We would portray the kangaroo in a drawing by showing the paw prints, so we know you think and observe in large and we will help you to see detail and also the invisible. The truths you are seeking are very specific, yet apply to the vastness of all mankind."

The group sat for only a few moments longer, then stood, one by one. Each person cleaned the area he had disturbed by sitting on it. When Beatrice saw Benala clearing away her drawing, she helped restore the rocks to the area. After they finished, the seven travelers began walking in silence out into the open terrain. The only sounds were of footsteps and the occasional scurry of some small creature darting for cover. Beatrice could not recall a time in her life when she had felt as she did now. It was almost a sensation of numbness. Her state of mind was an odd combination of anticipation and relief. It was difficult for her to understand. Perhaps, she thought, this is what peace feels like, a kind of nothingness.

In the silence youthful Karaween, Reed Basket Maker, was moving her left arm as if directing music. Beatrice looked at the young woman with a questioning expression. "We sing together in the voiceless way," the girl offered.

"The main method of communication among the Real People tribe is telepathy," Benala interjected. "It is referred to as speaking head to head, heart to heart. In time you, too, will be able to participate, but it takes training and practice. In your situation you will probably find, as I did, that unlearning is essential."

They walked in no precise order. No one was designated to lead. They carried no fire stick. It was not a season of difficulty in finding enough dry material to start each day's campfire. Later would come the season that required a protected glowing ember to be transported, but not that day, not under these skies.

As they traveled toward the setting sun, yam plants were pulled up for the tuber nourishment and other foliage because the leaf or stalk was edible. Two snakes, two rabbits, and a lizard also joined the day's menu. They would eat, but not together. Each took food as it became available. In the early morning, early evening, and after darkness much of the desert life made itself present. The act of gathering food was viewed as nature's way of developing the ability to throw, hit a target, kill painlessly, and perfect the talents of running and focusing sight and concentration. All youngsters in their growing years spent hours in animal, insect, and bird watching. They learned the sounds, and could imitate each call. They were able to duplicate actions down to the tongue flicking of the goanna, the stride-hopping variations of the kangaroo and the wallaby, and the pace and darting motion of the wombat and the possum. They taught that it was necessary for the human and life force of all food to be united in spirit before the essence of the two mingled to become one at a meal.

The sacredness of the earth giving man the gift of continued life is uppermost in each hunter's and each gatherer's mind. Beatrice was amazed at the volume of knowledge each person contained. They knew what could be eaten, where it might be found according to the season and weather conditions, how to extract poisonous chemicals and render a plant harmless, and how, in some cases, to dry poison for use later as medicine. The movements and sounds of animals were incorporated into nightly songs and dances. These were then used later as an actual magnetic lure for food. The life of the animal or plant was given in exchange for the life force to be continued on through the recipient. It was a deeply significant honor system. All things had an honorable purpose, a positive purpose, and this was never forgotten even when circumstances would make it appear otherwise. In what appeared to be a barren environment, there was nutrition available above and below ground, in the water, sky, nests, holes, dead and living trees, termite mounds, and caves. All food was asked for, anticipated, and gratefully received. It was not taken for granted, but the people did not feel that they must work to earn it. They were aware from moment to moment that the Great Spirit, a Divine Power, had spoken and acted through their ancestors and continued to do so through the yet unborn, through the elements, and through all of creation. The world and all of life were unfolding in a perfect way and each was a vital part of the puzzle.

There was a distinct difference between knowledge as Beatrice understood it and the wisdom the Real People tribe lived by. According to Googana, Rain Man, knowledge was education, learning that could come from experience or a teacher's instruction or, as the mutant world gained it, from books and other modern inventions they had developed. Knowledge was totally separate from wisdom, which the tribe believed was how one chose to use knowledge. Perhaps wisdom required an action, and perhaps the best thing to do would be to do nothing. The oldest woman, Wurtawurta, spoke to Beatrice. "Water running through cupped hands is a life without wisdom. Water confined to a vessel for drinking is different. Both are beneficial and have merit in certain times and places, but life without wisdom would, of necessity, need to be repeated at another time, in another place, on another level. Too much truth is lost."

31

One afternoon as they journeyed, Beatrice turned to Wurtawurta and asked, "Were you born into this tribe? I'd like to know more about you."

"You want to hear my story?" was the question coming from her gentle old face. "Okay, I will tell you exactly the way it was told to me so many years ago.

"It was a brilliant day. The ocean crashing upon the shore formed a rim of bubbles in the golden sand that inhaled and exhaled with each wave. Fishermen cast hand-crafted nets into the warm aqua water, and joyous shouts were heard as special specimens were retrieved. Young brown-skinned boys and girls played at the water's edge and took each prize back to the tree-lined shore where women, in readiness, prepared the meal. Everyone from the community was present, with the exception of three women. The most recent tribal bride was giving birth in a sacred place inland, and her mother and aunt were in attendance. They had been munching on fruit and dried turtle, but with the birth obviously only moments away, fresh fish would be brought to the new mother later in the day.

"The birth was not difficult. The young bride was very healthy and had prepared herself and the fetus for this entrance into the world. The tiny female infant was lovingly greeted by its relatives. The new grandmother cleaned the child using oil and the softest portions of large, split leaves that had been prepared that day before the first signs of labor were noted. As was the custom of these people, the mother and child would remain in seclusion for three days, allowing time for the new father and the community to prepare for the child's dedication and for the mother to cleanse and renew herself.

"Mother and child rested together on a fresh, green bed of grass. All the foliage used during the birthing process was ritually burned. An added ingredient was used to make the smoke very black. This would tell anyone nearby that it was not the proper time to come upon this place. The black smoke would also tell the invisible ancestor spirits in the sky that the child's spirit had arrived safely. The new mother was hungry after fasting for a day, so she ate after saying thank you to the spirits of the food and the female food bearers.

"The next morning mother and child walked to a rocky grotto where high ocean waves became trapped in a small lagoon. The water slowly seeped underground, enabling the plants and flowers around it to flourish to such a height the mother had to part stalks to reach her destination. There, she bathed herself and introduced her newborn daughter to the world of water outside the womb.

"On the third day the three adult females walked back

to the camping community, carrying the child in a gathering bowl lined with flower petals. They handed the baby to her father, who was seated flanked on both sides by older wise leaders. Grandmother watched the exchange, but was careful not to look into the father's eyes. Over eons of time it had proved to be best if mother-in-law and son-in-law did not have eye-to-eye contact. Now it was a tribal rule.

"There was a feast in celebration of the new human life. Usually, the people were not robust eaters; theirs was the dominantly lean and athletic stature of the Aboriginal race, but this day was special and the food was plentiful. After everyone had eaten, while some rinsed the serving bowls and cleaned the area others were busy preparing for the ceremony when all attention would again be directed to the baby. A musician picked up the hollowed limb of a tree and, blowing into it, made the drone begin. Clacking sticks set the rhythmic pace. Male dancers, with white cockatoo feathers glued to their thighs and tall palm leaf headdresses on their heads, moved in story form to remind everyone of the Dreamtime that created all spirit. One by one, dancers and singers played their roles. Women were painted with white chalk that sparkled because powdered seashell had been added, and they wore flowers since it was the season of blossoms. In the songs and dances, the story unfolded to say that in the beginning, in the time before time, there was nothing until the Dream of Oneness. The Dreamtime consciousness expanded to include a layer of energy that received the gift of free will. This allowed the layer of energy, the ancestor spirits, to join in the co-creation of the Dream. Men and women dancers dramatically depicted ancestor teachings, animal spirits, and earth's sacred inheritance. At last, the baby was ready to be a part of this society. She had heard the entire story. Her name would be Indigo, after the flower that bloomed only once each fifty years. The day the flower opened the expectant mother was looking at it, and that's when the fetus first moved. The tiny butterfly flicker in the mother's stomach was taken as a sign that the spirit was connected to the rare flower.

"Indigo lived with her extended family in this serene place for four years, moving back and forth between the nearby mountains and the shore with the seasonal changes. She slept each night cuddled against someone's chest or in a row next to another child. Her morning and afternoon naps were taken in the shade, with the sunshine playing peekaboo as a breeze lifted the tropical tree leaves. When she was old enough to sit and watch, the other little girls kept her entertained by playing with long slender blades of grass as if the blades of grass were people. They walked a blade of grass around pretending it was an adult doing its normal daily routines. When it was in season, the children also had dolls made from a flowering stick with branch arms. At other times the dolls were made from grass bundles tightly tied in the human shape. One child always used baby Indigo instead of a doll, so the baby was always included in the play. There was never any personal ownership of a toy. Each child had his or her favorites, but everything was shared and they worked out any differences among themselves.

"By the time Indigo was one, she could play two forms of hide and seek, hiding an object or hiding herself.

"At three she could help gather and prepare food and spent a lot of time with her grandmother, who collected and dried medicines for all varieties of injuries and discomforts. Education came from storytelling, tribal songs, dances, and ritual. During the first four years, there was no differentiation between boys and girls. They played together, slept together, and helped adults freely. Indigo preferred being with her grandmother to trapping little animals or birds, which the boys and older girls liked to do. Sometimes the search for a special medicinal plant took the two a great distance from the camp, which was the case when Indigo was four and the nightmare began.

"They had been gone all day. Grandmother had set the pace so they could return before the child became too tired and would want to settle down for the night's sleep. 'Something is not good,' Grandmother said as they walked around a marsh heading toward the community. It was quiet, too quiet. There was no sound of birds, a heavy smell of blood filled the air, and the presence of something unseen was almost palpable. Grandmother could feel the bad on her arms and the back of her neck, and it caused a knot in her stomach. She stopped and, turning, said, 'Be very quiet, little one. Stay close behind me. Something is not good.' They approached the camp area and the stillness became so disturbing even the child was alerted to something very different. In the distance they could see there was no large, lapping wave coming up onto the beach. It seemed even the sea held its breath in a hush.

"Then Grandmother saw them, two white men wearing long trousers and heavy boots and carrying guns. One man had orange hair and a full beard and the other wore a hat, but she saw blond hair protruding from it. They were talking to each other as the man in the hat kicked at something in the tall grass. The orange-haired man fired into the underbrush. Grandmother could scarcely contain a sound of surprise. It was the first time she had heard a gunshot, but she had already been told of the existence of such a weapon.

"Since the beginning of time her people had been caretakers of land farther south. Many white settlers had come, and, over time, the initial friendship had turned to violence. Ultimately, after trying to communicate peacefully with the foreigners, some of the tribe succumbed to the promise of daily food in bags and tins, giving them a life free of hunting and fishing. They voluntarily moved to a mission. Others, accused of crimes, seemed to die after being jailed for only a few hours. The remainder walked north to this land where the caretakers had mysteriously disappeared.

"Grandmother grabbed the child's head and held it against her leg, both bodies trembling. Slowly they began backing away, but she could smell the scent of the white man and it was becoming stronger. Grandmother held Indigo so close that their hearts were pulsating against each other's skin. Their next few steps were wet as they backed into the marsh. The ground gave way to thick mud, ankle deep. Grandmother picked up the child and placed her straddling her left hip. As she pulled the child from the sucking surface, she heard the pop of gooey mud and the sound of heavy boots coming toward them. The water grass was waist high, but thin, not dense enough to keep them from being seen. She no longer took a normal step, but kept her feet under the surface of the water and slipped along in a careful ski fashion. She didn't want to turn her back on the noise of the footsteps and the strange white man odor of alcohol, tobacco, and garlic, but there was no choice. She had to see where to hide. Part of the marsh was covered with this grass, then there was an open pool of water. On the other side was a bed of thick plants and a rocky cliff. Indigo was four years old and she could swim, but Grandmother knew her swimming involved an enormous amount of splashing and noise. She would have to swim and tow the little girl. Could she make her understand that this time she was not to swim, but instead to float in silence? The mud was deeper and deeper, her movement forward slow and strained. She heard the boots and the voice of one man, but couldn't determine how close he was. She sensed he hadn't seen them yet since there was no fluctuation in the tone of his speech. Grandmother looked at Indigo, piercing into her black eyes with thought. She put her finger to her lips in the manner indicating silence. She then shifted the child to her back. Indigo's arms went around her neck and Grandmother grabbed both of her little feet and placed them around her waist. Don't move, she thought over and over. Please don't move!

"She entered water deep enough to swim. Without breaking the surface with either her arms or her legs, she struggled, frog fashion, toward the opposite side. I should have taken some grass to hold, she thought. To cover our heads. It was too late. They were away from the surrounding growth and were clearly two human heads bobbing across the water at dusk. They had almost reached the other side when a shout came from the right. Grandmother looked over to see a third white man. More noise came from behind them where they had entered the water. The third man hadn't seen them, but he had seen his friends and yelled to them. She couldn't understand the foreign language. They had only a few feet to go to be in the reeds, but they were in clear view of the third man as she stepped out from behind a grove of small trees. If he simply turned his head, he would see the two of them. There was no time to warn Indigo, no time to think of any alternative action. Grandmother just forced herself underwater, and going forward under the surface pulled the child around to her front. As they surfaced in the tall grass and wild lilies, she clamped her hand over Indigo's mouth. The third man heard the sound as they surfaced but, looking around, he didn't see anything. Without breaking stride, he continued his walk around the rim of the muddy marsh to join his friends.

"The two in hiding were as motionless as the plants surrounding them. Grandmother held her hand over the child's mouth so tightly that a cough only puffed out her cheeks and forced water to run from her nose. The child was in pain and terrified, but Grandmother did not move a muscle until the third man joined the other two and all had turned their backs on the pool of water.

"They remained in the marsh for two more hours, until all sounds and smells of the cruel foreigners were gone, leaving behind them the bloody stench of death. Finally, they climbed out of the water and headed away from the sea. They had walked only a few yards when ahead they saw someone lying on the ground. Indigo, now walking and holding Grandmother's hand, saw the person too. Someone was sleeping on his stomach, she thought, but then she saw blood, still wet and leaking from a hole in the back of his neck. Near his head she saw feet and ankles embedded in the wild plants, little feet with a yellow-plaited anklet wrap like that worn by many of her friends. And off to the side was a hand where a body had fallen in a position now partially hidden in the grassy growth. The hand had prominent veins, an old hand, older than Grandmother's. Indigo could not keep her eyes from looking at the hand, at the child's feet, and at the dead man covered in blood. She didn't have to be told not to speak; it was impossible to utter a sound. Once in her young life an older man had died and she had witnessed the ritual of preparing the body, building the death raft, and releasing it, with a flaming torch, out to sea. She knew of death, but until now it had seemed okay. There was no talk of suffering and children dying. What she was looking at here in the grass was also death, but it seemed very bad.

"Grandmother had to make a decision. Should she hide Indigo and go back and see what had happened to the others? Would the child be safe alone? Would she stay by herself or wander off? If the men were not gone and they shot her, too, what would happen to the little girl? These men were baby killers, as the child at her feet proved. Guns seemed to honor no age barrier. No, they must leave. They must get away from this place of senseless death. So, without touching any of the dead, without any further investigation, Grandmother and Indigo walked away. That was in 1870, eighty-six years ago. I am Indigo and have lived with several different clans over the years, but the history has remained the same. Year after year the foreign settlers took more and more. It was a continued tragedy of gentle people being lured by candy into religious missions that sprang up as easily as pitching a tent. One by one, like plucked roses plucked from a bush, our language, customs, beliefs, games, and rituals were removed and left to die. People unaccustomed to sugar, flour, salt, butter, tobacco, and alcohol are now dying of the white man's diseases at a very early age. I don't know if some are still being shot for sport, randomly, as the new citizens have done with kangaroo and koala. Straggling refugees from various tribes found us banding together in the desert, which, for a while, appeared to be the one place the people of a foreign king didn't want.

"Yes, this is my story. I have changed my name several times over the course of my lifetime and am now known as Wurtawurta. I have explored eight different talents, learned wisdom from all my experiences, am a matron in the Real People tribe. Now, at ninety years, I am just ready to wear feather ornaments and boldly paint my body on less ceremonial days.

"I was already educated in the ways of my nation when Grandmother and I finally joined the mixed band of refugees and desert dwellers. Grandmother's body never totally adapted to the different climates where the temperature changed from searing sun to frosty moon within hours. She often said her bones were uncomfortable and sore, but she managed to live until I reached the age of thirteen. I remember as a child helping Grandmother into her deep sleeping trough so she could be covered with sand to contain the old woman's limited body heat. Now I am an old woman myself. My head is filled with stories, songs, and dances of the coastal tribe and also the knowledge of the people I now consider my own. Grandmother repeated over and over as the years went by, 'There were no conflicts from tribe to tribe. One sings that Oneness makes the sky and sky people first. That we are made from the dust of the stars. Others sing of animal people: It is not a conflict, only a difference. In the end, in the counting system of Forever, it has no bearing. All people are Forever spirits,' she said, 'even the blue-eyed Europeans who call this earth Australia and think they own it. For all souls, the same truths apply. They don't have to agree, but truth is truth, spirit law is law, and so, in the end, all people will wake up and know.'

"One of Grandmother's most frequently used phrases was 'Life is change. Some big, some little, but without change there can be no growing. And change and growth do not imply either pain or sacrifice.'

"When Benala joined us, we sat for hours, fascinated, learning about world events. From time to time, she has gone back into the modern world and returned with more information. Now here we have you, another refugee. I feel blessed that our paths have crossed. It is not an accident, it is in the highest good, and each day's events will reveal to us new spiritual opportunities."

Beatrice thought about the two worlds, the one in which she had grown up and this one from which mutants believed the Aborigines should be rescued. If they only understood!

32

It was decided that evening as they traveled that Beatrice would be taught the ways of the seasons, the weather, and would be introduced to each new life, either growing or crawling, that crossed their path. They would begin the next evening with the first of song and dance teachings that would take one year to tell. These teachings were normally repeated over and over for all growing children.

The six talked of their first meeting with Beatrice, and how they had felt comfortable with her sand drawing. She was not the first to come from the outer world and to see flat, as the white man did, to see only the skin of a kangaroo. The first time it happened they hadn't known what to think. All of the Aborigine artwork had views from the sky. One saw the billibong water holes, the sacred mounds, campfires, and people from the heavens. Or there were views of animals and fish showing the entire physical structure, exterior fins and eyes, interior spine and organs. They had a difficult time understanding how anyone could see the way the white man did, in such a flat way, seeing only the surface, but once it was explained, it was merely another interesting challenge with which to deal. Beatrice was not a personality who would argue or be demanding. That trait was evident from the lack of toes on her kangaroo picture or any other specific details. Her drawing was big and loose, which said to them that she had an open mind. They had each noted the line drawn across the kangaroo, indicating a pouch, but there was no baby's head peeking out. Beatrice, too, bore a line across her body. She offered no explanation. If it were to be offered, it would come later. Most likely it was woman's business. As an artist she had been hesitant and had even asked for instructions on what to draw. But she had participated in their screening process. That told them more about her. An individual's personality, characteristics, and actions, as well as the question of social influence versus hereditary characteristics, had not been of any concern for the original fifty thousand years of existence. Only during the last fifty years or so had it become an issue to observe and ponder. Only since the white skins had arrived and had taken their people did the captives sometimes escape and tell stories of cruelty, theft, and greed, which were all new concepts that appeared to smell bad.

In the beginning there were no irresponsible people. There were some with perpetual energy and others who seemed lazy all their lives, but each was responsible. In the beginning there was honor. People wore decorations of honor. Anyone could create wonderful ornaments to wear, but did not imitate or try to duplicate what another had been given in honor.

Since the Europeans had come and forced the tribes to

dissolve their nations, the new generations born in the modern places seemed to regard responsibility and honor as no longer a part of their culture. They had nothing for which to be responsible. The white man taught that everything they stood for was wrong, stupid, and evil. Certainly, little honor could survive such trampling upon one's heart and mind.

Later that night the group became six listeners and one speaker. Beatrice told of her life. With prodding from Benala, she updated the information of the world functioning around their periphery and told of faraway places named America and China. "There is a cloth," she said, "made of tiny and strong strands, the work of a worm."

"A worm that weaves like a spider?" interrupted Karaween with her fingers open and forming the shape of a circle.

"I'm not sure of the shape of the web," Beatrice acknowledged, "but it is like a long spider thread, only much stronger, so it can be worked together and woven into a fabric. The cloth is so smooth." She paused to think of a description and then continued, "You know what it feels like to run a smooth, polished stone across your cheek? Or the feeling when you just float in water, where there is no pressure or texture at all? This cloth is like being wrapped in the softest, smoothest cloud. Yes, it is like feeling the heavens touching your skin. It is to wear the polish of a rock. The cloth is called 'silk.' I held a square of it once. There are people in China who wear whole garments of silk."

She stopped, unable to think of anything else to add. The group sat under the starry night, each listener imagining in his own way the experience of this new idea, the touch of silk.

* * *

It was the new moon that gave way to the first rays of morning light. As they cleaned the camp area, each person was still full of the story of faraway places. Then old Googana summoned everyone to stand in a line one behind the other, belly to back, left shoulders facing the rising sun. Their left arms were down, palms open at knee level. Their right arms were up over their heads, palms open to the light. They bent slightly at the waist, forming a curved line, and each looked to the east. In unison they repeated the phrase they had used each morning, "It is today, Oneness! We walk this way to honor whatever is out there, for its purpose for being. Our purpose is to honor *the purpose*. If it is in the highest good for all of life everywhere, we are open to the experience of eating again today."

Mitamit, Spirit Wind Runner, finished cleaning the area used for the fire the previous night. While folding the ashes under the sand he talked to the wood and the earth. He explained how grateful the group had been for the warmth and offered now to give the burned wood a gift in return. The gift was the reunion with the earth so they could nourish each other and make preparations for new life, new trees to grow. "Why do you use the word 'gift'?" Beatrice asked. "I thought gifts were for people."

"They are," Mitamit replied. "But not just for people. And many times in the mutant world, from what I have heard, what is given is not a gift at all."

"What do you mean?"

"A gift is when you give something someone wants, not something you think they should have or something you feel obligated to give. Only when a person wants it and you have the ability to give it is it a gift." Benala chimed in, "But there is more to it than that. Your experience ends with giving, while the other person's experience starts with receiving and with acceptance. If you hold any emotional attachment to the item you have given, if you expect any certain conditions, then it is not a true gift. A gift given belongs to the recipient, to do with it whatever she desires. So you see, when a mutant gives something, and the receiver is expected to say thanks, or to wear it, display it, or repay it, that isn't a gift. It should be called something else."

"We love giving and receiving gifts," Mitamit continued. "It makes every day, every meal, every camping spot special, as you will see."

White-headed Wurtawurta spoke her thoughts. "There is so much to tell, but we must start at the beginning and each will add to the telling. Do you know how long Forever is?" she asked Beatrice, but she answered before the girl had had time to compose her thoughts. "It is a very, very long time. Forever has no beginning and no end. It has no tomorrow or yesterday. It is like a circle, and you must understand this enormousness before you can be told other things. Are you able to grasp and understand how long Forever is?"

Beatrice shook her head yes.

"Good," continued the older lady, "because you are Forever. You came from there, you go back there, and everything you do is reflected there. That is what we live for, our Foreverness. Do you know about the Dreamtime and the Rainbow Snake?"

"No, not really," Beatrice answered, looking intent. "Please tell me what I should know."

"Well," Wurtawurta began, "in the beginning, in the time before time, there was nothing. No stars, no sun, no earth, nothing. There was only the Great Oneness. And then Oneness began to dream. In this Dreamtime, Oneness expanded to make a layer of Oneness spirit. The layer was given free-will consciousness. The Rainbow Snake is the carrier of this spirit energy, and it enabled our ancestors to be. The world was created by invisible energy and ancestor Dreamers were free to design it in any way they chose. So you see, there are mountains, rivers, flowers, bandicoot, and people all made of the same energy. We cannot separate things and say that what we do to the trees does not matter. We cannot say the tree does not feel. I think the tree does feel. In a different way, yes, but it is alive and, after it is cut, takes a long time to die. Just as we have spirit looking after us, so there is spirit saying to each bed of flowers, "Grow, grow and bloom." We cannot swallow the meat of the red bird and say it is the same as swallowing the flesh of the crocodile. They are very different and add different energy to our bodies. We each have animal relationships with animals that are connected to the earth in the spot where we were born. We do not eat our totem animals. It would be eating your brother or eating yourself."

"Beatrice, you studied science, didn't you?" asked Benala.

"Yes."

"Well, do you remember reading about energy and how vibration and frequency variations make the difference between sound and ultrasound, color and invisible infrared color, and so forth? I think science is just now proving that what we have described for thousands of years and called the Rainbow Snake is absolutely accurate. Outsiders have laughed at our talking about what they pictured as a pink, yellow, green, and purple creature, but they simply did not try hard enough to understand what was being described. What our people have been saying all this time is that what makes up a cloud is also what makes up you. You are part sun, moon, star, water, fire, dingo. Do you understand what I mean? It is all one."

"Yes, I do understand," Beatrice acknowledged. "But people are different. We have souls, and others things don't, do they?"

"You can use the word 'soul' or whatever you want. I think humans were mistaken in believing they were superior to everything else, that evolution stopped with man and that he alone has a soul that in no way resembles the spirit of anything else created by the Source. The Real People concentrate on how to best handle having a human experience. We acknowledge each form of life as valuable and unique."

"I have to think about that for a while," Beatrice answered. "If everything has spirit connected to it, or everything is spirit, then what exactly is the human assignment we have?"

"'Assignment' is exactly the word to use," Benala commented. "The entire life of a flower unfolds in predictability. An animal is given the gift of movement and the opportunity to seek an environment where it might better survive, but it is not held responsible for how it relates to the world. But people, humans, do choose to accept an assignment and it is directly connected to the special abilities we are given.

"Our spirits were not incomplete in the invisible world before birth. We didn't have to come here to earth to be made whole. We didn't elect to be here to find that it is an all-or-nothing journey. It is not a fail-or-pass course. But unlike other life-forms, humans are held accountable. We have choice. We have free will and are aware of it. We alone decide our own degree of self-discipline and are accountable for that. We are creative beings. We have unlimited access to the creative. We are here for one another, to help, to nurture, to entertain, to interact. We are here to care for this planet. With our consciousness comes the knowledge of energy and the stewardship of it. We have a full array of emotions and ultimately discover that the key is quite simple. It really is to love without judgment. If anything appears to be complicated, it isn't love. It is something else. Love is helping, giving or receiving, whichever role proves helpful. Humans can achieve wisdom, but other life-forms don't have that opportunity. Emotional wisdom is a part of our earthly assignment.

"People are unique because we can laugh. We can understand and see humor in what we do. Our music is without boundaries. We alone are so blessed by the Source.

"I think that having lived for a period of time in mutant society, devoid of the natural connection to nature, has been a benefit for me. I have seen two worlds. I understand why the worlds appear so different, almost opposite, and yet are each universal law in action. It is a lot to think about, but we have plenty of time and there will be many days ahead for you to see the Real People way of life."

Yes, Beatrice thought as she moved her head up and down in agreement. I have time to learn and I have a family who will let me do that.

33

The seven travelers came to a water hole with only a few inches of water in the center and drying mud covering most of the surface. "We will gather food here," Apalie said. "Here, I will show you," and taking her digging stick she began probing the mud and turning over clumps of it. The other women joined her. Soon they were stacking up mud balls in a row. "We will stop and let these dry," she added.

Googana sat opposite Beatrice. His long white beard was tied today in a chin braid that swished back and forth from nipple to nipple as he moved his head in conversation. Once in a while, she caught sight of the scar that was usually hidden. Today's bright sun illuminated the large lump in the center of his chest. He saw her look and read her thoughts. "Would you like to know about this?" he said, placing a finger on the old wound. "Would you like to hear my story?"

Beatrice smiled and nodded yes.

"I am an initiated man, a Clever Man," he said. "All boys are initiated sometime between the time of their ninth summer to about their twelfth. If a boy is rowdy and a troublemaker, he usually goes at nine. Fragile boys aren't ready until they are twelve. I cannot give you details because it is man's business and not a subject to be put into a woman's mind, but I can say we have a formal ceremony where each mother must say good-bye to her son. It is very emotional because a boy hugs his mother in a farewell and several days later a man returns in his body. That is the end of childish things, the boy is dead. There are many lifetimes in a lifetime. Childhood is merely the first. We have found everyone needs help in growing up and our circumcision initiation does that for us. When a boy takes the guidance of mental imagery that is given to reduce pain, and learns it easily, that indicates this male has the ability to train and become a Clever Man, if he so desires, and has the passion to concentrate on one talent for a lifetime.

"I did. Other Clever Men can teach the techniques in a series of initiations over the years, but only the student can achieve the wisdom to determine when, why, and for whom he will provide service, and how to share his gift.

"When I had seen thirty-seven summers turn to winter, I heard a voice calling to me. It came from far away and promised, if I located it, that there would be an exchange of goodness. The voice led me across several tribal nations to a beautiful land where I found a tall cliff and roaring water falling into a very cold pool. The voice was deep in the water under the waterfall. It was the voice of a crystal asking to be removed, to see the sun, and then it promised to amplify my abilities. It has kept that promise and has ridden here under the skin, near my heart, for forty years.

"I now close my eyes and travel through the air and see activities taking place miles away. I travel underground and see what plants are growing, how much water is in the underground river, and where a new litter of animals is located and how many young there are. I have learned to use the senses of the birds and animals so, when summoned, I can help our people and all other forms of life. It allows me to see inside a person's body and know what is happening. Often conversation or music or color is all that is needed. There are no outside forces, no diseases or accidents that do not have a spiritual link. To cure any problem I must help the person determine the opportunity for spirit growth that is being presented.

"Earth is a place for learning by experiencing. As a Forever spirit you desired to come here and helped to create the way to do so. It was your energy that took the essence of food your mother ate and created a body from what was available. You were aware of the environment, the heredity, the situations you were setting up and agreed that it was the perfect place for you to experience a special sort of spiritual enrichment.

"If we could only remember our Foreverness, we would easily see that earth is the school of emotion. Our energy is combined differently from the energy of other things like rain or fire and is different from the energy of the other growing forms, the plants and animals. It is unique. We as humans are here to experience emotion and to use our bodies as vehicles to achieve emotional wisdom.

"The body is the way in which humans receive guidance from the spirit world, from the Source, from all our ancestors, from our own perfect Forever self. All the body senses—seeing, hearing, tasting, feeling, and smelling—are connected to emotion. Actually, I should say emotion is connected to the senses, because the emotion is the foundation.

"Babies are born in a state of emotional peace. What happens to their senses is linked to emotional feelings. As we grow older, for instance, the sound of the eagle's wings seems either to make us feel at ease or to feel apprehension, depending upon our experience with an eagle or what we believe from what we have seen or been told.

"I know as a Medicine Man that when people are aware of this they can live healthier lives, and I know as a Clever Man that knowing enables them to bring more Forever light into this human time."

Googana stood up and, borrowing a digging stick, he began to draw designs in the sand.

"This is the Rainbow Snake. It is the pattern coming from the Source and moving across and under the earth. It is part of the life force going through us like this,"

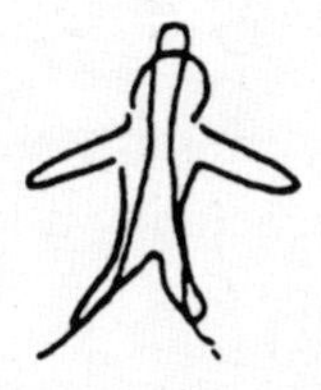

Googana said, pointing to one of the designs he had just drawn. "The emotion of anger is shaped like this spear.

"When a person becomes angry, instead of flowing freely like water over slippery rocks, the energy of life is pushed off to each side and becomes sharp and pointed. It digs into the body and injures your organs. Just as a spear will inflict a wound and is difficult to pull out, so, too, is anger.

"The energy of resentment is this," Googana continued,

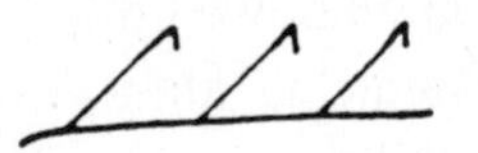

pointing to another design. "Resentment, too, has a pointed end, but it also contains a barb, so it digs into the person and clings much longer. Resentment is more destructive than anger because it lasts longer.

"When you worry, the energy pattern goes down like this," Googana said, drawing another design.

"Envy, jealousy, or guilt are more complex than worry and the knots can be in your stomach, under your skin, or can slow the life flow anywhere.

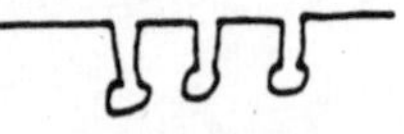

"Sadness is a very minor disruption. And grief is a form of sadness that is actually a loving bond. It can last for the survivor's lifetime.

"Fear brings things to a halt. It disrupts blood flow, heartbeat, breathing, thinking, digestion—everything. Fear is an interesting emotion because it isn't actually human. It was taken from the animals, where it serves a wonderful, very temporary survival role. No animal lives in fear. People originally had nothing to fear. They knew they were Forever. They knew any pain or discomfort was temporary. Now fear has become a major energy force surrounding our planet. This is the harm it does inside you.

"When you are happy, smiling, laughing, feeling good, this is how the body receives and uses energy," he said, pointing to another design.

"And peace, quiet, rest is like this drawing.

"Emotional detachment, such as observation free of judgment, is a smooth, complete, healthy, life-enhancing energy like this.

"So you see," Googana continued, "you are responsible for your energy and for the discipline of your emotions. Everyone experiences how it feels to be in a negative state, but to linger and not to learn from it is to be irresponsible, immature, and unwise. There is alive and non-alive time. Just because someone is breathing doesn't mean he is alive. Depression is not spending your time alive. It is necessary to mature, to live a long healthy time. Ultimately, we are all accountable for our time as humans and how we use our free-will gift.

"In mutant terms, I think they would refer to it as an eternal scorecard. There is an entry indicating how many seconds you were alive. The record is divided into how many seconds of your life you spent in peace, feeling fulfilled, feeling good, as you do when you help someone else, seconds spent in the joy of laughter or in the bliss of music. Also recorded are the times over your one hundred years or so of existence when you were angry and chose to stay angry, or felt hatred and harbored it.

"Every word you utter goes out into the vapor and can never be recaptured. You can say 'I'm sorry,' but that doesn't retract the first energy. Intent is energy. Action is energy. But a person may act one way with a very hidden intention. All human consciousness is cumulative. There is now such a thick layer surrounding Mother Earth that in some places people are fed by taking in the breath and thoughts of collective victimness, and in turn they replace the void with more of the same. There is also a layer that developed from the beliefs and actions of 'me first, nothing else counts, get what is wanted at any cost, it doesn't matter.' People's intentions have been to see what can be invented, what can be used, without any concern for the life left tomorrow or even if life will be possible tomorrow. Spirits of the newborns and young children are so wonderfully positive that many now come to earth and stay only a short time. They put all their energy into balancing and eventually removing the negative.

"We as individuals either add to this destructive force by everything we do daily, or we direct our energy into supporting the harmony, beauty, and preservation of life on this earth.

"Your life, your body, your future can be like this,"

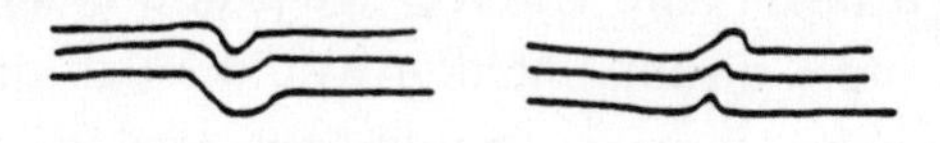

he said, pointing to a drawing, "or," he said, pointing to another, "this can be your world. You alone determine which it will be.

"Human life is a spiral, we come from Forever and we return there, we hope at a higher level. Time is a circle, and our relationships are also circles. As Aboriginal children, we learned early in life the importance of closing each circle, each relationship. If there is a disagreement we will stay awake until it is resolved. We wouldn't go to sleep hoping to find a solution tomorrow or at some future date. That would be leaving a circle open, with frayed ends."

"But," Beatrice asked, "what if you asked someone to do something? Say you asked a person three or four times, and he failed to do it. Certainly you would be disappointed in that person. It would not be easy just to say forget it, and close the circle on a positive note, as you say."

"Well, the alternative is to continue to associate the emotion of disappointment with that person. Ten years later the mere thought or mention of that name would cause the feeling, which in turn would cause physical distortion to your body. You must admit that that isn't very wise."

"So how would you handle it?" Beatrice asked. "What would you do?"

"Personally, I would say to the other person, 'Guess

what? I felt disappointed when you ignored my asking you to do me a favor. And I asked again and again and felt more and more disappointed.' I would laugh and add, 'I must be a slow learner. I should have realized after your first response that you weren't going to do this. It wasn't something you wanted to do. You probably thought it was pretty silly when I asked again. You are right. It was silly. I'm sorry it took me so long to see that you weren't interested.' We would end up laughing at my actions and both would be the wiser for the encounter. Then my circle would be closed."

"But what if it were a really serious matter? For instance, a relative of yours was doing or saying things that were very offensive to you. It really upset you. The person was truly acting in a manner that, as you say, didn't smell right for you. What would you do about the circle in that relationship?"

"I would say to this relative quite firmly, 'I love you, but I do not like the actions you take. I realize they are not a mistake. I know it is right for you to be this way because that is how you chose to express yourself. But I have tried and I cannot accept what you say and do as being right for me, so I must now release our relationship. I cannot put any more energy into it. I love you, but I do not like what you do, so you have my best wishes and good-bye.'"

"Wow," Beatrice said. "So you are saying that if I close the circle on a spiritual high, that's the end of it for me! If the other person accepts, then the circle is closed for him too. If he doesn't accept what I say, it doesn't matter because any circle left with frayed edges is strictly his circle, his spiritual challenge. He is keeping it open."

"Exactly. You don't have to like everybody. Not everyone is likable. What you did agree to do before you were born was to love everyone. It is easy to do. Love the Forever in all people, and put your energy into those who are of like consciousness. The only way you can influence anyone else is by example. They aren't going to change until they are ready. And remember, it is okay. In the scheme of Forever, it really is okay."

The old man's beard kept time with his speaking and his marking in the sand as he said, "You come into this world on one level of spiritual awareness and have the opportunity to leave on a broadened plane."

After a moment of thinking, Beatrice asked, "What about people from years ago? People I still feel resentment toward. Someone I may never see again."

"No matter. Have the talk silently and send it to them on a rainbow wherever he or she might be. It will find them. Turn your old judgment into an observation. No one has to be forgiven. We just have to be more understanding. Heal the wound in your mind, in your emotions, in your wholeness. Close the circle and walk forward."

Googana's sparkling black eyes seemed to act like a magnet as he faced Beatrice and explained, "The more subtle the energy, the closer it is to the Oneness Source. Rapidly moving arms are appropriate at times and are more physical, while slow, gentle moves are closer to spirit. Loud, fast music is physical. The long-drawn-out drone of one note is closer to spirit. The hunting of animals, depending on method and intention, can be more, or less, in keeping with our spiritual journey. Look at everything, including relationships, rituals, food, teachings, entertainment, even shelters, and observe subtle energy refinement. Soon you will see you can converse, soothe, support, and love with few actions and even fewer words. One can make love with the eyes. Nearness isn't always necessary either. Much can be influenced from vast distances."

Beatrice absorbed what she heard and she particularly liked the concept of a circle for relationships. She could imagine a necklace made of gold loops, each inscribed with a name. Close to her heart she could picture in her mind a circle, like a pocket-watch chain, and it was marked "Freda." That was without doubt the most meaningful relationship she had experienced thus far in her life.

34

It was the season when the moon ripens the berry to perfection and the people rush to beat the birds and four-legged creatures to the treasures. Mitamit had been gone and had returned with a handful of fruit to share. "Come follow me," he said. "I will show the way." After they had reached the place of this wonderful seasonal food and had eaten, Beatrice asked Mitamit if he would tell about himself and he agreed.

"My name, Spirit Wind Runner, was chosen because I have been given the opportunity to experience something not all people have. One day as I was running I suddenly felt like an emu and knew how to make my legs and feet barely touch the earth, like the bird does when it moves so fast. There is a rhythm to it separate from other movements. I think my heart, instead of going faster, actually slows, and the air in my lungs comes from a deeper place. I become a part of the wind. Without effort, I can be blown along, running all day. It is a wonderful feeling and I am grateful for this body of mine."

How refreshing it is, thought Beatrice, to find someone who genuinely does not take his body for granted, who appreciates it, and is so in tune with himself and the world that he can use it to the fullest.

Occasionally the mellow sun emerged from the thick cloud cover and shone on the travelers as they walked in the narrow opening, one behind the other, forming a line between the two tall walls of red-granite stone. The opening became so limited at one point that each had to turn sideways to squeeze through. It began to sprinkle rain. "Hurry," a voice said at the front of the line. "Before long this path will become the river that carries the rain down from the mountain. It crushes everything that stands in its way."

The seven hurried their steps, first walking between the walls and then climbing about fifteen feet above the path to stand on a wide, flat ridge in front of the entrance to a small cave. They had each picked up pieces of broken tree limbs during the day's long walk and these were propped vertically, one against another, to dry. The sacred place of rest had been prepared many years ago, perhaps hundreds of years ago, with soft white sand hauled from miles away and placed around the periphery to make more comfortable bedding. The precise location for a fire was identified by burned marks on the stone floor and by stones scattered from a circle. If located in this exact position, the fire would warm the interior and yet smoke and fumes would be released outside. Mitamit gathered up the bone fragments that larger animals had carried while eating their prey. Three of the women, each with a hair-and-grass net, filtered the sand a handful at a time, removing all undesirable components, and placed it back against the innermost wall. Apalie used a branch from a bush, heavy with thick strong leaves, to sweep the cave and placed the fire stones in their original circular formation. Googana surveyed the wall paintings, making a mental list of what was needed to repair and repaint the ancient ancestor portraits.

They would stay in this place for a while. There was work to do and food and water were plentiful. More than ten different species of birds visited there, and another assortment of at least ten different faces crawled, hopped, or slithered by. There were plants for eating, healing, and ceremonial use.

Within two hours the work for the day was complete, the fire was ignited, and each member was enjoying the nourishment provided by the flesh and spirit of one that had flown close to the stars and into the sunset.

As the gentle warm rain continued to fall, Googana stood on the front ledge, lifted his face to the sky, and swallowed as the water ran into his mouth. When he returned to the fire he addressed Beatrice by asking, "Tell me of the people who do not taste the rain. Is it true they live their entire lives and never stand in this glorious way? I have heard they run when the clouds open up and put a cloth upon a stick over their heads. Why do they do this?"

Beatrice looked at Benala and both women laughed. "Yes, it is true. Mutants don't often stand in the rain. Not by choice. They are usually wearing some clothing that would change in appearance if it became very wet. They also wear watches on their arms that quit working and rust if they get damp. Women have a way of wearing their hair that can't remain the same when it becomes moist. Mutants bring the water inside their dwellings so they can stand in it or sit in it at their choosing, not at the will of Oneness."

"How did they come to this belief that they know better when it is time to stand in the water and so made this change?"

"I'm not sure I can answer that question. It happened long, long ago when men first got the idea they could control nature and make life more comfortable."

"When our needs are met," Googana interjected, "we are content. What more does one seek?"

"The mutants seek comfort. Being content, being satisfied, isn't enough. They need to feel comfortable, and everything must be convenient."

"'Convenient,' I don't understand that word."

"Well, it means being in control. Like not having to gather today's food because you would rather do something else, so lots of food is stored, many moons of stored food. Convenience means not walking to a new place. If you want to go to a different place, you ride. First it was on a horse, then in an automobile, and now it is also in an airplane, a train, or a boat. But everything is always changing, so in the future, there will be something else more convenient and more comfortable."

"But Oneness rules. Don't mutants know that no man can stop the wind from dancing, the lightning from speaking, the flowers from blooming, or the fruit from falling? How can you take tomorrow's food ahead of tomorrow? How can you know what the world has in store for tomorrow?"

"Mutants don't believe the world has anything in store for tomorrow. They are in charge of the world. They believe humans are the only intelligence on earth, so people can do anything they want. The world was given to them to use in any way they choose."

"Humans the only intelligence? What about the talk and the thinking of dolphins and whales?"

"Oh, there are wolves, and parrots, and chimpanzees too," added Benala. "Animals and birds around the world that are extremely smart, but mutants can't see how these creatures could ever evolve or develop beyond what they appear to be today. They don't think animals have much to offer. Mutants really believe they are meant to conquer and rule."

Googana did not respond. The cave was quiet and all who had listened so intently now weighed the conversation in their hearts. They allowed the emotions that welled up within their bodies to be felt.

The next day was spent gathering material and creating paintbrushes from animal fur, human hair, and bird feathers. The following day ground powder was mixed to make black and white paint. "At one time only specially trained men were allowed to touch these images, but that entire tribe of people is gone, so now we have become caretakers. We will ask the ancestor spirits to grant approval for our work. Our intention is of the highest level. With spirit guidance, we can restore these cave dwellers' paintings for yet another period of time."

The original lines were painstakingly covered, stroke by stroke, in exact detail. Not a single line was missed nor a single extra brushstroke added. It was the patient work of dedication, by people with love and respect in each movement.

That evening Karaween and Apalie said they would enjoy doing a performance for the others, including the ancestors in the cave.

The audience of five sat looking out at the night while the two actresses used the flat area in the front as their stage. The moonlight was their spotlight because there were no trees overhead to block the direct glow on the sunken entrance and it was considerably darker inside than on the lighted ledge.

The theatrical performance was a comedy sketch in which the women made fun of themselves doing daily routine activities and acted out how they had grown from being clumsy to mastering certain feats. It had been a long time since this place of sacredness had such hearty laughter bouncing off its walls. Even an animal or two stopped to listen to a unique noise being welcomed by the world.

As the birds began to sing in the morning, Beatrice rolled over and opened her eyes. Karaween was already sitting up, leaning on the cave wall, listening to the world awaken.

"Thank you for the performance last night," Beatrice whispered. "It was such fun. It seems your name should be Artist. Tell me about yourself and why you are called Karaween." The sixteen-year-old nodded her head yes and pointed outdoors. Quietly the two exited and, climbing around the rocky cliff, found a comfortable area on top where they could hold their conversation.

"I selected my name not too many months ago because I felt I needed to develop interests in more adult matters. I have been a game master for a long time now. It was one of my games that became adapted as the sand-drawing introduction you received when you stood outside our circle. I know dozens of games using a circular border. There is one I call 'Around the Moon' that is a contest for as many players as want to participate. You start with two standing back to back, facing in opposite directions on a circle. At a signal to start, each begins hopping on one foot across the line in the sand, first inside, then outside, and so on. When the two players meet, it is determined who has proceeded the farthest and that person continues while the other is replaced by a new player. The original player waits for another turn. The game continues on and on, around and around, until everyone is laughing and so tired it must be called to an end.

"There is also the game called 'Drawing One,' played in a small circle. Players take turns drawing something inside the circle, but there can be only one of each item, and when the space is used up the game is over. Everyone tries to get more items and new and different ideas each time.

"Sometimes, when the earth is very soft and the sand granules extremely fine, we can play what I call 'Looking for the Lost.' Each player has a small stick and we sit around a mound of sand in which some tiny object, perhaps the lens off an animal roasted for dinner, has been buried. Taking turns, each one can move one stick full of sand, looking for the article. It is a wonderful game for keeping children focused, but now we don't have any children.

"Kids love to make up stories and illustrate them by drawing. Sometimes one child would first draw a part of something and another would tell a part of a story; it carried on so everyone had several turns and the story had an adventurous ending. I started a game using long sticks. A hot coal or hot rock would be passed between players. I have taught people how to take a stick with fire on the end and turn it round and round and behind their back and under their legs and so forth. Although games are good, and there is a time for that sort of laughing and fun, I felt I needed to take on more adult responsibility. Now I am learning to make basket containers, using reeds mainly, because they are most available, but I have learned to make containers using animal parts too.

"I was born here and have been here all of my sixteen summers. My parents and some others were taken away one day when a helicopter came. It was marked with the white doctors' sign. Since then, I have been with Wurtawurta. I am so happy you have come to join us. We seldom see anyone new."

The two females then looked around and began to gather supplies for the day. They returned to the cave just as the others were beginning to stir. Out in the open they all woke very early. In the darkness of the cavern, it seemed natural to sleep longer. Beatrice thought often throughout the day of sixteen-year-old Karaween and her growing-up project. "I hope she continues to retain her creative flare and some of her childish charm. I see now how important healthy minds and healthy bodies are."

The following day was clear and bright, and Beatrice and Wurtawurta gathered small stones for heating in the fire. "Wurtawurta, you have lived in both worlds, the modern one and here, isolated from others. What things are handled differently by the two cultures?" asked the younger female.

"There are many. Probably problem solving is a big one. I remember so many people arguing and screaming and even hitting each other during a dispute. The matter was usually not resolved either. People just got mad and walked away or parted from each other with ill feelings. I have learned now it was because there was no one standard to use as an agreed-upon goal. Here, we recognize that each of us is entitled to be open to our own expressions and ideas. We do relate deeply to nature, and we see that the tree does not break because it will bend. The taller it becomes, the more it bends. When two people disagree, we stop to define what direction we are speaking from. There are seven, you know: north, south, east, west, sky above, earth below, and within. In a disagreement, one might state that they speak from the west, from the past, something the person understood to be a certain way. Or are they speaking from the east, basing their point of view on the best interest of some future endeavor? Perhaps they would say that they speak from within, saying what is in their heart or in their gut. Then, if they cannot see the other person's point of view and come to agreement, they would trade places. Yes, physically move and stand in the other's footprints. They would then speak from that point of view. Just as aggressively, just as passionately as before. Usually, then they can come to an understanding. If not, they would stop and say to each other, 'What is the principle we are to learn from this?'

"Beatrice, for thousands of years our race has worked together. Everyone is respected, everyone participates, each is supported, but we are a team. You might say a human team on a spiritual assignment.

"Another factor that seemed so different to me at first and one I still feel is a vital difference between the two cultures is the concept of competition. In the mutant world there can only be room for one at the top and everyone else must fill in below, like a triangle, with most people on the bottom, supporting one person on the top. It is difficult for me to understand how a parent can tell a child that only one can win and everyone else must lose. They actually seem to believe there isn't enough prestige, enough places for leadership, so only one can be successful and everyone else must be in a lesser role. I think competition, by causing the belief in lack and limitation and feeding the emotions of envy and violence, has done more to pull people apart than any other factor."

"Of course," Beatrice interjected, "mutants would say it is the thing that has made the world so progressive and comfortable. People inventing things goes along with fame and fortune."

"That is true, but are we better off? Is the earth healthier? Are plants, animals, and people healthier? Does the future look brighter and more promising because of competition? I am not judging, since I know it is all part of the Divine Order. But as an observer, for me personally it does not have a good smell to it. I have to bless those who think in terms of not enough or superiority and let them go. The Aboriginal race has always operated more on the scale of a flat puzzle instead of a triangle. We feel that everyone fits into the puzzle and that everyone is a vital part of it. Without any one person we would be incomplete. We would have a gaping hole. When we sit by the fire, each brings a uniqueness. There is someone who brings to our group the expertise of hunting, someone else is a teacher, a cook, a healer, a listener, a dancer, and so forth. We have someone who is the leader, but we also know everyone has the ability to lead and should be allowed to do so when we want that adventure. We also have the ability to follow. One is not better than the other. There is a time and place for both."

In thinking about the racial disparity in the city between the current urban Aborigine and the offspring of transplanted Europeans, Beatrice wondered, Which side, or is it both, thinks in terms of lack and limitation? After all, we each live out our Dreaming.

35

The dawn brought Beatrice awake with this thought, continued from her sleep, Where do I belong? She had been thinking about taking a new name, but it wasn't an act to be rushed into. The name must be a word pleasant to the ear, and one she could quickly become accustomed to answering to. The name must reflect who she was at this stage of her life, so she asked herself again, Who am I?

> I am Aboriginal,
> a seeker,
> one who is already tainted in my perception,
> one who is now surrounded by friends, teachers,
>   love.
> I feel accepted, secure.
> There is no one talent I feel drawn to explore, yet I
>   feel full of talent. I feel I am developing, but I
>   certainly don't know what I will become.

A week later she said to Wurtawurta, "It is time for my celebration. I am ready to receive a new name." Wurtawurta in turn announced what Beatrice had said. The people were full of smiles and head-nodding. The ceremony would take place in three days. They would be at a special place then and have time to make preparations. As they walked the next two days, the air was light with festive feelings. They tried guessing what name Beatrice had chosen and the afternoon turned into a traveling guessing game.

On the afternoon of the name ceremony, they arrived at a very large and deep crater. There was a circle lifted from the ground about a hundred yards in width that would hold rows and rows of bleachers if, in the modern world, it were dedicated to holding sporting events. Across the bottom was a channel of shallow water that wound its way across the circle like a crawling snake. Whatever had pulled the ground to form this giant indentation had dug so deep it revealed the top of an underground water route.

"There are conflicting stories about the origin of this circle," Benala said as they began the descent toward the center. "It appeared here one day and was not here before. The tribe who were caretakers within this song line, in all their history, had no accounts of this place and, as you can see, it is too vast to have been overlooked. The tribe is gone now; they were all removed. The last man, forced off about five years ago, made no mention of this structure. The crater apparently developed after that time. It was certainly massive power that created it."

"As you know," Wurtawurta included in a joking manner, "all of our mountains, rivers, and valleys are named. Everything is identified with the spirits and their stories, but this place is like you, new and seeking a name."

Beatrice in her wildest imagination could not picture

how this giant hole came to be, but she was glad they had been so close when her decision had been made because it did seem most appropriate.

A purple layer streaked the sky at sunset, and each of the group thought it a beautiful color for Beatrice's party night. The fire was scented with a sweet smell by a sprinkle of tree bark carried for just such occasions. Karaween added salt grass to the portions of meat she handed out. Apalie had prepared an herbal drink by simmering a tangy spice leaf in a bladder of water she rotated in the sun during the day. After the meal each one took a turn telling stories. Later, using stick rhythm, they sang and danced and told of other naming events. Karaween and Apalie led Beatrice to the shallow water stream and, using their hands, smoothed the water on her body, telling her that the old life and present name were being washed away. Now she would wake in the morning as a new person with a new name.

Back near the fire, small feathers were dipped in thickened animal blood, then were glued, one by one, across her forehead. The finished look was that of a soft, fluffy tiara, and she felt as regal as a royal member of any society. Next, everyone sat around the fire and waited for Beatrice to whisper the chosen new name into someone's ear. Whoever was chosen to announce it would do so creatively. He would make up, on the spot, a song, a poem, or some action drama to introduce the information to all the others. No one knew who would be called upon, nor did any of them have any time to prepare. This was designed to keep the creative juices flowing in all their people for all their lives.

Beatrice stood and walked around the four women and two men. She paused and pretended to almost speak to

Wurtawurta before straightening up and walking on. Everyone laughed. Beatrice was a real joy to this family. She was making sure her party was fun for everyone and fun for herself. She skipped like a child around her friends, then stopped almost before anyone realized and whispered into Mitamit's ear. He was startled. He had never dreamed she would do this. They were friends, but since he was a single man and she a single woman, caution was always used in any actions between them. He did not want to give a false impression. He had no desire to take a wife. He stood and recited:

The heron has a long neck,
The penguin tiny feet.
The kookaburra a hearty voice,
Yet the eagle is our favorite treat.
What do they all have in common?
It is eggs within a nest.
And if you were to choose a part,
What name would fit her best?
She has left the white transparent world,
She is not a hard protective shell.
I introduce Minendie, the egg yolk.
Yes, it fits you well.

Thereafter, none would call her Beatrice again and they were pleased with Mitamit's poem. When he asked Minendie to explain her choice she responded, "I believe you have seen into my heart." Then, turning to the others, she said, "He told you exactly how I feel. It is as if I walk with your arms around me to show me the way and allow me to grow and change and develop. I feel nurtured and protected. I also feel that I don't know where this yolk came from and I have no idea what will eventually emerge. You are like the mother I have never known; you warm this nest every day and you accept what hatches without condition. I have never known such a wonderful feeling, and I shall always be grateful for your friendship."

The celebration continued with more singing and dancing until exhaustion finally took over and one by one they fell asleep.

Minendie looked to the heavens and released all hold on Beatrice. She was at peace with Father Felix, Father Paul, Sister Agatha, and the others. Tomorrow would be a new day and she was a newborn.

36

Some days there were conversations as they walked. Other days were quiet. But each evening was a time of sharing, usually with music accompanied by song. The group carried with it a set of clap sticks. They were two dried, porous pieces of wood about eight inches long, with rounded ends. Both sticks were decorated. The design had been burned into the wood. Each night different people used them, clapping them together to start a tempo. Sometimes other pieces of wood lying around were also used, or two rocks, or even clapping hands on thighs accompanied the desired sound. One instrument that has been used in Australia for thousands of years is called the didgeridoo. Mitamit found a dead tree where white ants had hollowed out the inside. He took one straight limb about four feet long. By blowing and forcing sand through it, he cleaned out the center. Then he used rocks, sand, and other wood to rub the surface smooth on one end, where he placed his lips. Different grains of various trees will render higher and lower pitch, but Mitamit could master them all. He could make the reedless wind instrument imitate bird and animal sounds. When the group was near a place where water grass grew, they made unique sounds by blowing upon the wild greenery. By using hollow reeds in varying lengths tied together, they fashioned a sort of harmonica instrument.

"Everyone is musical," they said. "Music is a part of our earthly assignment. If you don't sing because you don't think you can sing, that does not diminish the singer within you. You simply do not honor your talent." They sang of historical events. They sang of the Dreaming of the world into creation, and they composed at least one new song nightly. Certain songs had dance steps that involved the women moving clockwise or counterclockwise in circles or in a line. At other times they were encouraged to move freely and express themselves individually. "Men and women in many tribes never danced together, but that was a long time ago and before there were so few of us. Sometimes minor things must change due to necessity," Wurtawurta quietly explained, her dark eyes filled with remembering. After each concert they said thank you to the parts of nature they had used, and were grateful for having spent time in such an enjoyable manner. They dismantled the instruments and returned them to the earth.

One evening when Minendie felt the music was exceptionally moving, Wurtawurta said to her, "If a human being were born alone on an island and had no other human contact, she would develop two very specific characteristics, something we are born with as certainly as the bird is born knowing how to build a nest. Do you know what they would be?"

Minendie shook her head no.

"Music and humor. A lone person would learn to hum, to sing, and perhaps even find a way to make musical notes. The lone person would also discover the feeling of her own voice laughing. Yes, both music and laughter are medicine for the body and for the soul."

Minendie hadn't considered it before, but it was certainly true in her case; laughter always made her feel better and she resonated so strongly with music it could make her feel like marching, dancing, or crying. I wasn't left alone on an island, she thought, but almost!

The walkabout route they traveled was not a random wandering. They knew the seasons, knew what plants should be bearing fruit at what time. They were deeply committed to the obligations they had taken upon themselves to care for the land of the other tribes who were no longer available to do so.

Over the years they could also see the changes in the earth. When the rain came, the pooling water dried, leaving behind a residue on the rock. Each summer the temperature seemed hotter than before and each winter it was warmer. It had become so hot, they observed, that certain snakes had left their former habitats in search of a new place to live. The fish they caught had internal growths and, later, the disease was evident on their outer surfaces. One day at the edge of a marshy pool, Wurtawurta pointed out to Googana the malformed tadpoles and tiny frogs. Some had only one hind leg, some had a long side and a short side, and several had three hind legs. It was then the group decided to talk about what they were observing and what was happening to the earth at the next gathering of all twenty Real People.

It was to take place soon.

37

Minendie asked if the lives of male and female members had always been so congenial and equal. There seemed to be no demonstration here of male dominance, but she didn't know if that was simply how Googana and Mitamit handled themselves or if other Aboriginal groups living together behaved in a similar fashion. In the white world, white men were definitely believed to be superior, and black men felt themselves more intelligent than black women.

"We have men's business and women's business," Wurtawurta told her as they sat together in the shade of trees growing from a cliff side. "It isn't that one is better or lesser; our spirits are the same, but our bodies are not. Women don't participate in and don't speak of men's affairs. What exactly takes place we do not know. With head-to-head and heart-to-heart talk, there aren't any real secrets, but what they do is of no concern to us. How the men have handled the differences among tribal customs since everything has been ripped apart and refugees have banded together, I don't know. I think men have always wished they had a closer tie to giving new life, and that unfilled need bonds them together in their so-called men's business. It's their way of experiencing a separation in a society that is united.

"So women formed women's business and that I know. We are responsible for telling young girls what happens to their bodies as they develop, for teaching them how to handle this matter and explaining how wonderful and special these few days each month are for the channel of giving new life. Childbirth is women's business. Men are not present when the baby is coaxed to come out to see the place it has chosen to visit. We put great emphasis on grandmother wisdom and guidance. By the time a woman is a grandmother and a great-grandmother, she knows what is best, what is temporary, and what is long lasting. She has seen many different kinds of people and can help individuals and the community understand each other better." Wurtawurta then recited

"'An infant belongs to its mother.
A child to the community,
A youth to the teachers,
A bride with her husband,
A mother to her family,
An elderly grandmother to the people.'

"One very important part of women's business is the role of Keeper of the Answer Guide. I will ask Apalie to show you."

Two days later Apalie announced that she and

Minendie would go to a separate place and talk of women's business. They would return the following day. When they had separated themselves a goodly distance and made themselves comfortable sitting in the sand, Apalie pulled out a small bag, saying, "I am now the Keeper of the Answer Guide. It is something that changes hands when one feels the desire to express this gift. Reach inside."

Minendie did as instructed and pulled out a round piece of hide about the size of a large coin. It was smooth on both sides. There was a symbol burned into the leathery hide. When she turned it over, she noticed a different symbol on the back.

"There are thirty-two connections for guidance. Here, I will show you how it works. Put that back into the pouch. Now become quiet deep inside and ask a question that you would like some guidance about. I will also be quiet within. We both place our hands over the bag. When you have asked the question in your mind and in your heart, draw one out."

The same symbol that she had seen the first time was duplicated on her second draw.

"That is not unusual," Apalie commented. "After all, the world already knows your question and knows the answer before you think about it. But there is other guidance; not every piece in here is marked the same." With that comment she turned the bag over and the other leather circles fell upon the earth. "The symbol that you selected is the mark for maturity. It means someone or something is at the peak. It means the struggle of getting somewhere is over and the time has come to fulfill the purpose. How does that fit into your question?"

"I asked about our finding the other Real People and if

a meeting about our concerns for the earth would be successful. I would say the guidance means I should not worry about when and where and who. I should just know it is in the hands of Oneness and will happen at the appropriate time."

"That is a very good analysis of this symbol," Apalie commented as she moved the disks into rows upon the sand. "I think one day you will have an interest in being Keeper." The teacher spent several hours teaching the new student about the meanings, how to apply the knowledge, and how to repair or replace damaged circles.

38

Minendie asked Apalie if, before returning to the others, she would tell her story.

"I have now seen forty changes of summer to winter. Though I have been with this group for eight of these, I still think often of my own blood family and life before that last day together. I was born on a reserve. When I was eight years old, we left our original shelter and moved into newly constructed housing made of corrugated iron. It was a long wall with other walls placed periodically, and a door. Within each squared-off family space was a small open window. Possibly at one point it was meant to contain glass, but it never did. The room contained a bed, a table and chairs, and a few odd pieces of furniture, like a chest for clothing and a cupboard for dishes. In the center of the room was a single lightbulb with a long string attached. We sometimes plugged a radio into a socket. The furniture never lasted. My father either sold it, lost it in a gambling bet, or broke it in a fit of anger. My mother, too, was good at throwing and breaking things.

"My grandparents were assigned to live in the room, but they never did. They continued to live on government-designated land where older non-English-speaking people gathered, and provided their own shelter using the native tree and brush structure, sometimes adding cardboard, canvas, and wooden crates. The older people never really conformed to the foreign way of living. My grandfather covered his genitals, but never wore any garment that was sewn. And grandmother wore skirts and tied material around her breasts.

"Grandfather was a sad man who never smiled. He spent his time walking in the wooded areas or sitting in the shade under a tree. He rarely spoke except to acknowledge Grandmother giving him a bowl of food or a tin cup of tea. Often he fixed his own meals from food he located on his walks.

"Men usually went on Thursday to receive the food and tobacco supplies given out weekly, but that was not the case in this family. Grandmother and my mother completed the task. When I was about four, mother made her first visit to the truck bed of a white stranger. Four years later, when we lived in the room, mother had changed completely. I remember when my mother and father had first argued. He had taken her arm and literally pulled her away while I watched. I followed at a distance and saw them meet a white man who replaced my father's hold with one of his own. He forced mother into the back of his old red truck. My father kicked the ground as he walked away. He saw me and told me to leave. He was folding a dollar bill and putting it into his pants pocket.

"After that it wasn't uncommon for my father to

receive a dollar for the services of his wife. Mother was a pretty woman who played with me and made little toys, but that stopped when father started making her go with people she didn't like. Then it was grandmother who watched out for my safety, taught lessons, and tried to make sense of the world for me when I asked questions.

"Grandmother told of growing up in the open spaces. She talked about the wonderful forests full of colorful birds, the ocean shore, about beautiful waterfalls and deep blue lagoons. She talked about grassy plains full of kangaroo, and how at the perfect time her people would set fire to the dead area so the following rain season would provide all new green sprouts and new life. She described the vast open desert land and the beauty and peace it contained.

"When I was twelve, an illness swept through the community. Both of my parents died. After that I stayed with my grandparents and became a ward of all the older people and no longer lived in the metal housing. Grandfather died when I was sixteen, and grandmother when I was eighteen.

"At that point I just walked away. I went from place to place for years. I never had any interest in getting married or having children. I never could make any sense of the world until one day I stumbled on a runner who had come to the urban area temporarily. I returned to the desert with him. That was eight years ago.

"I selected the name Apalie, meaning Water Person, because an old woman who is no longer with us had taught me the art of smelling water in the air, hearing water under the ground, feeling for water with my body. Her deep reverence and respect for the life-extending fluid inspired me. Water asks no questions, it accepts and conforms to whatever the shape of the container happens to be. Water can be hot, cold, steam, rain. It is very adaptable. It nourishes plants, animals, fish, and man. It respects all life and gives of itself freely. Water is weak, yet a drop at a time can make a hole in a stone. Man can make it muddy, but when left undisturbed it clears itself. I am proud to be connected to water."

Everyone everywhere has a story to tell, Minendie thought. If only the world was considerate enough to listen. I'm sure the understanding levels between individuals, between countries, governments, and religions, would take a giant step forward.

39

The Aboriginal people often walked in total silence because they were speaking in the ancient way, with telepathy rather than voice. "How is this done?" Minendie asked the companion walking beside her. "Can I learn to do it too?"

"Of course," Benala replied. "The only reason it is not done in the mutant world is because it is blocked by fear. Mutants keep secrets and do not always tell the truth. They are afraid to have someone walk through their heads and hearts and find out what is deeply hidden inside. They tell themselves it can't be done, and if it could, that it would be undesirable, actually evil, because tapping into the supernatural is frightening to a lot of mutants. They believe this is beyond the normal range of human ability. It isn't. It just takes practice and concentration."

That evening when the campfire was lit, Benala taught Minendie how to look into a flame and concentrate so forcefully that she had no inner dialogue taking place in her head and she didn't hear any sound or see anything happening around her. She went into a self-induced trance state. Then the entire group concentrated on sending her the color red in mental telepathy. She was told that when she could receive five colors accurately, she would graduate to becoming the sender. She had difficulty that first night. In trying to analyze what blockage she might have, she admitted she still secretly did not want to deal with the issue of nakedness.

"You must realize," Wurtawurta said to her in the gentle manner of the old woman, "that there is no right or wrong. There will be no applause for a correct answer or frowns because you feel differently than most of us. The world is not black and white. It is all the colors in between. What might be so repulsive to you that you would become ill over the thought may be held as sacred by others, even by yourself at another time, in another place, in another situation. Honesty is the answer. Just be honest with yourself. Recognize how you feel about things. Observe yourself. It is perfectly all right to feel uncomfortable, just don't deny or hide how you feel. From this we learn people can have differences and each is right for his or her own path. If you can't honor your own feelings, it would be impossible to honor those of another. It is the law of the universe that no one can get inside your head and read your mind without your allowing them to do so. It is an art of openness."

Once Minendie understood, the lessons went much more smoothly. They began by teaching her to mentally receive and transmit color. She visualized the color red—the texture, the feel, the smell—using all her senses. Then they progressed to shapes. She learned to deal with circles, squares, and triangles. The material became more and more complex, with the addition of colored spheres, until she could send and receive abstract thoughts. Telepathy was not a voice she heard in her head, not words written across her brain, but somehow a knowing. Daily practice made it easier. Eventually, she did not have to stare herself into a trance state to carry on silent conversations. She also began to develop a sensitivity to mass collective outbursts of thought from vast distances. When the others pointed in a direction and said they felt great pain and suffering or a burst of happiness being released she, too, began to feel the subtle energy being transmitted.

Minendie decided the advantage to telepathy was that it forced people like herself to get rid of thoughts tucked away and to bring everything out into the open. I feel good to know where I stand. Where I have placed myself, she said silently.

The earth was warm, but somehow the world kept a gentle stirring in the air, taking pity in such a hot climate.

"When will we find the others?" Minendie asked as she pulled her long hair to the top of her head and struggled to tie it.

"Very soon now," Apalie answered, placing a finger on the tie so a knot could be finalized.

"Earlier someone mentioned that our people could become undetectable. Mutants coming to save, civilize, and rescue us from ourselves could not see us. Years ago I was told that in former times our race could perform illusion and disappear. Is that what was being referred to?"

"Yes," Apalie answered, watching Minendie's head; with each step the tuft of hair on top waved back and forth like a cock's comb.

"How is it done?" the new Egg Yolk asked. "Can I learn that too?"

"It isn't a trick. It is a basic way of life that developed into disappearing because of the consciousness of warriors and aggressors. If someone came to harm you, someone with a gun, and you were one of the Real People, what could you do? You had no weapon. You wouldn't use it if you did. You were in control of your energy distribution and knew you could not die. You were Forever. So you did not even entertain the emotion of fear. You did not judge this person pointing a gun at you as being wrong. You realized that he was expressing himself at the highest level he would allow himself to be. For him, it was perfect. He was not making a mistake. For him, that was his rightful place at that time. You did observe what was taking place but refused to feed what smelled and tasted unpleasant to you. So you selectively channeled your energy and felt what you believed was right for all of life everywhere. Whenever possible, the best posture is standing, your feet slightly apart, your hands at your side, palms open, facing the challenger. Then you envisioned sparkling light, the spirit energy, coming from the earth up through your feet and legs, filling your whole body. Every cell was full of this perfection. You sent this beauty out, beamed it out to the gun bearer. You did not move a muscle yet you hugged and surrounded this person intent on taking your life. You sent him total acceptance, respect, understanding, and love. You talked to the person silently, in head-to-head, heart-to-heart talk. It was important that you explained in this silence, to this man, that he was not making a mistake. That he had never made a mistake. No one can make a mistake. We are traveling from the same Source back to the same Source and all are given the same gift. In every circle there is always one last portion of the line to be completed and so it is with us. He, too, was a part of the perfection and it was okay for him to choose this action. That does not mean you agree, or condone it, but you do not judge him. You love the person, not his action.

"When you can accept unconditionally and love this person regardless of the circumstances, his deepest level of awareness is awakened. There is a conflict between his spirit consciousness that knows the truth of who he is, and the limited earthly brain consciousness that believes he is capable of murder. The situation is resolved by the use of the animal emotion taken on by people. His reaction to absolutely unconditional love is 'phear,' which is different from the temporary survival emotion taken from the four-legged animals. Humans have added tremendous complications and made fear into this new phenomenon phear. They are afraid of imagined situations, anticipated future events, reoccurrences, anything unexplained, and are terrified by the purity of true unconditional acceptance. Whatever is pheared the most, manifests, such as a deadly snake. If he has no self-worth and feels he is no one, that his existence doesn't matter to anyone, he won't see anything. Some hunters see snakes or wild boars, and still many have reported that we simply vanished.

"Illusion is in the eye of the beholder. Protection comes from never choosing to believe you need any."

40

They walked toward the sea and the northern coast, seven brown, shiny bodies reflecting the glow of Mother Sun. This was the best place for twenty non-law-abiding Aborigines to convene for a few days without being detected. The last runner into the urban world reported the latest rules that, under penalty of law, must be followed by all indigenous persons. This group had no intention of complying with any of the official government laws. They were ruled by a higher court, by higher laws.

The area where they were designated to meet was not out in the open. It was a swamp where tall trees and full foliage prevailed. There was little actual ground for walking upon. Instead, to get from place to place, they would have to walk on thick ropes of tree roots, each extending in a ten- to fifteen-foot spread around a giant tree trunk. The water in the swamp was at least waist high and usually much deeper in the main inlets where saltwater crocodile and water snakes made their home. It was a safe haven from two-legged hunters for the people. They couldn't be seen from an airplane and they could hear any motorboats canvassing the channels. It was also a place of abundant food. They would have access to fish, frogs, eggs, turtles, snakes, leeches, and numerous plants.

All twenty of the Real People would be there. Minendie was eager to meet the other thirteen. They traveled in three separate groups, two groups of four members each and one of five. These three groups and her own met four times a year.

As they came closer to the swamp, the plant growth increased, until they were entering a dense sort of jungle. It stayed shaded all the time, so was cool and damp. Moss in varying shades of green seemed to grow everywhere. The ground covering began to feel slick and moist under Minendie's feet. It wasn't a place she would want to stay for long. Already she missed the bright sunshine.

They heard the voices before they saw the people. Voices even in a hushed whisper resonated through the cavernous space under the trees. The group would not be using telepathy. Experience had taught that it was confusing when so many people were communicating at one time.

Minendie, who so recently had gone through the process of selecting a name, was most interested in what the other thirteen had named themselves and why. She decided to ask each one to explain his or her name as each was introduced. That way she felt she could put a face with the name and remember them better. After all, she joked to herself, I am accustomed to writing things down.

Her group approached two women who smiled and hugged the new arrivals. Minendie introduced herself. One woman with scar decorations on her shoulders said she was Timekeeping. When Minendie asked her to explain why that was the name she'd chosen, she said, "Well, it represents a responsibility. We have had someone for several hundreds of years who is responsible for recalling once each year all meaningful events, such as births, deaths, the first sighting of an airplane, and so forth. Along with another person who actually records the information by painting, we work on a mural of our history, located in a cave. The responsibility of timekeeping is something that is passed from one person to another. While I have had the name, it has become significant to me in a different way. There are three ways of speaking about time. There is the past, yesterday, behind us. The future, tomorrow, out in front, like a straight line. Then there is the circle of time. We come from Forever and return there. For me, I have related to time as represented in our art by a mere dot. You cannot change the past. You are not guaranteed a future. So our artwork is filled with dots; each stands for time. The only time that matters is now, each moment, each dot. If we live each day to the best of our ability, doing everything with our highest level of integrity, we will be successful on this journey as a human." She seemed genuinely pleased that Minendie cared enough to ask about her name. She finished by adding, "Welcome to our tribe."

The next woman's name was One Who Talks to Ancestors. She had a long thin face and wore a serious expression when she explained, "I selected this name because I wasn't sure how I felt about life and death. For me, it has been difficult to remain positive when so much was happening to our people. I wanted to learn how to communicate with the spirit world, if there was one. I guess I questioned if guidance was really available for the asking.

I started off with the name Interested in Talking to Ancestors, but now I can say that I do. Each of us is guided, if we pay attention. It is hard for me to imagine a life without talking to the invisible world and to the unborn. It certainly helped restore my positive frame of mind."

A group of three, two men and a woman, approached Minendie. She repeated her introduction and unusual request to hear an explanation of everyone's name.

The first man was short, stocky, and seemed very happy. He said, "I am Chest Plate Maker. It is what I like to do. Have you seen one? They are only worn as decoration, not for protection in battle. I've been making them for years. I have used almost everything in their crafting: fur, grass, hair, stone, bone, wood, feathers, teeth, claws, snake. When I first started, it was men's business. There was a crafter for women and that was her business, but now there are so few of us that somewhere along the line I was asked to make the first woman's piece. I now make both styles. If you've never seen one, you wouldn't know how they are used. We use them to express ourselves. Sometimes they symbolize the feeling that we need protection, that we are vulnerable people. We need a shield from the sad talk that comes from the city. The shield can represent a heart that is not ready to be exposed. I enjoy creating them."

Next was a man who called himself Kin to Water Buffalo. He was without doubt the largest man in the tribe. "I like my name because the animal does not really belong in Australia. It isn't native, you know. It was brought here by boat people. It has enormous strength and endurance and learned to adapt and survive when it escaped from captivity. In my eyes, our situation is reversed. We belong here, but we are uprooted, so rugged brute strength may be required in order to live."

The next tribal woman had white streaks that looked almost as if they had been painted running through her otherwise dark hair. She was enthusiastic and bubbly as she said, "I called myself Three Beings Within. I realized," she continued, "that as I grew older and looked out upon the world, the view I was seeing was sometimes still that of a child. Other times I saw and felt as a woman, and I try more and more each day to see from the wise elder inside. I won't give up any part of the three. I like being a responsible adult and I pride myself on making some wise decisions, but I still enjoy laughing like a child. My curiosity about the world around me has not faded. I think my name says, 'Accept me as I am, I'm not going to grow up.'"

The next man was in his mid-forties, tall and thin. He was named Divided Path. "I selected this name thinking it would be for only a short time. I was unsure about what talent to pursue. I was unsure about getting married. I didn't know if we could, as a group, keep up all the responsibility as caretakers for so many abandoned nations. My naming ceremony was years ago." He laughingly added, "I'm still Divided Path."

A woman then approached Minendie and introduced herself. "I am Instant Bloom," she said. "My name comes because I see nature has a magical way of keeping order in the world. Nights turn cold so little seeds can store enough power to burst forth when the hot sun shines. Nature sees the faded petals on flowers, the wilted branches of trees, stirs up the air, and, selectively, plant by plant, strips off the dead and sends the debris tumbling to collect in a ravine. The old leaves become the shelter for the tiny frightened rodents and lizards. When everything becomes very, very silent, the birds come down from the sky and hide, clutching their wings, sitting motionless. The air gets heavy, the sky turns black, and then it is time to prepare for nature's great show. I see a flash of light with spider legs running out in opposite directions. Many times one leg runs down to the ground. As quickly as the light was exhaled, it is sucked back into the blackness and there is a moment of silence before the loud clap stick sounds. Sometimes it is so loud it sounds as if the earth is broken in half. The ground rumbles, and the noise skips over the surface of the sand. The rain comes in big drops. Sheets of water march across the horizon, bending everything in their path. Every indentation in the ground or rock is filled with water. There is such an excess that the water rolls across the soil like an ocean wave. With the very first rays of light following the heavenly water, as far as the eye can see is a vast field of flowers. It is so inspiring to me. It has become my motto. I think of our tribe as those little dormant seeds, blending into the surroundings, no one paying any attention, but at the right moment we will burst into color. I've always felt there must be a certain amount of apprehension on the part of the little seed. It strives so hard to remain fertile and has no control over the elements. The seed is made perfectly for its surroundings and so are we. Every time the sun rises, I feel like blooming." Minendie liked her immediately.

Next came a very serious-faced, older white-headed woman called Sees Through Water.

"That's an interesting name," Minendie said. "Are you a swimmer? Do you search for certain things under the water?"

"No," the older, slowly speaking female replied. "The water I see through is tears. I feel the sorrow and hear the tears of our people as they fall upon the land far away. I hold them in the light of my thoughts. I send them

Rainbow Snake energy and see for them when they cannot. I daily remind myself I am not here to understand the Dreaming that is unfolding. My role is in the knowing that Mother Nature will find the solution that is the best for all of life."

A very thin, very serious young man explained that his name was White Owl. "There are many different owls, but the white one has become very rare. The owl is usually silent, a characteristic I understand. I usually say things in my mind a couple of times before I say them out loud. Maybe I lack confidence in expressing myself. Maybe it's because I'm not always tolerant with people who talk all the time and never say anything."

"My name is Sister to the Ant," said the middle-aged woman standing nearby who wore a strand of seeds around her ankle. "I selected it because it is a constant reminder to our group that, over time, tiny creatures can build monumental structures that are not destructive and are in keeping with the harmony of the earth. There are few of us Real People, but we are patient, have stamina, and are willing to do our part to devote our lives to saving our land and preserving our culture."

A very dignified and stately, attractive man about sixty spoke next. "I am One Called from a Distance. I spent a period of my life feeling very resentful about how the European invaders came and conquered our people without our resisting or putting up any united struggle. I feel now I was meant to come here and be with this group to get an understanding of my role as a human. This support system saved my life. In turn, I am trying to be protective and aware of my responsibility in being steward of my energy. I am devoted to doing my best not to add negativity to the consciousness and the world Dreaming."

A short, unusually small man introduced himself next. "My name is Keeper of the Record. I am the artist who works with Timekeeping to continue our story on the cave wall. It is a responsibility that changes hands as someone new expresses a desire to experience this important role. I love drawing and painting, so I really enjoy who I am at the present time."

The last member of the tribe to whom Minendie was introduced was the most handsome man she had ever seen. His smile revealed a mouth full of perfectly shaped white teeth. His black eyes were so kind and friendly they seemed to cover most of his face. He appeared strong and his skin was smooth and unblemished. He swallowed Minendie with his gaze as he nodded his head and came forward to say, "I am Boomerang Maker. Welcome to our tribe. My name is self-explanatory. I feel a deep connection to our brothers and sisters, the big family of life-giving trees. There are so many kinds, no two alike, and the spirit of each is as different as their locations. The boomerang is a wonderful helper when you deal with the tree spirit within. There are many different shapes of boomerangs. Some are for sport and some are for the original intent, which is to kill painlessly and unsuspectingly. As long as there are Aborigines on the face of this earth, there will be someone like me called Boomerang Maker."

The group mingled and exchanged small talk, then they went about the work of securing and preparing food. After the meal Minendie sat upon a huge tree root and looked around at the gathered people. She was pleased that she could recall each of the thirteen names. She also felt she knew the person and that a bond had been established in a very short time.

41

Googana was sitting some distance from Minendie, on a stump that was slightly elevated so that he was in clear view of everyone. Somehow the body posture of the group had shifted so that all faced him. He appeared to have evolved as the leader for this meeting.

White Owl was across from Minendie. She didn't expect that he would say much. Sees Through Water was next to him. Minendie wondered if the discussion ahead would add to the tears that she held in her heart. She smiled at Instant Bloom and nodded to Keeper of the Record.

"It is good to see you again," Googana said, looking around and making eye contact with each one. "I suggest we go around the circle and each one can tell of the earth changes you have observed and comment on any other concerns you have."

One by one they spoke of the very obvious and mysterious things that had taken place during the past months and years. There were fewer birds, and they less healthy, with sparser feathers. There were fewer eggs per nest and more fragile eggshells. Whole species of birds had disappeared. There were fewer plants, fewer blooms, smaller in size, paler in color. The temperature was fluctuating in an unpredictable way. It was getting hotter and hotter in the summer and warmer in the winter. One entire species of snake had vanished. A fish that was once so large it took two men to carry it was now small. Wurtawurta reported her sightings of the abnormal tadpoles. They didn't know what was causing all of this. The fact that kangaroo, dingo, and koala were being massively slaughtered could be directly connected to the white population. The imbalance in nature caused by the introduction of such foreign animals as sheep, cattle, camels, horses, water buffalos, rabbits, cats, dogs, toads, rats, and insects was a direct result of the European presence.

"Something else to consider," Googana interjected, "is the latest list of rules that are now law for all indigenous people." He proceeded to recite the laws.

Aborigines must:

Fill out a census form and be counted.
Register for the tax rolls.
Report every birth.
Report every death.
Bury the dead and bury them only in authorized places.
Send all children to school.
Immunize all children
Apply for licenses to work machines.

"How do we deal with observing all of this and not judging it?" came the question from One Called from a Distance.

"It is not a matter of how," Googana answered, "it is that we must do it! What is the principle involved here? It is our responsibility to direct our thoughts, our actions, our words, all our energy into that which we wish to see grow. That which smells good to us and which with guidance tells us to focus, so harmony with all of life can be continued."

Others spoke. "What has happened cannot be reversed. Only Mother Nature herself could restore these things."

"They won't be restored, but maybe something new and stronger will be the replacement."

"The black man cannot save the world. It is questionable if he can save himself."

"Maybe saving is not the issue. Maybe we are trying to keep things as they once were and believe this is saving the earth. Perhaps the world is not being lost, it is only changing, drastically changing."

Googana addressed Minendie. "You are the most recent person to know firsthand of the mutant world. Some say they are responsible for much of this. How is it possible that they can control the feathers on a bird?"

"I don't know," she answered. "There are new inventions coming all the time. Once in a while, there is some small opposition, which protests that the object or factory puts poison into the air and into the water. I don't know if it is true. The white world is not keen on telling the truth. They say, 'Of course, it is not true.' They say, 'Why would we poison ourselves?'"

Heads bobbed up and down. Yes, it was a good question. It seemed true that the mutants had no regard for their role as caretakers of the earth. They were busy putting cement everywhere, killing animals for sport, but would they go so far as to poison themselves while doing so? And would such poison affect animals and birds miles away?

The discussion continued. “It does no good to live at the missions. There our ways are trampled upon. It would do no good to go to the city to speak of our concern for these new rules. I am sure other Aborigines have done so already. Let us not forget there are Aborigines who agree with the rules. They chose to become like the white man and live as he does.”

In the end they came to the agreement that one principle involved was not to accept the illusion of lack and limitation. They would not take up arms to defend themselves. They would not give up honoring all of life and living in harmony with nature. They would continue as they had been, each group covering a different part of the land, each taking care of sacred places for those who had been removed. They would meet again in three months in the best place for that season.

The group stayed in the swamp for four more days. Minendie became better acquainted with all the others. One evening Benala was sharing a turtle leg with her and said, “If you wish to walk with others in the coming months, you are free to do so. We love having you with us, but I feel I should tell you that you are not obligated in any way to remain with us. Karaween is going to go and be with Talks to Ancestors. I think that she and White Owl have become interested in each other. There has been a system of what is called ‘skin barriers’ in the past. People could marry into certain tribes and not into others, depending upon to whom they were related. These two young people are not related in any way, so they are free to learn if they wish to marry or not."

Minendie had found Instant Bloom to be someone with whom she enjoyed talking. Instant Bloom was married to Water Buffalo. Would it interfere if she walked with them? she wondered. After several discussions, people regrouped and it was decided that Minendie would join her new friends as a third party. The fourth in the group was the man called Divided Path.

"'Fire Blessing
May the fire be in our thoughts,
Making them true, good, and just.
May it protect us from accepting anything less.
May the fire be in our eyes.
May it open our eyes to share what is good in life.
We ask that the fire protect us from what is not rightfully ours.
May the fire be on our lips
So that we may speak the truth in kindness,
That we may serve and encourage others.
May the fire be in our ears
So that we hear with deep listening,
So that we may hear the flow of water
And all creation and the Dreaming.
May we be protected from gossip and from things
That have the ability to harm
And break down our family.
May the fire be in our arms and hands
So we may be of service and build up love.
May the fire be in our whole being,
In our legs and in our feet, enabling us to walk
The earth with reverence and care
So that we may walk in the ways of goodness and truth
And be protected from walking away from what is truth.'"

"That is beautiful," Minendie said as she watched the beaming faces of her friends. "No wonder our people were so puzzled when the missionaries kept saying what a bad place hell was, and described it as an eternal pit of fire. It is fascinating how the same objects can be regarded by two different groups as such opposite extremes. One set of eyes sees only the negative and spends its life praying for what it truly believes is not attainable, man born without sin. The other group has eyes that see infants born innocent and pure, a world of abundance, where we are guests invited by the Source. There is no word for work. Instead each expresses himself doing what comes easily, and is of interest. The terms 'primitive' and 'civilized' don't seem appropriate to use."

43

During the next years, as the tribe gathered every three months, people changed walking companions until everyone had experienced being with all the other nineteen members. The responsibility of sharing all year long the song and dance lessons, for Minendie's benefit, was graciously accepted and continued.

Tribal people did not celebrate birthdays. For them, the word "celebrate" meant special, a personal accomplishment. All agreed that getting a year older was not something that fit this category. They did, however, celebrate. The difference was that the individual to be celebrated announced when it was time to do so. The others supported by acknowledging, listening, and giving attention in a festive setting. One didn't say "Celebrate me" unless he had earned it, and no one was challenged or denied.

Minendie remained with the name meaning Egg Yolk for three years. One day she was alone collecting broken birds' nest shells, which she would later pound into fine powder for using as food and as paint for body designs. "I've been a yolk long enough," she said out loud, to no one. "I have had time to develop into a finished product. I must now consider who I am and receive a new name." She pondered the question mentally for a week before she announced to her traveling companions that it was time to celebrate her new name.

This time the group was not near a supply of water for the ritual of washing away the old. Instead, they used smoke. It symbolically burned away the remnants after a fruitful season. A new woman, like new life springing up from charred soil, would be sitting in their circle. Minendie whispered her chosen name to Sister to the Ant. Within a few seconds, the creative words had formed and Sister to the Ant rose to sing her announcement.

"You expect our Egg Yolk, Minendie,
To hatch into a bird.
For her to emerge as something else,
Might be a bit absurd.
After all, there are cockatoos,
Kookaburra, and parrot to choose.
With hundreds of two-legged,
Finding kinship, she couldn't lose.
But Minendie surprised me.
Platypus, Mapiyal, is her name.
A dweller in two worlds,
Unique to us she will remain."

"Why Mapiyal?" someone asked. "Tell us what is in your heart."

"I do often think of the two worlds, the mutants' and

ours. The platypus goes between the water and the land. She is most at home in water, and spends her life in quiet still pools, but she can't remain underwater. She must visit the land, she must leave the safety in order to breathe the air. I gave it much thought and it is right I now become Mapiyal. Thank you, Sister to the Ant, for the song and announcement."

44

Days and years passed. Life in the open was peaceful and fulfilling. There were new sights, new discoveries, and new ways to express while walking along familiar terrain with old friends and continuing ancient traditions.

When Wurtawurta became 102 years old, she announced at the seasonal gathering of all tribal members that she had asked Divine Oneness if it was in the highest good for her to return to Forever. She had received an affirmative reply.

It was the first time Mapiyal and several others would witness the deliberate spirit release from a human body. The members of the group, who so strongly held to the belief of Forever and who knew that life consciousness did not begin at conception, were also advocates of a death that need not be painful and undetermined. Each had already learned many of the steps needed to achieve the final act. They had learned how to use inner mental pictures to make their bodies warmer during chilly nights and cooler when the world remained stiflingly hot after sunset. They had been schooled about the power centers running in a straight line up the body, from between their legs to the tops of their heads. They knew how to sleep for short periods with their eyes open if necessary and to reduce the bodily functions to those in a state of deep, relaxing sleep. They had each mastered the ability to leave the body and project their consciousness elsewhere.

Several days were spent in preparation for Wurtawurta's transition. When the dawn came that special day, Mapiyal wondered if her long unanswered question, Do people, when they die, have any inkling as they wake the morning of their last day?, might be answered that day. Perhaps it had bothered her so deeply and had been so troubling because the inherent energies in her being were saying, "You do not die, you simply honor a belief in your heart and return to our Source. You made the decision to come, you are entitled by choice to leave. There are no accidents, only spiritual connections from which we have not distanced ourselves far enough to see."

The celebration honoring Wurtawurta lasted all day. There was a special herb potion brewed and extra care taken in gathering and preparing the food. Every tribal member had an opportunity to perform and tell about Wurtawurta's life and the times they had shared with her. The honoree spoke and said everything she felt that would be significant for the others. She told Mapiyal she was grateful that the woman years ago had told her about the feeling of silk. She had used it in her visualizations and would use it today as she returned to Forever. The group called upon the spirits of the plant and animal world to share in the day.

As the sun was setting, one by one, each person held Wurtawurta and each repeated the same phrase, "We love and support you on the journey." Then they walked away as the old bent woman sat down, cross-legged. She mentally shut down each power point, cooled her body, slowed the circulation and heart rate, and, at last, used a traditional final breathing technique. When her heart stopped, her head fell forward and her body slumped to the side. She had exited, projected herself as she had done many times before and had taught the others to do, only this time she did not return. Her body would be devoured by whatever life-forms found it to be sustaining. There was no burial.

A month later the party of five with whom Mapiyal was living came upon the wreckage of a small aircraft. It was almost hidden. Out in the vast open space there was a large collection of giant boulders. The plane must have hit on an angle because the debris was forced between the stone, making it difficult to spot from overhead.

There were the remains of two men. The group buried the bodies because they honored the way these men believed, and they marked the spot in case someone found the wreckage someday. Mapiyal suggested the marker be two sticks forming a cross since, for mutants, that seemed to symbolize a grave. They took some of the torn cloth from what appeared to be one man's jacket, the other's shirt, and a piece of cloth from a seat and ceremoniously burned them. Each sent smoke energy over a mental rainbow to the deceased and to a worried family somewhere.

Mapiyal thought, They were probably men flying over to see if any other Aborigines remained in the outback and needed to be rescued from themselves! But they are just doing what they believe is right.

45

Mapiyal grew more stately, peaceful, and dignified with each passing year. She changed occupations and helped add to the community life in a variety of fields but was not drawn to again change her name. Every few years Benala would leave the tribe and go to the nearest community for a few days. On her return she reported her findings about the condition of the world beyond the Real People. Each time Benala left she asked Mapiyal if she wished to accompany her. Mapiyal, curious, was tempted, but each time a feeling would come that it was not the thing to do. She would decline.

Prisoner number 804781, known as Jeff Marsh, also grew to be a dignified peacemaker in his older years. His hair, by the age of forty, was sprinkled with gray.

He had access to all the library books he wanted, so he studied various forms of artwork and the lives of many artists. He gave a lesson to one inmate that, in turn, over the years grew into a program he directed. Ultimately he taught and participated in doing arts and crafts, gaining such a degree of recognition that the prison had an annual sale for the prisoners' hand-crafted items.

The acknowledgment of his existence and his creativity at these yearly sales became his focus in life. To do better each year was his goal. The man who had lived twice as long incarcerated behind institutional walls as he had spent free in the world as a youth had found his place. He had settled into a routine and was at peace.

In the Australian outback the people sat on the ground looking into the velvet-black night. Two nights before they had seen a bright glow move across the heavens. They did not know if it was a star or something new from the mutant world. On the following night, when it appeared again, following the same path, they were mystified. Surely it would not come again but, yes, it did. Three nights in a row it could be seen moving among the other brilliant beams of light.

"What is it?" came the question. "Do you think it is a sign?"

"We must ask for some guidance. I will ask for a dream."

The Real People did not ordinarily dream at night. They believed sleep was the time for the body to rest, to recover, to heal, to recharge. If part of one's consciousness was busy dreaming, it would be a physical distraction. They understood that mutants dreamed at night, but of course that was understandable. In that society one wasn't allowed to dream during the day while awake, as Real People did. Tonight, as suggested, several members would ask for a message dream.

Mapiyal used the same procedure as the others. Taking a seashell container of water, she swallowed half and made her request for information about the object in the sky. The other half of the fluid would be consumed upon awakening to connect her conscious mind to the memory of the dream. She could then have better recall for finding meaning and direction.

In her dream there was a young child straddling a turtle. It seemed to be a boy, but she wasn't sure. At first he sat patiently riding the creature. He then began to cry. He begged the turtle to move faster, but it continued in the same slow pace.

In the morning, when the group helped her study the dream, she was asked, "How did you feel about the child?"

"I felt as if he were mine. I loved him, as if he belonged to me!"

"And what does the turtle feel like to you?"

"Timid, withdrawn, a slow, steady pacer. Not an animal you could entice or whip to make it move any faster. It wasn't one of our turtles. It wasn't a water turtle. It was a land type."

"How do you feel about that?"

"I feel comfortable with my kinship to turtles in general. Quite frankly, I have not spent a moment that I am aware of thinking about land turtles. This was definitely a foreign sort, I would say from America. But I see no connection to the object in the sky. The dream could mean that any child for me will be a long way off. It has been slow in arriving." Then she laughingly added, "That is certainly true; I am fifty-four years old."

The group of women turned to another member and asked about Mapiyal's dream. She felt it indicated the need for a member to visit the mutants' society to find an answer firsthand. Another felt her dream was saying all of the world was changing, first it was the earth and now it was also the sky.

It had been thirty-four years since Mapiyal had walked away from city life and joined the tribal people. She had never regretted the change and missed nothing from her former existence. She had grown older, that she could observe by looking down at her body, but she had no occasion to see her own face. There had not been a time when they had visited any pool of water clear or still enough to give an accurate reflection. She hadn't considered the idea for such a long time that it amazed her that it would pop into her mind now. She didn't care what she looked like. What she cared about was how the others looked upon her and she felt at peace with their expressions. When Benala traveled back and forth the reports were not favorable toward any restoration of the Aboriginal way of life. Perhaps it was time for her to go. Not out of curiosity, but because now she felt she might have something to offer her people. She would consult Keeper of the Answer Guide and then make her decision.

Later that day she and the Keeper went off alone. When they were isolated from the others, Mapiyal went into a deep, quiet state of mind. Reaching into the pouch containing the women's business of answer guidance, she selected a round leather disk showing a symbol that stood for seven directions: north, south, east, west, above, below, and within. It implied that Mapiyal must now carefully study the direction she had come from and the direction she was pointing toward. In the past, she was aware of what way they were walking, but wasn't a part of charting any course. Over the years they had traveled in all four ways of the compass. She thought about the other three directions: the sky above, the earth below, and the personal inner self. She felt confident in hearing her own inner voice, and consulted the upper spirit world and the lower animal world with ease. The symbol seemed to indicate that she should look carefully at one of the four wind directions. It was her own personal decision to make to walk with the others or walk toward the cities. She intuitively sensed her future step.

That evening she announced to everyone that she would leave. She would travel to the closest community known to have an Aboriginal settlement. Unless things had radically changed, she was confident she would find allies who would provide clothing, shelter, food, and friendship. Centuries of sharing and helping each other seemed embedded in the very matrix of the Aborigines' being. It was foreign to them to turn their backs on a fellow traveler.

The sun crept up slowly the following morning, as if it were giving Mapiyal a second chance to think over her decision. But she had made up her mind. Now was the right time, it was in the highest good to go.

She said good-bye to everyone and expressed her desire to return someday. They had estimated the distance to be a seven- or eight-day walk to the nearest indigenous group. It took Mapiyal nine days. When she arrived she sat in the bush country at dusk watching from a distance. There were five makeshift dwellings that gave the appearance of being in either some stage of construction or demolition. It was hard to tell which. Three had wooden steps to the front doors. Two did not. Only one house had glass in all the windows, but they were shoved up so air could circulate. Although some people went in and out of the residences, most seemed to be sitting or standing outside. The buildings were nestled in tall green trees. She saw an older woman, with a double chin and a little protruding belly, who looked near her own age. The lady mingled with the others and later cooked on a barbecue in the yard. She seemed the best person to approach.

Mapiyal waited for an opportunity. She hoped the woman would be alone later that night. The community of people did not retire at an early hour. They were still gathered together, talking into the wee hours before dawn. Mapiyal slept off and on but couldn't rest for very long at a time. Just before sunrise the woman came out of her house and sat on the front step drinking a cup of tea. Mapiyal stood up and walked toward the community. She dusted off the hide wrap she had made to cover herself. As she approached, the woman looked up.

"It is today," she said, having totally forgotten what greeting people used.

"G'day," the woman answered, looking at Mapiyal in bewilderment from behind her dark black eyes. She asked, "Where did you come from?"

"I belong to the Karoon tribe. I walked here because I would like your help. It has been many years since I left the city. I need something to wear and I need to see a map to get some idea of where I am."

The woman had a gentle manner. She shook her head in agreement as she said, "I can give you something to put on. You look about my size, and everything I have has elastic at the waist. But I don't have a map. I've never even seen one. No bother, though, I'm sure we can find what you need. Come inside. I'll make you a cuppa." She stood up and headed indoors as she continued talking. "I had no idea there were any people left in the bush. We were told everyone was gone. I want to hear all about what you do."

The woman first made a cup of tea. After handing it to her guest, she went into another room and came back with two dresses. One was blue and the other had a print pattern. Both had short sleeves, were buttoned down the front to the waist, and had elastic stretchable waistbands. They were homemade, from the same pattern. "Here, you can try these. I hope one will fit. My name is Sally. What is yours?"

"I'm Bea." Mapiyal had no idea why she said that. She hadn't been Beatrice in years. Now it was out, so it would have to do. If she were back with her family, this change in interests would certainly be appropriate for a name change, but she wasn't with her family. Bea was okay. She would think of it as "Bee," the little creature that is so busy taking pollen from place to place, helping the flowers continue to grow. Bee's help constructed communities for its kind. It did so with sweetness, but there was always that stinger available if needed. She hoped she had learned never to use any stinger.

For the next few hours they talked. Bea had walked away from her employment in 1956; it was now 1990, and nothing had remained the same. Sally told her about television, wireless telephones, computers, satellites, and rocket ships. She didn't own any luxury items, but she knew all about them and had friends who did own them. She couldn't explain the object in the sky. "But the Americans and the Russians have activity out there." Bea in turn told Sally about life with the Real People; soon it was late morning. By this time everyone in the community knew that Sally was entertaining a desert dweller. One by one they came to the kitchen, looked, and introduced themselves and both asked and answered questions. When it was mealtime Bea realized she had forgotten about beans in a can and white bread in a plastic wrapper. She was grateful for the hospitality, but ate sparingly, not sure her stomach was ready for this kind of food again. That evening a group gathered under the trees and Bea sat and listened to each one express their opinions of what was happening to the Aborigines in Australia. Ninety percent were unemployed. The dole welfare system was inadequate to meet their needs. The young people did receive a good education, but there was no incentive for higher education because jobs were not available. There were token Aborigines in government and working for newspapers and other media, but most of them were lighter in complexion. One man felt the color of the skin remained an absolutely negative factor. The health of the general Aboriginal public was a major concern. Diabetes and alcohol addiction were taking such a toll that living to be eighty years old was rarely achieved.

The heaviest weight upon the shoulders of their culture was land rights. There was no one in government who understood or stood up to protect sacred sites. The people had been given some land designated for Aborigines only, but mining companies had obtained rights to destroy the earth even there. Every beautiful place on the continent was now designated a national park, but even that land was not free from mining and exploration.

The people lacked pride, they said. They had nothing left to be proud of. They had lost contact with their heritage.

Later Sally made a bed for Bea on her sofa, but sleep

was slow to come since she was not yet used to sleeping on a pad again. Finally she went outside, where several others slept, and found a comfortable spot on thick grass. She did take a sheet and put it down because she was warned of tiny insects that bit their way under the skin.

As she looked up at the planets overhead, it was difficult to imagine how two so very different ways of life, not all that far apart geographically, could exist under the same Milky Way.

I don't know if I'll find an answer to the object in the sky, but maybe that was what Oneness used to get me here, she thought. I feel now that I was called here not to get information and report back, but instead, to give information. I feel pulled toward helping in some way to remind people of our heritage and restore pride and dignity. Perhaps the time has come for us to influence the mutants instead of buckling under to their power and demands. Maybe it is time for Bee nectar!

Birds chirped and children giggled as Bea stirred from her sleeping position. Sally had spoken to a neighbor and arranged for Bea to have a ride from the settlement into town. There was a library facility there and also a town office where Bea felt certain she could locate a map to study. After a breakfast of tea and cake, Sally hugged her and with misty eyes said, "I hope you will come back, but somehow I feel you won't. I wish you success and I want to help. This is for you." She handed Bea paper money that had been tightly rolled and clutched in her fist.

A car sat idling nearby and the thin young Aboriginal driver dressed in blue jeans and T-shirt waited. As soon as Bea started toward the car the young boy got into the driver's seat next to a woman passenger and looked ready to leave. Both the woman in the front seat and a man already occupying half of the backseat were people Bea had met. No introductions were needed. She climbed into the back. The man was going to see a doctor and the woman to visit friends. They talked all the way, and Bea felt less and less like an outsider.

At the city hall a helpful man using a cane got several maps out and opened them on a table. In schoolteacher fashion he pointed out the front door and oriented his new pupil about what was located in each direction. He told her about offices for Aboriginal affairs and Aboriginal hostels. When asked, he had no knowledge of any objects seen in the sky two weeks before.

She learned that a government-funded one-room office for Aboriginal affairs was set up in almost every small town. Rarely did she find the room occupied, but someone nearby could usually tell her where she might go to find the local director. Directorship was viewed as a position of prestige, but paid a minimum salary. The government intention appeared pure. White supremacy had put her people down two hundred years ago, but what was keeping them there? She didn't see racial hatred any longer. If anything, what she was observing was white indifference to blacks. In the stores she entered the clerks spoke to her just as they did to a white customer. In each town she found a place to sleep, could wash and change her dress, and was able to eat economical meals.

After thirty days she found herself on the western coast. She was sitting on a bench outside the Aboriginal affairs office when a woman came out and called her in.

"Sit here," the young woman said, looking over the top of her glasses. "There are some papers we need to fill out. What is your name?"

"Bea."

"Last name?"

Bea sat motionless. She had no last name. None had been assigned at the orphanage. Mrs. Crowley didn't require it nor did Mildred at the milk bar, but that had been thirty-four years ago. Now it seemed the time had come.

"What is your last name?" the woman asked again, slightly louder in case Bea was partially deaf. What would have been done in leisure in the desert and with great deliberation was now approached in keeping with the modern pace of life. Quickly, she scanned her feelings of where she was in life and how it could be reflected. She remembered the phrase "We rise and decline racially as a group just like the water in a lake."

"Lake," Bea replied. "My name is Bea Lake."

"What is your tax file number?"

Bea gulped. "I don't have a number."

"Another one of those! Well, we will fill out the papers for that too. Can't work and not pay taxes."

"Work?" Bea questioned.

"Yes, you are in luck, my dear," the woman said, removing an earring and rubbing her aching ear as she continued to write. "A very nice family is interviewing today for the position of nanny. They will provide a room, all meals, and a salary. There is one child to care for, a boy. What is your address?"

"Well, I really don't have one."

"I'll use the hostel's address. You can stay there for a few days. It's a good place for me to contact you. Now, you can do child care, can't you?"

"Well, I love children but I—"

"Oh my goodness," the blond interrupted as she looked at her watch. "I have to close for lunch and you need to scoot out of here and catch the bus. Here are the directions to the Carpenters' house. Take bus number forty-four, then transfer to bus number sixteen. It's only six blocks from this stop. Here is my phone number. Call me after your interview. Here's the address and phone number for the hostel. If you don't stay there, be sure to tell them where you will be so I can reach you if Mrs. Carpenter decides you will do. Frankly, I think you are the best one so far, but then, I'm not hiring you, am I?"

With that the clerk stood up, pulled down her short skirt, which had crept up around her hips, and staggered across the room on spike heels. She opened the door, indicating that her new client should leave.

It had all happened so quickly that Bea wasn't sure what to think. As she looked around she heard the key in the office door click. She turned to see the white plastic sign hanging inside the glass window turned to read CLOSED.

Above the bench outside two firms were listed. "Office for Aboriginal Affairs" was first and, under it, "Baker Employment Agency." She shook her head and laughed to herself, thinking, Isn't it interesting how the universe works? The Aboriginal office was still closed. The more she thought about it, the more appealing the idea of the nanny position became. She could become better acquainted with the modern world. It was a job she could leave at any time. She walked to the corner and read on the sign posted there that this block was a stop on the route of bus number forty-four, which came shortly. She had no trouble finding the Carpenter residence by following the instructions on the note from the Baker Employment Agency representative.

The residence was in an upper-class neighborhood and looked to be newly constructed. She rang the bell once and waited. A shadowy figure could be seen through the etched and beveled glass door. The handle turned and Bea found herself facing an Asian woman.

"G'day," Bea said to the smiling face on the tiny female. "I've come from the employment office."

"Yes. Please come in. I will tell Mrs. Carpenter. You can go in there and wait," she said, pointing to a lovely big lounge with tall windows that faced a side garden. The room was very bright, having white walls and ceiling and a light-beige marble floor with white rugs strategically placed on it among pastel, upholstered furniture. There were touches of gold in candlesticks and photo frames. The sun coming through the spotlessly clean windows was reflected off a large crystal bowl on the center table where a white rose floated in the bowl's blue-tinted water.

Bea walked around a grand piano in one corner and looked at the photographs on display hanging like marching soldiers in a straight, uniform line. She blinked and looked again. A little boy with curly hair, just like the child she had seen in her dream, was looking back at her. The only difference was that in her dream the boy on the turtle had been an Aborigine. This child was Caucasian.

"G'day," said a gentle voice behind her. "I'm Natalie Carpenter. Who are you?"

"My name is Bea," she said, looking for the first time at the decorator of this magnificent room and the mother of the lovable-looking child. "The employment office asked me to come."

Natalie Carpenter was perfectly groomed. She wore icy-pink slacks and a matching top, a gold chain adorned her neck, and gold and pearl earrings dangled just below the bottom of her freshly brushed light brown hair. She looked ready to model in a fashion show. She was pleasant, bubbly, and Bea liked her immediately. Although the little boy, David, was taking a nap, Bea was escorted upstairs to peek in his nursery. Natalie showed her the guest room, for the nanny. She explained that Kuno, the Japanese woman, was their cook and housekeeper. When Bea left, Natalie told her she would call the agency with her decision. Bea was too aware of the power of the universe not to believe that this door was being opened by Divine Spirit. She spent that night at the hostel. The following day she received the phone call telling her that the Carpenters had selected her for David's new companion.

He was a bright, well-mannered four-year-old. Bea knew they would get along well when on their first day together he insisted that, along with him, she enjoy a bowl of ice cream as her afternoon snack. He loved to read stories to her and she appreciated the refresher course on written language. He liked to visit the park and run in the open space. Finally he had a nanny who felt as at home in the open air as he did. Bea was free each evening after David went to bed at seven, so she became involved in local Aboriginal politics and attended evening meetings.

She had been with the Carpenters for two months when she learned Natalie's father was coming to dinner. Kuno asked if Bea and David could go to the store and make a purchase. She wanted to prepare a dessert the guest of honor especially enjoyed.

That evening after dinner Bea was called into the lounge when it was David's bedtime. A tall, stately, white-haired man was just coming in from the garden. Natalie said to Bea, "I'd like to introduce my father, Andrew Simunsen. Dad, this is our nanny, Bea."

"Happy to meet you," Andrew replied. "My grandson has become very fond of you. That is nice to hear."

Bea would have recognized Andrew anywhere. He

hadn't changed much at all. He was still thin and athletic-looking, with slightly protruding ears. The white hair only added to his already distinguished looks. "It's nice to see you again," Bea remarked. "It's been a long time."

"I'm afraid I don't remember," the man offered in return as he rotated the empty cocktail glass he was holding.

"Mrs. Crowley's place. I left after the fire."

"Oh yes, of course, Beatrice. Well, isn't this a surprise. You look well. I'm glad you are doing so well. My, my, isn't this a surprise."

Bea took David upstairs after he'd said good night to everyone. When he had fallen asleep, she went outside and sat in the garden. As she looked up at the stars, which only numbered one fourth as many as were seen in the desert, she wondered what door was opening tonight. Shortly after that, Andrew and the Carpenters emerged, each carrying a full glass of wine. "So, Bea, tell me about yourself," the old acquaintance said, taking a large gulp of his drink.

"Oh, there isn't much to tell, but you seem to have lived an interesting life. I'd love to hear your story."

"Ha, ha," he snickered in merriment. "My story, you say. Well, yes, I have done well. Mining business, you know. Done very well in mining. Your people were a big help in the beginning. I listened to a fellow one day talking about this special place, a place with special power, and I got to wondering if such a place really existed. If so, why? Maybe it could be a mineral deposit, making the water high in mineral content. So I got him to tell me where it was. Then I had the place assayed and immediately filed a mining claim. Can't tell you how much iron, uranium, even gold I found from asking about Aboriginal power places. Of course, now we pay for the mining rights.

Started doing that quite a while ago. There is still a little legal entanglement from time to time, but nothing major. Your people have come a long way. Just look at you, Bea. It's wonderful to see you looking so well." His diamond ring sparkled in the moonlight as he tipped the glass and finished its contents.

That night in bed, her window open, Bea listened to the city night sounds and thought, So Andrew Simunsen thinks we have come a long way. It doesn't smell and taste that way to me. Without judging anyone as right or wrong, I need to observe where we are and put my energy into the highest good for my people.

47

Judy was a thirty-five-year-old Aboriginal woman Bea had seen at some of the political meetings. She seemed to be well-educated and was very articulate in voicing her opinion. Bea felt she would be a good source of information. The following evening there was a brief get-together of nine people regarding a dump site officials wanted to add at the edge of the city, next to an Aboriginal settlement. Bea asked Judy if she could stay to talk. Bea learned that Judy was a schoolteacher and was most concerned about the young people, particularly the teenagers, who were drinking and sniffing glue to get high. She told Bea about the number of blacks who were incarcerated in jails and prisons and that she was devoted to making a difference for them.

"I know our people are not inherently bad; we rarely had a crime before the Europeans came to our shores. In fact, they were the criminals, who came in chains. Why is it that now our people far outnumber theirs, percentage wise, in being institutionalized? I have asked offenders, and they tell me they steal to get money because the dole isn't enough. Some of them, at one point, did try to get employment, but most stopped trying. The majority of the offenses happen when the person is under the influence of alcohol. The young people say they drink because there is nothing else to do. It is an adventure. It feels good. It is fun. When I ask about their future, they say, "What future?"

"What would you like the future to be like for Aborigines?" Bea asked.

"I would like to see us have our own businesses. If we made furniture and bought only from our own, in time we could perfect it so people of all colors would prefer our styles, our colors, our finishes. Maybe even export it someday. Furniture is just an example. We have wonderful artists, but they don't get paid for their work. We need to have our own galleries and handle our own promotions. We need clothing factories, shoe manufacturing, cosmetics companies, flower shops, grocery stores. I cannot think of one single Aboriginal restaurant. Look at the foreign people who move here and start a business and do very well. We are already here. Why can't we do it too?

"I have also given great thought to our ancestral ways and how our culture seems in between worlds. It is a fact that we have problems paying our taxes. Once a worker receives money, it is difficult to put some of it away for a future tax situation. Also, many of our men are addicted to alcohol and cannot be depended upon to have good judgment about how the family income should be used. I would suggest we set up professional accounting firms to handle the small businesses' finances and that we incorporate each family business, making the grandmother the person who heads the corporation. She would be in charge and would receive the payroll money and be the one dispensing it. I know it would work!

"It is possible to have a successful, modern, Aboriginal society. One with integrity, honesty, pride, and so forth. It doesn't mean we have carpets on the floors of our houses if we don't want to, but we can manufacture the best carpets in the country and sell them to those who do. We can honor the spirits of the wood as we build our buildings and maybe even find a way so that they will be maintainable, mendable, and repairable, but also of material that will return to the earth if the buildings are left abandoned.

"People will be coming to the Olympic games in the year 2000. They could see a proud, prosperous race of people by then if we get organized.

"I am also concerned because we have Aborigines in foreign countries who are living in prisons because they didn't fit into that society and thus committed a crime. Some were never given a chance. They had no say about being taken to a foreign place as children. They don't even know what it is to be an Aborigine. We must do something. We can't turn our backs and pretend they don't exist. They are our brothers and sisters. We must find them and bring them home."

"You have very ambitious plans," Bea commented to Judy, who had stopped to take a breath.

"That is why we have been given the emotions and feelings of ambition. Not as some self-serving device but for the goodness of all. Will you help me? Can I count on you?"

"Yes," Bea answered. "I will do everything I can possibly do."

The two stayed and talked for another hour. When Bea finally returned to the Carpenter home, she was full of both questions and possible answers.

The first person on her agenda was Andrew Simunsen. A visit to his office would be the best approach. She waited for an opportunity, which occurred the following Tuesday. Natalie and David were going on an outing, so Bea had the afternoon free.

She wore the nicest housedress she owned and took the bus to the heart of the financial district. As she stepped down the vehicle's six steps and the folding doors opened, she saw the world Andrew had created for himself. The building was made of smooth cement, with shiny silver pillars, and more than 70 percent of it seemed to be of spotlessly clean glass. The entrance was a massive double-size glass door. She read Andrew's name and office number in white plastic letters inserted in a black velvet case upon the wall, then took the elevator up to the fourth floor.

His office occupied the entire floor. A young woman with short auburn hair held back by pretty gold combs in each side sat behind a desk in the center of a rounded semicircular reception area.

"May I help you?" she asked.

"Yes, I'd like to see Andrew Simunsen."

"Do you have an appointment?"

"No, but I am a friend. Please tell him Bea is here, Beatrice."

"I'm sorry," the receptionist replied. "But you need an appointment. I can make one for another time."

"Please just tell him I'm here."

"I can't do that right now. He is in a meeting. Let me give you another time."

"No," Bea said, shaking her head. "I'll just wait." She walked over to a set of wingback chairs, upholstered in floral material, and made herself comfortable. She was determined to stay. An hour later the elevator door opened and Andrew and another man exited.

"Mr. Simunsen," the receptionist called as Andrew turned to enter a door at the left. "This woman is here to see you without an appointment."

Bea stood up. Andrew recognized her from across the room. He turned and walked in her direction. "Bea, is anything wrong? Is David hurt, or Natalie? Is everything all right?"

"Yes, yes," Bea answered. "Everything at the Carpenters' is just fine. I've got something else I need to discuss with you. Something very important!"

"Sure, okay, all right, fine, yes," he answered, taking time to arrange his thoughts. "Cindy, take Beatrice into our conference room and get her a cup of tea. I'll be there very shortly." The girl motioned for Bea to follow and the two men walked through the other door.

The conference room was a large narrow space, one wall made entirely of glass, looking out at a parking lot dotted with small trees planted in soil squares within the black asphalt surface. A long table dominated the room and matching padded high-backed leather chairs on rollers lined each side.

"Have a seat. I'll bring you some tea," the girl said over her shoulder. Very shortly after the beverage arrived, Andrew appeared. He walked to a place just opposite Bea. In taking that seat he made the big open room suddenly seem to shrink down to kitchen-table size.

"What's this all about?"

Bea told him about her time in the outback and what

kind of people Aborigines were. She told him of her observations of the inequality in today's society. She shared Judy's ideas for training and encouraging self-sufficiency by privately owned and managed businesses, and her concern for anyone of her race incarcerated in a foreign country. Last, she appealed for his help in both administrative skills and monetary funding. She asked him to look at the help he could give now as a sort of return for being led to sacred power places by an innocent, trusting people who were not aware of what they were giving away.

Andrew actually seemed relieved. Somehow he had feared there was another matter of graver concern to him personally that she might bring up. "Help your people? Yes, I can help you help your people."

They spent another thirty minutes together. Bea left with Andrew's agreeing to meet Judy. Their meeting took place the following week.

Of all the concerns, and all the projects to be launched, Bea found her interest most keen in working toward the return of all Aborigines held in foreign prisons and jails.

She continued to be David's companion during the day. The Carpenters taught her how to drive so she could take the child on outings more easily, and she even went to the driver's license bureau, where she passed the tests and was given a valid driver's license. Holding it in her hands, Bea broke out with a loud "Wow!" In this society, it meant she had arrived. She was now proved to be a real person.

In the evenings and on weekends, Bea wrote letters and gathered information. The biggest obstacle she ran into was that many countries had no central record office. Each institution kept separate files and most had no classification of Aboriginal prisoners. She found that America only listed Negro, Hispanic, Asian, Caucasian, or Indian. Her countrymen would be categorized as "Other." So over the months she wrote to each of the fifty states in America asking about all men and women in the "Other" column of their computer lists and ended up writing personally to some of the named and numbered entries.

Then, in June, she received a document from the United States identifying one Aboriginal man. His sentence was life in prison without parole. He had already served thirty years. She was given permission and instructions on how to write directly to Jeff Marsh, prisoner number 804781.

Dear Jeff:

I wish to introduce myself. My name is Bea Lake. I am a fifty-six-year-old Aboriginal woman who is making a project of communicating with any fellow brothers and sisters incarcerated around the world. I understand your nationality to be Australian Aborigine. I would like to hear from you, to get to know you, and to be a friend. I am enclosing an addressed envelope for your reply. I hope to hear from you soon.

Sincerely,
Bea

Dear Bea:

Thanks for your letter. Personal correspondence is rare for me. I occasionally get a thank-you from someone who purchased art, which I produce and sell at a yearly prison event. Yes, I am an Aborigine. I was born in Australia and am also fifty-six years old. I lived there until I was adopted at the age of seven. I don't remember a lot of the details, but I have fond memories of complete freedom and no worries. My hell began when I left.

I would like to write to you but the cost of stamps may be a problem. Right now I have some money in my fund because I earn 5 percent of any money collected from art sold each year. I haven't used all of it yet. I don't know the cost of a letter mailed overseas, so if it is expensive, I won't write often.

What should we talk about?

Sincerely,
Jeff Marsh

Over the next two years, Bea and Jeff exchanged letters until they each knew the other's life story. Bea told of changing her name and Jeff revealed that he had too. They were amazed that their birthdays were so close. The official documents showed them born one day apart. The birth location for Bea was said to be the city where the orphanage was located and the birth location for Jeff was Sydney. Bea also worked diligently in forming a committee, extending it to international interests. She finally received a government hearing and proposed a prisoner exchange program. The long-term goal of the Aboriginal population in Australia, as presented by Bea, was to regulate themselves. They felt that, given the power to punish, incarcerate, and rehabilitate their own, they could also influence and prevent the young from committing crimes. Eight months later Bea received an answer. The Australian government would consider accepting the Aborigine with American citizenship, but there were many questions and details to be worked out. Was he in agreement with the exchange? What concrete details were in place for dealing with this prisoner if the Aboriginal people were sincere in punishing and rehabilitating by their own standards? How could they safeguard society against any additional crimes committed by this now-convicted criminal?

Bea called upon her old friend Andrew, who had remained a loyal supporter. She told him of the government hearing and asked him what advice he could give. "Well, I think you need to visit this Jeff and ask him how he feels about returning to Australia. You need to go and size him up. See what sort of bloke he is. I know you are very optimistic, but maybe he isn't salvageable. I will pay your airfare and expenses."

48

Bea rented a car at the counter displaying a yellow Budget rental sign. The young uniformed clerk handed her papers, one single car key with a tag showing it was parked in space thirty-three, and a map of the local area that she marked with orange felt-tip pen, outlining the highway and showing the desired location of a nearby town. Following the signs pointing to the rental-car garage, Bea located space thirty-three; the key opened the door of a white Ford so new the odometer read only forty-eight miles. She climbed behind the steering wheel and felt uncomfortable on the left side of a car, so she clumsily groped around, pulling out knobs and pushing buttons until she located the power windows and windshield wipers and adjusted the seat forward for better reach of the foot pedals. Last, she turned on the headlights because the parking facility was an underground garage. It was necessary to wind up three levels of parking to reach the toll booth exit, where she was waved through without question by an attendant busily eating a smelly tuna fish sandwich. Once outside, the sunlight was brilliant and she squinted for just a moment, letting her eyes become adjusted to it.

The rural scenery driving to the prison was very similar to the roadside views she was accustomed to in her own country. Both climates were warm all year long, so the houses had porches hugging their frames, open windows, and rutted dirt marks acting as driveways. Periodically a yard would sport a nonfunctioning vehicle, long ago abandoned and forgotten, always encircled by tall dry weeds. She tried the radio, but found nothing to her liking. After forty miles she spied a wooden sign with peeling paint and faded letters, the remnants of an arrow pointing to the road leading to the maximum security institution.

Bea drove up a paved entrance, around a circle with a tall guard tower, and into the area marked "Visitors." She parked the car and walked to a small crowd of people standing across the street from the prison entrance under another tall glassed-in tower where a uniformed police officer could be seen looking down. Just as she was about to ask a question of the women standing near her, a loudspeaker bellowed, "Next three. Next three enter." The three women in the cluster closest to the entrance broke away and walked across the paved street to the prison entrance. Bea fell in place and waited to be called. She saw no men in the visitors' crowd. It appeared to be only women and a few children. Most of the women were Negros. After intervals of about twenty minutes, the voice would again resound with "Next three enter," and the herd would shuffle forward. Finally it was Bea's turn. There was an electronic gate inserted in the center of an imposing fifteen-foot-high wire fence, barbed wire stretched upon the top. Once inside, a visitor was confronted with another duplicate fence and gate. The space between the fences was completely filled, right to left, with rolls of razor-sharp wire glistening over cement carrying inch-wide water trenches, which apparently were there to enhance the electrical conduction of the perimeter. The building ahead was painted pale apple green.

Inside Bea was asked for her passport as photo identification. She signed the visitors' log and handed the attendant the permission slip she had received in the mail. As she pulled the paper from her purse, she noticed the stamp across the left corner, "Death Row." The guard stared at the passport photo and then at Bea's face before finally accepting the match. "Why is this marked 'Death Row'?" she asked the guard behind the counter. "Because that was his sentence, lady. He may still be alive by some quirk of fate, but he ain't supposed to be." With the same sober look he instructed her to hand over her purse, remove her belt and shoes, and show the bottoms of her feet. Then she had to remove everything from her pockets and take off any metal objects she was wearing. She was frisked, flat-handed, by a sweaty stern-faced officer weighing more than three hundred pounds. The man could barely bend over, so the search ended at his arm's length. Next she was told to put all her belongings in a locker and bring the key and her shoes to the next room. After passing through the doors she entered a long hallway with a wire cage midway to the exit. She walked through this metal detector. Once past it she was told to put her shoes on. When the exit door was unlocked, she found herself in another long hall and followed a new guard, making several twists and turns until they came to a room with a partition down the center. The top of the divider was Plexiglas, the bottom solid metal with a small shelf every six feet and chairs facing each other on either side of the Plexiglas. Telephones sat on the shelves. The occupants of the room demonstrated that all conversations were going to take place face to face but via the phone.

"Four," the guard muttered and Bea moved to the fourth chair. She had been seated only a short time when a door on the opposite side of the room opened and Jeff Marsh entered with his hands and feet in chains.

The room was gray, with cement floors, stone block walls, and a dirty ceiling with paint flaking off the wire covering the light fixtures. It had been thirty years since Jeff had last seen this room, thirty years since anyone had requested a visit with prisoner 804781.

Bea was already sitting down when the door opened. Jeff's first emotion was one of disappointment. He wished she had been standing. It had been so long since he had seen a female that he longed to take in the entire view, from head to toe, in one long visual sweep. She looked heavy. She had a round pudgy face and her broad flat nose blended with dark black eyes not much different from what he observed of himself on the occasions he glimpsed in a mirror. She had come from Australia, one of his race, so he guessed she was okay. What had he expected? A long-legged, thin, scantily clad poster girl? Yes, that's what he had dreamed of.

He had dreamed for years of having a visitor, then when he was told Bea had requested permission to speak to him, his thoughts rekindled his deepest desire and for over two months he had anticipated this moment. He had pushed aside in his mind the fact that in one of her letters she mentioned being his same age. It was much more enjoyable to think of a young and beautiful visitor.

The moment she saw him, she smiled and stood up. "Hello," she said, nodding her head yes, yes.

She didn't have a model's figure.

The guard removed Jeff's arm restraints and he shuffled over to chair number four.

"You're not what I expected," he said as he lifted the telephone receiver.

"Why, what were you looking for?" she asked.

"I don't know. It's okay. I just thought you'd be different."

Bea smiled and asked, "Do you know why I'm here?"

"Sure," Jeff replied. "Somebody's pipe dream that maybe there is a chance you can spring me from this hellhole before I get so old I die in my cell!"

"There are serious negotiations taking place on a United Nations level to return citizens to their countries of origin. Special consideration is being given to people like yourself who had no say and were put up for adoption to foreigners. It is felt that life might have been very different had the person been reared by his own people. The exact procedures for rehabilitation are not worked out, but the emphasis is on rehabilitation, not incarceration. We are asking for you to be returned to tribal leaders. You would be the first, so they can't afford for you to fail. It is important for you to realize that leaving here would not mean you were set free. Your situation has caused us to question our splintered connections among fragments of tribes. In a very positive way it is forcing unification. Where once hundreds of tribes existed, we are now trying to stand as one united people. You would be turned over to a group of men, probably eight to ten in number. Men handle men's business and women handle their own affairs. They would ask you to tell your life story, including the day and details of the crime. Also, they would want to hear about your life behind bars, up to the date you left.

"I cannot tell you what would happen. In the ancient days men were isolated, shunned, or even speared in the leg as punishment if found guilty of wrongdoing. Each tribe acted as its own nation. Today, of course, all that has changed. We hope that if we are given the right to regulate ourselves, it might be possible that a police department would not be needed. If that is not the case, we would work toward a system that is fair and would listen openly to each case presented. We would strive to have police and governing officials who were honest and not susceptible to their egos being inflated by power or influenced by corruption. Before I can proceed any further, Jeff, I have to know if you are willing to be exchanged for an American held in the Australian penal system."

"Bea, I can't give you an answer at this moment," Jeff said, looking at her across the cradle of the black telephone. "It would be a dream come true to get out from behind these walls but, in all fairness, I cannot say I would do it without some sense of the treatment in store for me at the other end. I have no freedom in here. I am told what to wear, what to eat, when to shower, when to exercise, even when I may speak. Everything is controlled. I am powerless. But it has been so long since I was responsible for myself, it is really frightening to think of surviving with the limited skills I possess. And maybe these tribal leaders will have some outrageous penalty in mind. I don't know enough about being an Aborigine. I have tried to read some books, but I can't really relate to much of anything recorded there. Can you help me? Where would I start?"

Bea listened intently to the man on the other side of the glass wall. She understood what he was saying and hoped she understood what he was feeling. "I will help you, Jeff. I will write down for you the philosophy of the Real People tribe as it was taught to me. I think when you read what I write you will see that your life has not been completely devoid of the factors they deem most important.

"Our connection to Oneness has always been in the way we live our daily lives. We are connected to all of nature and to all of mankind. Our people refer to life before birth and life after death as being in the Forever. There is a message from Forever. Just as Christians have a list of 'thou shalt not' rules to guide their behavior, we, too, have a guide." Laughing, she continued, "Ours is more of a 'you should'/'thou shalt' list. As it was explained to me in the desert, what souls are supposed to do with the experience of being human applies to everyone, everywhere, at all times in history. As incredible as it may sound, it applies to you, in this place, as well. It will remain appropriate if you leave and return to Australia, or if you elect not to do that.

"I am sorry we have so little time together, but I am happy that I was able to come and visit you. I feel like we are more than acquaintances, that we are true friends, really connected. I hope you feel the same."

Jeff's gray head nodded in understanding. With a puzzled look on his chubby face he said, "You wrote in one of your letters that you were an orphan too. We could be related."

Bea smiled in response. She had thought about that too. "My tribal people would say it doesn't matter. We are to treat everyone we meet with the same respect and honor. Later, if the person turned out to be a newly discovered relative, it would be your reward."

"Hmm," he muttered, thinking about her answer. "Guess I got a lot to learn!"

Over a loudspeaker came the announcement, "Time is up, number four." As Bea stood up to leave she said, "I support you on your journey and look forward to hearing from you again."

"Yeah, me too," Jeff answered as he, too, stood, his stooped shoulders bending forward. He shuffled to the back exit where a guard again affixed chains around his wrists. Bea sadly walked away.

The day ended with two people united, one circle closed, perhaps another circle ready to open. Two spiritual spirals broadened upward. Bea could envision a return of dignity and respect for all Aborigines by the influence of this one man. Someday she hoped to see him walk with his head held high, proud of who he was, understanding and living the truth of his heritage.

With this thought in her heart, she returned to the motel where she was staying for the night, and sat at the small wooden desk by the window. She began to write. The following morning at the airport, as she boarded the plane for her return flight to Australia, she mailed the papers.

Two days later the prison guard who distributed mail to the prisoners gave Jeff a thick envelope. Inside was a document of several pages, stapled together in the corner, and a letter.

Dear Jeff,

Like you, I was raised to adulthood without any knowledge of my heritage. Fortunately, I found the desert nation of Real People. By living with them, I learned the values most important in life. Their beliefs are ancient, but are just as appropriate today. They apply to you and me. They apply to everyone.

If you return to the land of your birth, I cannot guarantee what will happen to you. I can offer you what our people offered to me—an understanding of our connection to Oneness and of ourselves as Forever spirits.

I have written down what they taught me, and I call it the "Message from Forever."

The decision to return to Australia after so many years is a decision you must make alone. I will honor whatever decision you make.

Please know, Jeff, you are loved and supported on your journey—by me, by the Real People tribe, and by all the universe.

Sincerely,
Bee

MESSAGE FROM FOREVER

Written by Bee Lake

The following message applies to all souls everywhere. It has been appropriate in every period of time, from caveman to the present. There is no distinction between male and female. The task is not worldly success, it is spiritually oriented.

This is a standard that has been held by my people in the Outback Nation since the beginning of time. They have never been farmers, merchants, or herders. They have always been gatherers, musicians, artists, and poets; they lived in oneness with the earth, all its creatures, and each other.

This is one of their ritual chants:

Forever Oneness,
Who sings to us in silence,
Who teaches us through each other,
Guide my steps with strength and wisdom.
May I see the lessons as I walk,
Honor the purpose of all things.
Help me touch with respect,
Always speak from behind my eyes.
Let me observe, not judge.
May I cause no harm, and leave
Music and beauty after my visit.
When I return to Forever,
May the circle be closed and
The spiral be broader.

You are a spiritual being here on earth having a human experience. You elected to come. It was not an accident nor by chance that you were born of the two people who are your biological parents. You were aware of who they were, of the circumstances under which you were conceived, and the inherent genetic pattern of both. You said, "Yes!"

You are a spiritual being evolving into enlightenment. Earth is a classroom in which lessons and demonstrations are available. It is a unique planet with unique life-forms. It is the only place in the universe where six senses—sight, hearing, taste, touch, smell, and intuition—are used with the field of energy, identified as emotions, to connect a visible body to the invisible spirit.

Every physical thing on planet earth comes from the One Divine Source and all are made from identical fragments of energy. We are one with all creation.

You are probably familiar with the ten commandments, or the "thou shalt not" laws. They have been available to mankind for thousands of years.

There have also been laws of "thou shalt," which have been around even longer. If the thou shalt rules had been followed, there would not have been any reason for the second set.

Your being here is voluntary, self-assigned, and long awaited. Your eternal progression will reflect this human journey.

Here are the "you should"/"thou shalt" rules for all humans:

1: *You should express your individual creativity.*

Each individual sees things through his own set of circumstances, and so has a unique expression to offer the world. Creativity includes the arts, but is not limited to that, nor is painting, composing, or writing in any way more significant than the creative measures taken to comfort someone in distress, to bring order to conflict or chaos, or to tell a child a story.

People are not taking advantage of the opportunity to enrich their souls if they believe they have no creative talent or believe some situation in life prohibits this expression. Indeed, it is quite the opposite. When one rises up against the odds, when we strive to release our creative consciousness, it carries great merit.

Society is formed in such a way that not all people have the opportunity to be leaders. Since there are many more followers, expressing our creative flair becomes even more significant. Creativity is meant to be positive, but we are each given free will. It is possible to use it in a manner that proves negative to oneself and to the world. We can be expressive in the way we comb our hair, select our clothing, arrange our residences, plant a garden, make a craft, or even mend something. The key seems to be to let your actions express you and work to make everything you express something you are proud of.

2: *Realize that you are accountable.*

You are a guest on this planet and, as such, are expected to leave it as you found it, or in better condition. You are accountable for caring for the other life-forms that cannot speak for or help themselves. You are accountable for promises you make, agreements you enter into, and for the results of all your actions.

It is important to explain that spiritual evolution does not stop and start. It isn't like turning a water faucet on and off. When a person dies, there is only a pause at some interesting activity while the physical debris is discarded. It is actually impossible to kill anyone. People are Forever beings, although Death does stop the physical expression. You are accountable for your thoughtlessness, as well as all pain and suffering you may have caused to the victim and the reflected influence it has on all others connected to anyone harmed. The deceased person does not hold ill will. It is society that does.

In order to help balance the scales, you must become responsible for everything you say and do. You must learn to honor and cherish life and try to help sustain it.

You are accountable for your body. It is a gift borrowed from the elements that your consciousness helped form and gave life to. To neglect it or to abuse it is to be irresponsible.

Each person is accountable for his sexual actions. You are held responsible for guiding the souls of any children conceived, for protecting their bodies, and for setting positive emotional examples.

This rule goes hand in hand with creativity. You are held accountable for what you create and share with the world, for safeguarding others and not harming life.

3: *Before birth you agreed to help others.*

The human existence is not one meant to be spent as a sole traveler. We are designed to support and care for one another. Everything we do should be done with the thought in mind, "What is in the highest good for all of life everywhere?"

Service to others means bringing aid, sharing knowledge, and providing a positive addition to someone else's life. All people are born with the right to be treated with respect and dignity. Being of help is extending a hand to the elderly, the children, the ill, and the dying. Service is the opposite of doing things for oneself, for the glory or the economic income. It means being aware that you are a part of a team, the team of human consciousness, and the fate of planet earth rises or falls depending on the team activities.

4: *Mature emotionally.*

We each express all the emotional feelings, including anger, frustration, depression, hopelessness, guilt, greed, sadness, and worry, as well as joy, happiness, hope, peace, love, and so forth. As you mature and gain insight into what it is to be human, the goal is to grow, to discipline and select your emotions. As someone famous once said, "You are as happy as you will let yourself be."

Relationships and incidents are circles. They start, continue, and stop at some point. If you mature emotionally, there is no difficulty in closing each circle, leaving no frayed edges, no negative feelings.

It is hoped that you experienced being angry as a child, early in life. You can determine how it feels physically to have your body filled with rage compared to how it feels to use understanding, flexibility, and inner peace. The only way your soul has to connect to your brain awareness is through feeling. If your back hurts, for instance, you should ask why. What does it represent? What can you do to change it? What can you learn? Then take care of what needs to be done physically to correct your body, but don't overlook the thought process and spiritual lessons.

There is also the place of honoring your emotions, especially joy and grief. To suppress either of these can cause physical health challenges to emerge.

One of the most important emotions for the health of any individual and for the health of our planet is the use of laughter. As a human, you are given the awareness, the gift of humor and the ability to express it. Through laughter and lightheartedness, the body can remain healthy and health challenges can be corrected. Humor is a problem suppressor; it adds strength to relationships and brings joy to others. The things we consider humorous and laugh at are to be analyzed closely. The challenge is to avoid being destructive in any manner. Humor is so important to your well-being, do not close your eyes for the night's rest unless you have experienced some laughter or joy during the day. If you haven't, get out of the bed and find something to be happy about.

Clowns are special people, found in every culture. There is a clown in each of us and an appropriate time in our life to expose that aspect of ourselves. We never grow too old to enjoy ourselves as clowns.

But truthfulness is the key. You can't seek the truth about who you are, why you are here, and how you are doing unless you speak only the truth. Always.

5: *Entertain.*

Yes, part of your earthly task is to distract and redirect the focus of other people as well as yourself. Entertaining is deliberate and is meant to cheer the weary, to soothe the frustrated, to comfort the diseased, and to be an outlet for creative expression. Entertaining yourself can aid in self-discipline and in maturing emotionally. The challenge comes in partaking only in positive entertainment and not always remaining in the role of the one being entertained. Entertainment can be an extremely strong influence, but it cannot be separated from accountability.

6: *Be a steward of your energy.*

Man can neither create nor destroy energy. We can only use it, change it, and rearrange it. All the energy that exists was created in the same instant in time. Every word, every action, every thought you focus on carries with it energy. Everything in our world, both seen and unseen, is a fragment of this stuff called energy. Our world is made up of nothing else.

Why is it so important at this particular time in history that all humans are reminded that their task is to become stewards of their own energy? Because it is collective energy that results in what we see, and in unseen layers of consciousness that surround people and places. Everything in our world is in the process of building up or eroding away based upon energy level. Each word you utter is released, and goes out into the vapors. Our words are never recaptured, never corrected, never retracted. They become a portion of the layer encircling the planet. Over time, the layer has become so filled with victims' screams, with violent actions, with selfish, limited thoughts that a layer of victim consciousness has now formed. People on earth find it easier to tap into that negativity than to bore through it and reach above it. More than half the souls visiting earth today are in the victim-consciousness mode. We created it, and we must dispel it. This can be accomplished by each of us becoming aware of our stewardship and setting an example. Whatever you focus on grows. Feeling like a victim, blaming others, and wallowing in self-pity only add to the negative vibration. You must change your attitude, forgive and forget, become more optimistic, look to the positive. Put your heart into the other thou shalt tasks, and let all the victim relationship attachments be severed.

7: *Indulge in music.*

One of the great gifts given the human race is the ability to vocalize in a range of tones more far-reaching than any other life-form and the ability to make instruments that will also produce the sounds of music. Creative expression and entertainment can involve music, but it is so important, it ranks as a separate and distinct task of its own. Music influences all mankind, and, indeed, the energy of music can be healing for both body and planet. Listening to peaceful music set to the pace of the human pulse can have a profound positive influence on one's nerves and mental state. Everyone is musical and is influenced by it. Music is your soul speaking. It is the voice of our planet communicating to the universe.

8: *Strive to achieve wisdom.*

Wisdom is a very separate issue from knowledge. Knowledge is learning that can be obtained from many sources: books, schools, the media, and experience. It is what IQ is based upon. A person can be extremely intelligent and not possess one ounce of wisdom. Wisdom is how a person uses knowledge. It is the deliberate, selective decision to act in a certain way or not to act at all, considering the welfare of everyone concerned.

There is no earthly requirement to attend school or to get a degree. Reading and writing are helpful, but they are not necessary to have a successful spiritual journey as a human being.

You must strive toward wise action, bearing in mind that all souls are having the same human experience, all are visitors and guests on Mother Earth. All are one with the Creator. All of creation came from the same One Source. It is a show of wisdom to honor the purpose of all things and to do that which is in the highest good for all life everywhere.

9: *Learn self-discipline.*

It isn't anyone else's obligation to see that each of us chooses actions that are compatible with peaceful, productive, joyous life on this planet. Unfortunately, laws have been found necessary because people did not live in ths way.

It is possible to overindulge. It is possible to become addicted, to be negligent, to be greedy. It is possible to be cruel and to be destructive. Self-discipline will keep these things in check, and help toward the task of gaining wisdom.

Self-discipline can help keep your body

healthy. The state of human health is a barometer showing us the state of the earth's health. It is necessary to develop self-discipline to experience any inner connectedness of body and soul. Listening to your heart will tell you when something is enough. Learn the difference between hearing what your head says and listening to the message from your heart. Head talk is a product of society. Heart talk is from Forever.

10: *Observe without judging.*

Observing without judging is sometimes called "unconditional love." All humans are spiritual souls. All were created in the same instant. No one is older, smarter, or better off than anyone else. Each was given the same one gift, the gift of free will, freedom of choice. The Source is perfect, and everything created by the Source is perfect. We were created spiritually perfect and have remained so, but our gift lets us believe and act otherwise. We allow ourselves to see ourselves and others as less than perfect and have the adventure of acting less than our potential peaceful selves.

There are no mistakes in terms of Forever. You can't make a mistake because human life is your gift and you are exploring. You can observe what is taking place and, without judging it as wrong, decide that it doesn't smell, taste, or feel intuitively good for your path. You then bless it and walk on. That is how you can fulfill the requirement to love everyone. It doesn't mean you like their actions, or how they choose to conduct themselves. But you don't judge the person as being wrong. It is simply not a part of your path. You put no energy in that direction. No words, no actions, no thoughts.

If you judge, you must also learn to forgive. Forgive others, forgive situations, forgive yourself.

By using observation without judgment, there is no forgiveness necessary. Observation is linked to understanding, to knowing the truth that all is in perfect Divine Order, that we as humans are only choosing to live less than our perfection. On a daily basis, we can become closer to our potential and reflectively the world will become a more godly place. Ultimately, we will witness the closing of a beautiful golden circle.

Jeff sat on the bunk in his prison cell holding Bee's letter and the document she had sent with it. He thought about the faraway land of his birth. For the first time in years he thought of his first home and first memories at the Willetts' sheep station. He remembered the insects on the farm, the flies, the grasshoppers, the spiders and ants. He recalled his favorite hiding places in the barn, and up in a tree where he could sit for hours, quiet and still, until the birds would come and land on the branches nearby, as if they thought he, too, was another bird. From his hiding place in the tree he could watch the adults working below and knew that he was invisible to them.

It had been so long ago, another lifetime it seemed. He had forgotten what it was like to be a whole being. Now he saw his years in Australia as the only time in his life he had felt harmony and balance with the world around him, with all its life forms and creatures, including the tiny ones. In that place he was out in the open where he knew he belonged, where he could think and feel, instead of being confined inside a building, or trapped as he was here in prison, where he had ceased even to think.

He had not thought about his youth for years and had given up the idea of ever walking in freedom. He had wondered years ago about his own people, the Aborigines, but only about their art, which he could never make any sense of. He realized that, although he had lived among the Americans all his life, there had always been a void existing within him that longed to be connected to the spirit of his ancestors.

What he could not know was that when he entered prison life, he did exactly as his mother had done the day her babies were taken from her, when she had said, "Whatever is in the highest good, I am open to experience. What has happened I do not understand, but in sadness, I will accept it."

He looked at Bee's "Message from Forever," outlining the ten most important things for a human being to spend his life doing and thought about his own life. He had expressed creativity. He had helped other prisoners through his art program. He had overcome his temper and matured emotionally. He was self-disciplined and self-entertaining. He appreciated music and indulged in singing occasionally. But he still needed to become accountable and to balance out any harm he might have done. Becoming a steward of energy was a new concept and so was the notion of observing but not judging. Eventually, he hoped, would come wisdom. Yes, he thought, I'm batting fifty percent. But I can make up for lost time. I can leave planet earth batting one thousand. The question now is where and how to learn and live these principles.

Jeff did not know what to expect from the tribal men should he return to the land of his origin. All he knew, as he sat on his bunk holding the papers and listening to his cell mate snore, was that he now had perhaps the most important decision of his life to make. Almost every major decision in the past had been made by someone else—the Willetts, the Marshalls, the judge, the guards. Now he had to decide about his own life, and he was frightened.

He read again the pages Bee had sent. She had said that she, too, had been lost in the white world until she came to know the ways of the Real People. Quietly, so as not to wake the man in the bunk overhead, Jeff began to speak out loud the chant that she had written down for him: "Forever Oneness, who sings to us in silence, who teaches us through each other, guide my steps with strength and wisdom . . ." He felt a stirring within him, as if something long asleep had been awakened.

He reached down under his bed and took out a drawing pad and a pencil. After sitting for some time and staring into space, his hand began to move. He was drawing what he was seeing in his mind's eye—a bright sky full of stars, and the vast, barren, dusty land beneath it, a circle of singing people around a small fire.

Now he understood Aboriginal art. It wasn't meant to be hung on a wall. It was meant to be viewed from above. It was drawn as a scene would be seen from the sky, the eye of Oneness looking upon creation.

When he had finished the drawing, he sat looking at it, not sure what had made him answer Bee's question in this way. He got an envelope, wrote her name and address on it, and put the drawing inside. Then he lay down on his bunk and closed his eyes. He thought about the journey ahead of him—the most important journey of his life—and about the brave man he would have to become to return to a people he did not know and face their judgment. He was no longer Geoff or Jeff. He would change his name to reflect this new man, in the way Bee had said she changed her name when she herself had changed.

In Australia, the land called down under, on the opposite side of the earth, Bee continued her work for the betterment of her people, and made plans to return to the desert. She dreamed that someday the modern world would be open enough to receive the ancient wisdom that was already in its midst, waiting to be shared. A world ready, like Jeff, to read and live the "Message from Forever."